THE QUIET WOMAN

Also by Priscilla Masters

The Florence Shaw mysteries

UNDUE INFLUENCE *

The Martha Gunn mysteries

RIVER DEEP
SLIP KNOT
FROZEN CHARLOTTE *
SMOKE ALARM *
THE DEVIL'S CHAIR *
RECALLED TO DEATH *
BRIDGE OF SIGHS *

The Joanna Piercy mysteries

WINDING UP THE SERPENT
CATCH THE FALLEN SPARROW
A WREATH FOR MY SISTER
AND NONE SHALL SLEEP
SCARING CROWS
EMBROIDERING SHROUDS
ENDANGERING INNOCENTS
WINGS OVER THE WATCHER
GRAVE STONES
A VELVET SCREAM *
THE FINAL CURTAIN *
GUILTY WATERS *
CROOKED STREET *
BLOOD ON THE ROCKS
ALMOST A WHISPER *

The Claire Roget mysteries

DANGEROUS MINDS *
THE DECEIVER *
A GAME OF MINDS *
AN IMPERFECT TRUTH *

* available from Severn House

THE QUIET WOMAN

Priscilla Masters

**SEVERN
HOUSE**

First world edition published in Great Britain and the USA in 2024
by Severn House, an imprint of Canongate Books Ltd,
14 High Street, Edinburgh EH1 1TE.

severnhouse.com

British Library Cataloguing-in-Publication Data
A CIP catalogue record for this title is available from the British Library.

ISBN-13: 978-1-4483-1309-9 (cased)
ISBN-13: 978-1-4483-1408-9 (e-book)

All Severn House titles are printed on acid-free paper.

MIX
Paper from
responsible sources
FSC
www.fsc.org   FSC® C013056

Typeset by Palimpsest Book Production Ltd., Falkirk,
Stirlingshire, Scotland.
Printed and bound in Great Britain by TJ Books,
Padstow, Cornwall.

Praise for Priscilla Masters

"A captivating tale"
Kirkus Reviews on *Undue Influence*

"An excellent choice for those who enjoy intricately
plotted British mysteries"
Booklist on *Almost a Whisper*

"Fans of traditional police procedurals will find a lot to like"
Publishers Weekly on *Almost a Whisper*

"A riveting police procedural focusing on guilt,
frustration, and the many varieties of love"
Kirkus Reviews on *Almost a Whisper*

"Well-plotted . . . Fans of character-driven police
procedurals will be rewarded"
Publishers Weekly on *Blood on the Rocks*

About the author

Priscilla Masters is the author of the popular DI Joanna Piercy series, as well as the successful Martha Gunn novels and a series of medical mysteries featuring Dr Claire Roget. She lives near the Shropshire/Staffordshire border. A retired respiratory nurse, Priscilla has two grown-up sons and two grandsons.

www.priscillamasters.co.uk

ONE

There are times when a consultation is over but incomplete. Even as the door closes behind the patient you wonder, 'Why did they really come? What was the underlying agenda? What was it that they did *not* say? As you fill the consultation in on the computer, you recognize how vague the text is, that whatever you've written, you've left out the most important part – the parts unsaid. Your fingers hover over the keyboard remembering the words she'd used, trouble getting to sleep, waking early in the morning, tiredness that lasts all day, but you know these words glide over the subtext, while her husband stands over her like a sentry. You spoke; she answered. But something was lost between your questions and her responses. Cracks between the paving stones where weeds can grow. There had been a subtext, but I had missed it, skating over the surface as though it was ice. But ice reflects what is above it while concealing murky depths. You can kneel down, feel the chill on your knees, while you try to peer through, but you can never see right to the bottom, to the pond life, the weeds, mud and pebbles that lie, shifted around by swirling water under that thick sheet of impenetrable ice. And so you abandon the attempt, stand up and walk away.

Because it is easier.

It was a week before the start of the new school year and I was busy, catching up with delayed vaccinations, syringing ears, checking rashes and temperatures, taking endless blood samples. Pumping up the sphygmomanometer cuff time and time again. Reading results and logging alerts on to the computer. Asking questions and filling in the patients' responses.

Some of it the truth, some of it observation, others incontrovertible test results.

Patient claims to have stopped smoking.
Patient omitted medication this morning
Patient gained 5 pounds in weight
Patient complains of . . .

I'd met the Clays on a number of occasions – more frequently
this year, I realized, scrolling back through the consultations. But
it is always that first impression which sticks with you, the one
I'd formed from five or so years ago when I'd first met them.

He was a tall, spare man with hard, unforgiving, blue eyes
and an upright military bearing, sharp-suited, thin to the point
of emaciation.

Impatient.

She was small and plump, soft, in a heavy, shapeless, woollen
skirt which seemed to reflect her personality. Brown, I think, and
too wintry for the day.

Subdued. Suppressed.

His voice was sharp, suited to barking out orders, while hers
was hesitant, questioning and polite. That morning, years after
I'd first met them, I'd run through the usual questions. Simple
tick box exercises to fill in the algorithms the computer dictated.
Her responses were cued in by her husband. She shook her head
when I asked whether she'd skipped her breakfast before I
checked her blood sugar.

'Yes,' Richard barked. 'As instructed.'

I looked at him, met his cold eyes while he stared right back
at me, his face uncompromising and impassive as a statue's while
Christine dropped her gaze to the floor, her body seeming to fold
in on itself, shoulders drooping and head bowing. It was as though
she wanted to disappear into the chair.

I continued with my questions. 'Alcohol?'

'She drinks a glass of wine sometimes in the evenings. Never
more than one.'

I filled in the template and studied my patient, trying to divine
what really was the problem this time. In the last two years Mrs
Clay had made numerous visits to the practice, each time with
a different, minor complaint: headaches, trouble sleeping, aches
and pains. She'd been referred to various consultants: the general
medical physicians, the gastrointestinal department, even the

chronic pain clinic for a stiff neck. The letters back from the hospital were all the same.

NAD. Apart from a few minor issues put down to the aging process, Nothing Abnormal Discovered.

Nothing had *ever* been found. And these were the tricky patients – the ones when it was all too easy to miss something. Because at some point you stopped listening. I trawled through X-rays, scans and blood tests, hospital letters and the results of investigations. Nothing.

I met her eyes, lids sagging as though it cost too much effort to hold her eyes open. Faded blue and tired looking. There was hardly a spark of life. I thought then it was as though all hope had been extinguished.

'I think you might have lost some weight.'

'Well, she will have, won't she? She doesn't *eat* properly.' It was as though she wasn't there.

I looked up – at him first, then at her.

'Why?'

Christine dropped her head even further and murmured something I couldn't quite hear.

'I think I should check.'

Her husband looked impatient while I led his wife towards the scales and verified my guess. From my memory she had been nicely rounded, almost plump, a woman with a quiet manner and a sweet face. Now she was heading towards gaunt. Her cheekbones stuck out and her hands, trembling slightly, were bones and veins. My instinct was right. She'd lost almost a stone and when I looked at her, I realized there was something more. She'd aged too quickly. I glanced at the blood bottles and decided on a couple of extra tests I could add to the fasting blood sugar.

I realized she was depressed. But something else was disturbing me.

He hadn't noticed it. He was unconcerned, detached. Chin in the air. Shifting from foot to foot, his hand gripping the back of her chair, obviously impatient with the pace of this visit. I looked at him and wondered why the hurry. In their early sixties, they were both retired – he as CEO of his own company – and she from a clerical job in a local solicitor's. I remembered her as being quiet, but now I realized she had crawled inside a shell, as a snail does, for protection.

'I suggest you watch your diet,' I said.

'She does. We both do.'

I looked up at him. 'I didn't mean like that,' I said, touching her hand to connect with *her* not *him*. 'I wouldn't lose any more weight if I were you.' I tried out a smiling comment. 'Treat yourself to some chips – now and then.' I stepped out on thin ice. 'Do you think you might be a little depressed?'

The look she returned was uncomprehending.

I took another step. 'Have you had thoughts of self-harm? Suicide?'

'No,' he barked out. 'Don't. Be. Ridiculous.'

She looked at me then, lifting her eyelids with effort, and I was taken aback. Her look held a mute appeal. Combined with the degree of her hopelessness, I wondered if a psychiatric diagnosis rather than a physical illness was what was needed. I would check the results of those blood tests very carefully.

He gave a little twitch of annoyance. 'Come along, Chrissie. Time to go.' He picked her handbag up from the floor and handed it to her – or rather thrust it at her.

'Before you do leave . . .' I addressed her now very directly, '. . . have you any other symptoms that you haven't so far mentioned?'

She looked at her husband.

'No. She hasn't.'

'I'll ring you with your results. They'll take a day or two.'

And they were gone, leaving me with an empty room and an uncomfortable feeling of something unsatisfactory and unfinished. I wished I could have seen Christine Clay on her own.

I knew I'd failed her as I logged the consultation: *sleeplessness/ mild depression with no red flags – no thoughts of suicide or self-harm.*

I made a note to check the blood results next Tuesday and was briefly thoughtful – until the next patient arrived with their problem.

TWO

Late morning was punctuated, as usual, by the exotic flavour of Jalissa O'Sullivan, who waltzed in with her basket of sandwiches, cakes, fruit and desserts. It was one of my favourite encounters of the morning. Not just because she made the most delicious lunches, but because she was loud and cheerful and, it being the week before school started, that morning her two children accompanied her. Jalissa was the result of a diving holiday in Jamaica ten years ago, taken by electrician, Brett, with his mates. He had fallen in love with Jalissa and when he had returned to the UK he'd broken off his engagement and courted her from afar. Eventually she'd followed him back to the UK and they had two of the most delightful children you could possibly imagine: Petronella, eight years old, a pretty child with coffee-coloured skin and her mother's wild hair tamed into cornrows. She had the longest, curliest eyelashes I'd ever seen outside a mascara advert and large, darting eyes. Where his sister was merry, Charles, her five-year-old brother, was solemn, observant and intelligent, with the dignity of a politician. To be honest I loved the little boy and his sister but had to refrain from picking them both up and hugging them, which was my instinct.

'How you today?' Jalissa made no attempt to speak anything other than her native patois.

'I'm good,' I said, adding pointedly, 'but very hungry.'

Petronella put her finger to her chin and carefully selected a chicken mayo sandwich before hovering over a slice of carrot cake, but Charles stopped her. 'You don't want to get fat, Nurse Florence,' he said. 'I'm sure your boyfriend will feed you plenty.'

He gave a very straight look, first at me and then at his mother who was standing, hands on hips, laughing at my embarrassment.

She pretended to cuff the boy who wasn't fooled and didn't even bother to duck away. 'Sometimes,' she sighed, 'I think this boy is psychic. What you seein', Charles?'

He smirked as though he had a secret. 'Nurse Florence,' he said. 'You got a boyfriend?'

I gave a despairing look at Jalissa and paid for the sandwich but left the cake as per Charles's advice. And now, judging by the giggle that she couldn't hide behind her hand, Petronella was in on the secret.

12.30 p.m.

I was alone in the staff room that lunchtime. The others had either wandered into town or else were scuttling home to feed the dog or enjoying half days.

I had no dog and a full afternoon's surgery and, to be honest, I was glad of the work that took my mind away from some uncomfortable happenings in my personal life. Let me fill you in.

Four years ago, my dear husband, Detective Sergeant Mark Shaw, left me for his worktime squeeze, Police Constable Vivien Morris, who had proved ready and willing. While I had nursed dreams of a leisurely life post-retirement, funded by our combined pensions – making friends on cruises and various other holidays in the sun – my husband had revived his sagging libido. However, his plans of nonstop sex on the beach had been scuppered by her secret plans for a baby. PC Vivien Morris, the goofy-toothed wannabe siren, had subsequently become pregnant. I'd learned about the impending happy event through two sources. The first was my dear ex-husband who, hating the thought of another child (our own two having flown the nest a while ago), had confided in me, spending almost the entire six months whining about having been trapped.

And my second source of information? Young Vivien was so overjoyed at having her man plus imminent baby that, blind to her lover's discontent, she was in the habit of sharing the joyful news on all of her many social media platforms, holding baby-grows to her expanding abdomen. And because she wanted the whole world to know about her darling Mark and her happiest news, she shared the details with every single one of her friends, including one of my few allies in the Force, PC Rowena Barrett. So I was 'in on the act' from both sides.

Mark's abandonment of me had given me pause for thought and a new perspective on the marriage state. Which, as I chewed on my sandwich and drank flavoured water that morning, brought me neatly back to ruminating about the Clays and marriage in general.

Joined at the hip, do everything together. Sometimes seen as a sign of closeness. But a doctor's appointment together? Really? Even in our closest phases I wouldn't have wanted Mark to stand there, answering personal questions in my place, as though I was dumb or mentally impaired. No, I decided. Richard Clay had been intrusive, controlling and domineering. I would have learned far more of her fears and symptoms had I seen Mrs Clay on her own, without her overbearing husband. There are plenty of those – and some wives too – who do not allow their spouse to have any independence of deed or thought. Mark and I hadn't been like that. We had grown into that most mundane of states: comfortable rather than competitive. I felt my face twist. And look where that got us. But Richard Clay . . . I bit into my sandwich thoughtfully, disturbed by the memory of her weight loss. It was always a worrying sign. For years Christine Clay had maintained the same weight. Was this a result of depression, as I'd thought? I'd combed through her medical history, searching for any previous episodes, but there was nothing. And so I fell back on instinct. The best I could come up with was to slide past her and focus on her husband. Maybe the real problem was that he was *afraid* of letting his wife have any say in her own life. Maybe it wasn't dominance but underlying insecurity. He was frightened to let her go. If he opened his hand and let the little bird fly, he thought she would fly away.

That was when I smiled. Christine Clay might fit the description of a little brown sparrow but the thought of her flying away was nonsense.

THREE

My first patient of the afternoon was Ryan Wood, booked in for his fourth – or was it his fifth? – anti-smoking clinic appointment. As usual he made me smile as he sauntered in. With his deceptively earnest, honest manner and guileless blue eyes he was the town's anti-villain. More victim than villain, who had somehow got into the habit of petty pilfering. I'd witnessed his light-fingered behaviour for myself, as had the town's police force, who had charged him more than once with the offence. But put him in front of a judge and a row of jurors and he inevitably got away with the lightest of fines or, in the past, a brief sentence to a young offenders' institution. Maybe they could see into his heart, which was not bad. Not really. He was one of those boys who means well but never quite makes it. Just like his attempts to give up smoking. And yet – and yet – I couldn't dislike him, though I doubted he'd ever quite kick 'the tobacco habit'. Still, we both played the game, acting out the sequence of expected moves.

'So have you been smoking since I last saw you a week ago?'

He drew in a deep, regretful sigh accompanied by an eloquent apology in those blue eyes, which told me everything, before starting on one of his apologetic excuses of which he had a repertoire as vast as an entire library. 'See, it's like this, Nurse Florence.' Another flash of his eyes accompanied by a wide grin. 'I was with my friends and they' – he opened his eyes very wide, a trick I figured he must have learnt in the crib – 'sort of offered me one. I couldn't say no,' he added quickly. 'They'd have thought I was being rude.' Another grin. 'Standoffish, see?'

'Oh well, Ryan.' Still slightly distracted by worrying over the Clays' consultation, I was in a forgiving mood. 'Not to worry. I suppose you want another prescription for Nicotine gum?'

Now he grinned, all discomfort behind him with the chance of some free gum. 'Hey, thanks.'

And then, head on one side, he observed me for a moment before asking, 'You all right, Nurse Florence? Looks like somethin' botherin' you.'

I was hardly going to confide my concerns about another patient to Ryan, but I was touched by his concern. This was his other side exposed, the sensitive, kind and perceptive underbelly. And he was right. I did feel unsettled and odd. Off-kilter. It was the same uncomfortable feeling I had when I suspected I'd missed a significant diagnosis. I tried to laugh it away. 'I'm fine, Ryan. Fine,' I repeated, trying to convince myself with a hearty tone. 'Now then. Do you want to book an appointment for next week?'

He screwed his face up. 'I'll do it on the way out, Nurse Florence. Thanks.'

Which meant that was the end of his attempt of stopping smoking – until the next time.

4.10 p.m.

My afternoon ended with a visit to The Oaks, a residential home where a few of my aged patients were lodged – amongst them Nora Selleck, a lady in her late eighties who had moved into the residential home a year ago. Nora was in festive mood as fourteen residents of The Oaks were having a trip to the Regent Theatre in Hanley to see *Swan Lake*. 'And I love ballet,' Nora confided as I dressed a wound on her leg, checked her blood pressure and, as Nora knew everyone and everything about the residents of Stone over the last fifty years, I asked her, casually, whether she knew the Clays.

'Not really,' she said, eyes bright as a sparrow's and, as always, eager to chat. 'They're quite a bit younger than I am but I know *of* them.' She screwed her face up. 'Was he a military man?'

'Maybe once long ago. I think he was the CEO of a business somewhere in the Potteries.'

'Oh, that's right.' She smiled. 'Bathroom company, I think.' She giggled. 'Toilets, ceramic basins. That sort of thing.'

'What do you think of him?' I'd tried to keep my tone casual, but Nora was a perceptive woman.

She gave me a hard look. 'Why do you ask?'

I shrugged. 'No real reason.'

'Florence.' Nora touched my hand. 'There's always a reason for asking these questions.'

'He seems a bit—'

At which Nora smiled. 'Don't always believe what you see.'

'Meaning?'

'Christine Clay was one of the brains behind our local am-dram group. Bloody good at it too. She made a stunning Beverley years ago in *Abigail's Party*.'

It didn't really tell me anything. Neither could I connect the timid woman I'd seen that morning with the monstrous character in the well-known play. I secured the end of the bandage with a strip of Micropore tape and studied Nora's face. As always it was bright and engaged. But I could also read mortality and a fear for her future. Nora, like all of us, was aging. And that thought followed me back to the car where I sat, reflecting on my own future – and something I'd been reluctant to face.

A year ago I'd made the acquaintance of a detective constable who worked, as my ex had, out of the Stone station. I'd thought then that he was nice. But no more than that. However, he had texted me a week ago mentioning a possible dinner 'date' which had unsettled me. When Mark had left I'd settled into a sort of acceptance that, as far as a love life went, it was more or less over. Being realistic, my self-confidence had taken a knock and I'd been forced to confront a different view of myself. PC Vivien Morris was significantly younger than either my ex or me, by sixteen years, and I wasn't sure I could take rejection a second time. I'd spoken to plenty of friends who had tried Internet dating, and the consensus was that you had to kiss a lot of frogs to find your prince. And even after that, a few had found their prince only to have the prince find someone else. And so the hurt goes on, the knocks and the puncturing of self-confidence perpetuated. I wasn't sure that I wanted the possible bruising of a relationship. I wasn't even sure I could be bothered. Again, the image flitted through my mind of the Clays, the way Richard appeared to control Christine's thoughts. A contrast to the image Nora Selleck had just described. So had the unevenness of their relationship existed from the start or had it developed over the years? Was this simply a rut they had got stuck in and the longer it went on the deeper the rut and the harder it would be to heave out of it? Was being subservient a necessary component in a marriage? No, I thought, with passion. Not these days. But a couple in their early sixties – I corrected that to, *some* couples in their sixties – stuck to the guidelines their mothers had probably dished out to them years ago.

And now, I thought sternly, as I started the car and headed for home, to return to the question you've been avoiding. How are you going to respond to DC Summers' invitation?

FOUR

A nswer? I didn't. I couldn't make up my mind whether to or not and if I did what to say. I agonized over a response over the weekend and still couldn't decide. So rightly or wrongly, I did nothing leaving my response to DC William Summers' invitation for another day – and then another day – and so on.

Tuesday 5 September, midday

The results of Christine Clay's latest blood tests were all normal. I scanned through them but, as before, there was not a single blood test out of line. I rang her landline to deliver the good news and received a curt response from Richard. No relief, no thanks, nothing. I sensed a complete desert of emotion. So much so that I was tempted to challenge him. Is this good news to you? A relief? That your wife doesn't have some unpleasant disease but is healthy?

Mr 'Sympathetic Not' said coldly, 'I'll pass the message on. Thank you for calling.' And he put the phone down. He could have been an automaton. In fact, I would have preferred to deliver the good news to an answerphone.

Thursday 21 September, 11 a.m.

It was almost three weeks before I saw Christine Clay again, her husband still dancing in attendance, though dancing was hardly the word for the way he stood stiffly, like a clockwork soldier or a marionette. I'd run through her blood test results again, double-checking. Had I missed something? I even discussed it with her doctor. In the light of her frequent visits – sometimes three in a month – I knew we *were* missing something. If not physical then mental. Depression?

But the relief was that there was no evidence of any sinister pathology behind her weight loss. It was always an alarming symptom.

A diagnosis of depression, however, takes time. It could be difficult to achieve with her husband watching every word she said.

As I pressed the buzzer to call her in, I wondered. What symptom would she produce this time? Headaches again, muscle weakness, tiredness? I watched her clumsy entry, bumping into the door and dropping heavily into the patient's seat, almost knocking it over, while her husband, behind her, tut-tutted at her awkwardness, fussily straightening the chair as she sat, almost causing her to miss it altogether.

He couldn't have drawn my attention to her lack of coordination with greater emphasis, even catching my eye and nodding as she sat. She drew in a sharp gasp before swivelling round to look up at him and apologizing. While she was all humility, he was unforgiving, with that same disapproving, granite-like expression.

I watched the tableaux without comment, waited while she settled down and he took up sentry duty behind her, which meant she couldn't read his expression. But I could. Still impatient, increasingly bored, disdainful as his eyes skated over the top of her head to meet mine.

'So, Mrs Clay.' I used my cheery voice. 'What can I do for you *today*?' I knew the *today* I'd tacked on was a deliberate reminder of the sheer number of consultations she'd requested over the past two years. I watched Richard's mouth twitch as he picked up on the none too subtle admonishment.

She didn't respond straight away but swivelled her head around to look up at her husband, waiting for him to cue her in. But he didn't. He simply stared at her, hostility in his eyes. 'Richard suggested I come,' she said timidly, still looking up at him, waiting for some assertion. 'I've been having some dizzy spells. In fact, I fainted getting out of the bath last week.'

That was concerning. I knew she wasn't anaemic so as I watched the sphygmomanometer screen I ran through the various possibilities, postural hypotension being top of the list. 'Did you hurt yourself?'

She made a weak attempt at a laugh. 'Got some bruises on my leg but nothing more than that. Nothing serious and I suppose it's to be expected.'

It was that uncomfortable phrase. *To be expected.* Why? If she meant her age I begged to differ. However, I said nothing and focussed on the computer screen, sneaking a swift glance at Richard who was staring ahead, snorting impatiently.

I should have followed up on her comment; I was taken aback, thrown off balance and puzzled, but I asked her to stand and focussed instead on the sphygmomanometer. Her blood pressure had dropped a little but not enough to cause her to faint.

'Has this ever happened before?'

'No.' His mouth was a straight line.

I advised her to take her blood pressure tablets at night rather than in the morning, to drink more fluids and to return for another check in a week or so. 'If you have another fainting attack maybe we should get some further tests done.' I was wondering now whether she might have some neurological defect which could possibly thread together her symptoms. I reassured her and, as though she'd expected nothing more, she was already standing up, her husband holding open the door. His eyes rolled over me with a message I had no hope of deciphering. I watched them go and decided then that I would discuss her case with her GP – again.

I still had that disturbing instinct that I was missing something. Tripped over one of those awkward sentences. *To be expected.* Misinterpreted a sign, not only in Christine's health but in the way her husband had looked at her when he'd held open the door, unmistakably ushering her out. It wasn't dislike. More an angry tolerance. But then, I suspected, that could well be his default expression. Maybe all these trips to the GP surgery were boring him. Many couples, retiring after fulfilling careers, take a while to adjust to less fraught lives. I watched him and wondered. Was that it? He'd been a company director. Spending his days trotting along to the GP surgery, sitting in the waiting room, listening to his wife's tales of minor ailments must be unfulfilling. And now his pale eyes had registered the fact that I was focussing on him rather than her. And he didn't like it. His shoulders twitched and he shook himself, his movements brisk and assertive. At the same time his expression changed. Now he was guarding against me reading him. He deliberately turned his back and followed her out of the door.

I sat back and sighed, then filled in the consultation on the computer and pressed the buzzer for a patient who had turned up at the front desk requesting an urgent appointment with me. 'He wouldn't take no for an answer,' Darcey said apologetically. 'I'm really sorry.'

And so I'd tacked the patient on to the end of my morning surgery. If it was that urgent I'd better see him.

12.20 p.m.

Ryan Wood peered round the door, his face chalk white. 'Thanks for seeing me,' he said before dropping into the chair. He was nursing an arm padded out with cotton wool. I could see blood starting to soak through his shirt.

'What the heck?'

'I got into a little problem,' he said, avoiding my eyes. 'I didn't wanna go to the hospital.' His skin was starting to take on a yellowish, greenish tinge. I reached across for a cardboard vomit bowl and started to peel the cotton wool away to expose a long, straight knife wound about nine centimetres long. He looked at it, retched, then eyed me, his face taut with fright. 'It's bad, innit?'

I didn't respond but started to clean around the wound. It was still oozing, but less so.

'I don't usually carry a knife.' It was a protest made through pain, his eyelids about to close. He was actually swaying in the chair.

'Put your head down.'

He did that and his breathing steadied before, true to form, in a few moments, he raised his head and managed a thin smile. 'You want to see the other guy.'

I was already assessing the wound, which was not as bad as I'd first thought. It was clean and not too deep. I met his eyes. 'No, Ryan,' I said. 'I *don't* want to see the other guy. One victim of knife crime is enough.' I wanted to say so much more. Like couldn't he see how this could escalate? How easy it was when you had a knife in your hand for a threat or defensive action to prove fatal – even accidentally? I wanted to lecture him on where carrying a knife could lead but he was in no fit state to listen to a sermon. He'd be lucky if he didn't end up on the floor.

'See, Nurse Flo,' he said, beginning to recover, fixing those innocent blue eyes on me to do their work. His grin was suffused with a childish, naive trust. 'I knew I could trust you. If I'd gone to the hospital they'd have told the police and they'd be askin' questions.' He moved his head nearer, giving me that hopeful, childlike, trusting gaze. 'I thought you might be able to fix it.'

I was still assessing the injury as he continued, 'See, Nurse Florence. If *they's* carryin' you gotta match 'em. See?'

I shook my head and fixed him with a direct and questioning stare. 'Ryan,' I said softly, not sure I wanted to hear the answer, 'what have you got yourself into?'

I couldn't be medic, police, judge and jury.

The slash wound was still oozing blood. But it wasn't too deep and it appeared clean. No underlying tissues appeared to have been involved and, stroking the skin around it, as well as his palm, wrist and fingers, told me there was no nerve damage. It wasn't serious . . . this time.

'I can stitch this up for you, Ryan,' I said. 'So you can avoid hospital, but you need to tell me who did this.'

He didn't answer but stared at the floor, his face set in a determined frown and giving a slight shake of his head.

'Are you in trouble?'

He gave a slight nod this time. His eyes slid left, then right, and then he looked straight at me in that blue-eyed, I'm telling the truth (particularly when he wasn't), *honest* stare that could be so deceptive. But sometimes they did hold the truth.

'I don't *usually* carry a knife, Nurse Florence,' he said quietly. 'But lately things have got a bit . . .' He hesitated. 'Out of hand.'

'Slipping a knife into a person,' I had heard Mark, my ex, say in the days when we had sat and talked, 'can feel as soft as a knife slipping into butter. That is the danger. There does not have to be absolute intent. A knife in your hand and enough force and a six-inch blade can reach the vital organs even in a grown man.'

I was finding it difficult to respond. I'd seen the results of street crime during my student nurse days and I never wanted to see it again. And yet here it was, in a market town in Staffordshire, somewhere I would have classed as safe.

I should have realized safe is a dangerous word, like a promise, all too easily sprung apart.

He managed a wan smile. 'I'll be OK, Nurse Florence.'

I remained unconvinced, snipped the stitch with some sharp scissors and challenged him. 'Seriously?'

He shook his head then looked away.

'Ryan,' I began, as I dressed his wound, but he held his hand up.

'Don't start lecturing me,' he pleaded. 'Just leave it.'

Maybe he was right. It was the wrong time. Maybe what he needed now was an ally. Not a preacher.

'A week,' I said. 'Make the appointment on the way out and I'll take the stitches out for you. Try to keep it covered and dry.' I gave him a couple of spare dressings. 'Keep an eye out for signs of infection.'

I sensed I didn't need to tell him what the signs of infection were, the classic *rubor* – redness, *calor* – heat, *dolor* – pain, one of the medical students' favourite trios. Ryan Wood was streetwise. He'd know.

'You'll have a scar,' I added. Now he'd had his 'little problem' sorted his response was predictably jaunty. 'Battle wound.' He shook a fist in the air. 'The mark of a warrior.'

I opened my mouth to say something then shut it because his bravado suddenly deserted him and he looked like the boy he was.

'See you in a week,' he gulped, and was gone.

So now I had two patients to worry over.

FIVE

B efore I ate Jalissa's sandwich, I felt I should talk to Christine Clay's GP to get some perspective. Something about that most recent consultation had jarred, leaving me with an unpleasant prickling down my spine, the feeling of something hinted at but unsaid. I'd witnessed something but missed the subtext. On the computer I'd scrolled through her past medical history searching for a clue and noted three things. She had well controlled hypertension for which she was on minimal therapy, and had had a hysterectomy in her early forties for fibroids. She'd had one normal pregnancy and been delivered of a daughter. There was nothing sinister here. Nothing that would account for the fact that in the last couple of years she'd bounced in and out of the surgery thirteen times with minor complaints: headaches, indigestion, lassitude, sleeplessness. She'd had a plethora of tests: gastroscopy, an MRI scan, CT scan, X-rays. None had resulted in a serious diagnosis. This sort of history always makes one wonder. Was the underlying problem related to the mind? Depression? Boredom? Neuroticism? When behaviour changes, one looks for an external factor, maybe in the patient's lifestyle or family circumstances. Either way, frequent attendances can be more a cry for help than a medical condition.

Her husband came to mind. I turned my focus to him, scrolling through his consultations. If his wife attended frequently, apart from accompanying her, Richard Clay seemed to avoid the surgery altogether, ignoring invites for health checks. And he was as he appeared – healthy, on maintenance doses for borderline hypertension and a statin for a raised cholesterol, again borderline. But when I searched farther back I read a few consultations for vaccines prior to foreign travel cited as 'business trips'. I checked the dates against Christine's notes. No corresponding business trips there. He'd gone alone.

And so I returned to Christine, wondering why I felt so worried. Lots of patients come to the surgery often with the same symptoms without any serious underlying cause. So what was I picking up on? I returned to Christine's notes, this time focussing on the subtext. *Husband says, husband claims. Attended with her husband. Mr Clay says . . .* He'd been present at all her consultations. Why was he constantly at her side, guarding her, feeding facts into our system, often relating her entire history himself, without a word from her, sometimes diverting her claims with contradictions of his own, disclaiming her symptoms or at least minimizing them. The phrases: *husband says not that bad* and *she still managed to go out for the day* cropped up more than once.

He wasn't the first spouse to control his wife's thoughts. Sometimes it is even the other way round. You might recognize the situation but, as a nurse, there is nothing you can do about it. Tuck it away, Florence, I said. Ryan's case is different. There you might have some influence. You might even be able to get to the bottom of his behaviour. But when the Clays attended surgery again the most I would be able to do would be to gently steer Christine into speaking for herself.

I did wonder whether an explanation might lie further back in the Clays' past, so scanned right back, realizing that in the past the Clays' registered GP had been Dr Morris Gubb, who had been an old-fashioned, traditional GP who showed a keen interest in all aspects of his patient's lives and knew their family history for generations. He would have known the ins and outs of the Clays' lives – each nuance and past influences on present behaviour. But Dr Gubb had retired a year ago and his vacant post had been filled by Dr Jordan Bannister, a doctor who seemed more interested in profit and loss than his patients. He had an eye permanently focussed on the bottom line and was constantly checking all staff had submitted their claims for enhanced services and used free prescriptions to restock our dressings cupboards. He was medically competent but his mentality was that of a businessman. His patients' health – or ill health – was less of a priority than the balance sheet and he was constantly looking for ways to maximize practice income. That was where his focus was, not on the minutiae of their personal lives. Maybe, I thought,

I could use this business brain of his to my advantage. The plethora of unnecessary expensive tests on Christine Clay might persuade him to focus on the patient this time rather than the budget. If there was nothing seriously wrong we could, in the future, save money that was currently being squandered on unjustifiable hospital tests and consultations. I suspected Dr Bannister had a reason for being so focussed on money. His wife, Denise, was one of those excessively thin women who spend their life running marathons, playing tennis or some other Olympian pursuit and wore clothes even I recognized as expensive, with designer labels. They lived in a large, sterile house. (I'd been there for 'parties' which had felt more of an endurance test than a knees-up, any joy or free spirit sucked out of them by terror of spilling red wine on the pale, plain carpets.) Unsurprisingly they had no children and no dog, just a smug-looking Siamese cat who twitched her tail and looked down her whiskers at the unruly intruders.

I didn't want to ask *him* about the Clays' marriage. I would have to work on the other angle.

I could hear Dr Bannister moving around his surgery which was across the corridor from mine, our doors opposite each other. I hesitated but the rule was set in stone: any concerns about a patient must be addressed to the patient's registered GP, and so I knocked on the door and waited.

SIX

12.45 p.m.

He was sitting at his desk, frowning into the computer screen, a tall, thin man with dark hair, already thinning, and a pale, intense face, eyes framed by heavy glasses. He hardly looked up and his expression was not welcoming. 'Florence,' he said. 'What is it?'

I related the story of my morning consultation with Christine Clay, mentioning the frequent appointments and plethora of hospital referrals and unnecessary tests, Somehow I led into the dominance of her husband and the way he answered for her. As expected, he looked bored. But he did flick through her medical history before looking straight at me. 'I don't understand what you want me to do.'

Which left me floundering because he was right. I put forward my theory that she might be depressed which led to him shrugging. His interpretation and perspective were different from mine. His frown deepened as I watched him mentally tot up the cost of the number of tests and investigations she'd had, together with the results. Apart from pathology put down to the aging process, *nothing abnormal discovered.* NAD. Of course doctors are famous for always leaving a loophole or referring to another speciality, so a few suggested another port of call. Interestingly not one of these had suggested a psychiatric assessment. The last in the long line of results was my collection of normal blood results from the first of September. Dr Bannister studied everything for a while, taking it all in, while I watched him tot up the price to the NHS in general and the practice in particular. Then he turned his head towards me, puzzled, and repeated, 'I don't quite see what you want me to do.'

Then he waited while his finger traced the report on her recent brain scan. 'Doesn't seem we're missing anything.' He tried to make a dry joke, perhaps to make up for his lack of interest. 'She's practically glowing with the amount of radiation she's had.' And when I didn't return his smile, he made another attempt. 'MOT, maybe?'

Some people simply aren't suited to making jokes.

'I think she's depressed.'

Had I been speaking to any of the other doctors I would have said something like, *I would be, if* my *husband gave his own version of my medical history, interrupted when I was speaking to my doctor and attended all my appointments.* But I didn't know Jordan Bannister well enough to share such flippant comments with him. I'd already been divorced when he'd joined the practice so he'd only ever known me as a divorcee and might interpret any comments as post-divorce sourness. So I skirted round my response delicately. 'I wondered about referring her to . . .'

I could see the way his mind was working as though his skull was made of glass. As well as a community psychiatric nurse called Kelly, we have a clinical psychologist visit the surgery twice a week for counselling sessions with patients suffering from various mental disorders. The trouble is that both of them have long waiting lists of patients so wouldn't get to see referrals for months. And a drum was banging out a phrase in my head. Too late. Too late.

And, I argued to myself as I watched Jordan Bannister toss the alternatives around in his head, there was nothing to justify an urgent referral and certainly not a hospital admission. Besides, I wasn't sure how Christine – or Richard – would take the progression from physical ailments to a possible mental problem. I could almost see his lips, even thinner when pressed together. But I could read Jordan Bannister's internal cerebral workings. It just might be a solution for a patient who was taking up an inordinate and unjustifiable amount of professional time, while I could see an added bonus. Surely our psychologist would insist on seeing Mrs Clay alone?

I wished I could feel as pleased with myself as Jordan Bannister appeared to be. He was actually smiling as he leaned back in his chair, breaking the connection with the computer screen. 'Psychiatric referral,' he said, 'to our clinical psychologist. I'll make the referral.'

'Thanks.'

I only wished I felt as smug as he obviously did at the solution. But I had observed the Clays up close. While I would have liked to feel that I could wash my hands of their marital imbalance I still felt uneasy, fearing there was a pathological element to their relationship.

'That all?' His tone was dismissive and I felt disarmed. I left the room feeling dissatisfied. I'd left behind unfinished business.

It wasn't the first time I had resented the sticking to the patient's-registered-GP rule. I work with five GPs: two women who job share and three men, all of whom work full time. The two women, Gillian Angelo and Suzie Carter, had both trained at Birmingham, and had been friends before they joined the practice. Next in line is Dr Bhatt, a softly spoken, ultra-polite Indian doctor. His wife is a radiologist and they have five children, all privately educated and with the same soft, polite manners. Until Jordan came our junior partner had been Sebastian. Sebastian Timor was a beam of light which shone right through the entire practice. Charismatic and handsome with a mop of curly dark hair, he is the life and soul of the place, full of fun and with a sharp sense of humour. We all adored him.

In my opinion any one of those doctors would, at least, have discussed my patient more fully, picked up on my concern, and maybe, together, we might have formed a plan.

I missed Dr Gubb.

But he had finally been beaten down by the demands of General Practice. The shame was that his retirement had not been the Shangri La it should have been after a lifetime of hard work and devoted service. Five years ago, after a long and contented marriage, he had been widowed, so the cruises and holidays he and Sylvia must have promised themselves had not materialized. I had seen him wandering round the town or along the canal towpath, Doric, his Labrador, on a lead. And what had struck me was my description. Wandering? A word that implies aimlessness, something his life had never ever contained before. He had entered General Practice not long after qualifying and it had been his (busy) life. I had thought he looked lonely, though I guessed plenty of his one-time patients would have stopped him for a welcome chat – and probably a quick consultation. Certainly, when I'd bumped into him he'd always been anxious to talk and asked affectionately about his patients – particularly the ones we'd called (in the privacy of the surgery) 'the heart-sinks' – patients who attended surgery frequently with insoluble, sometimes imaginary problems. His loneliness wrapped around him like fog, a soft grey cloak isolating him from people, even more so as his son, Tim, worked for Médecins Sans Frontières and was usually working abroad. The issue of the Clays was exactly the sort of interpersonal problem Dr Gubb would have dealt with, gently asking them questions, spending time discussing the best strategy, teasing out some sort of intervention. He knew everything about his patients, their past problems and difficulties, old tragedies that might be influencing their current behaviour. Maybe there was something in the couples' past that had been missed off the computerized records – an old tragedy or drama – that might have affected her and which had been suppressed for years only to surface in later life, retirement allowing time to ruminate.

And so I missed Dr Gubb even more.

The Clays would turn up again soon. In the meantime, I worried what Ryan Wood's latest venture was. I wouldn't be surprised if there was a link with criminality.

SEVEN

6 p.m.

And so on the way home I bought a local paper. The *Sentinel* covered news for the Potteries as well as Stone, and I scanned the pages half dreading reading about a stabbing. If Ryan admitted to carrying a knife and had been wounded by someone else 'carrying' I worried that his joke about 'the other guy' held a more sinister meaning than I'd realized. It had concerned me at the time but puzzling over the Clays had pushed the consultation from my mind. Now the memory of that slash wound surfaced. I recalled his insistence that he couldn't go to the hospital. Was I now implicated in a cover-up? I didn't wait to go home but sat in my car, scanning through the headlines, as well as the stories below. But, although a fracas was mentioned outside one of the local pubs, there was no mention of serious injury, no phrase claiming 'the police were investigating'. Whatever Ryan Wood's bravado had implied it seemed it prob-ably was just that and he was the one who had ended up worse off. I folded the paper, telling myself I'd known his boast had been fake. But then my smile faded. *He* was the one in danger. *He* was the one with the wound. And carrying a knife indicated different behaviour from his previous self. Ryan was not, by nature, a violent sort. The knife meant protection. Why? And from whom? It didn't take much imagination to know he was in something a little more serious than his usual petty pilfering. I headed for home trying to put my patients out of my mind. One more day and then I could enjoy the weekend though I had nothing planned. I prepared myself for two quiet days.

And yet as I unlocked my front door I was still wondering which patient I would see next. The Clays (because now I felt it impossible to separate them. In my mind's eye they had morphed into Siamese twins), or Ryan, who was due to have his stitches out in seven days.

If he didn't pull them out himself with a pair of scissors.

Or slice them with a knife.

That evening I made the mistake of logging into my Facebook account. PC Rowena Barrett, former colleague of Mark, my ex, had become my 'mole'. She and I were Facebook friends and she regularly shared information and images of Mark's new life from there. The latest posts from PC Vivien Morris shared by Rowena displayed pictures of Vivien, looking hugely pregnant and very smug. There were captions such as *not long to go* followed by a snowstorm of emojis, exclamation marks, love hearts and kisses galore. But what was missing, I noted with some pleasure as well as curiosity, was my ex, of whom there was no sign. Not a whisker. No proud father-to-be picture, that awful, look-what-I-can-still-do expression, hand on pregnant mistress's belly. Initially I'd wondered if he was the one who had taken the picture and that was why she was looking so pleased with herself. Gazing at her lover. Unwisely I'd studied the picture with mixed feelings, most of them sour. Some drip once said that women look their most beautiful when they're pregnant. Bullshit! And it certainly didn't apply to Vivien. She'd always had crowded teeth that should have been straightened, a couple removed and the others braced into line. She'd also had a plump face but now, with her puffy cheeks, she resembled a hamster. In fact . . . I peered closer and enlarged the picture. Her face looked bloated and swollen. Had she been one of my patients I would have kept a close eye on her blood pressure and tested her urine regularly. She looked to me as though she was heading towards pre-eclampsia. I felt some concern for her. But I left the site without replying to Rowena and toyed with the idea of finally ringing DC Summers to tell him I'd love to have dinner with him.

Which led me down a different track.

DC Will Summers.

So far I'd put him off. I liked him. He wasn't really a good-looking guy. He was OK. He had nice brown eyes. He was kind, polite and gentle – there was nothing overtly offensive in his features – he just didn't have the charisma that Mark had displayed when I'd first met and fallen for him. Maybe that was a good thing. No, what Will Summers exuded was not sex appeal but kindness. It shone out of those toffee brown eyes and his open, honest face, one where a smile hovered always near. I liked his understanding eyes that displayed both perception and intelligence. There was something else that was just starting to hit me. I realized now that for years I'd seen Mark as he *had* been, rather than as he actually *was*. I'd still seen him as fit, charismatic, sexy, without seeing the middle-aged, slightly tacky man he'd become, responding to a much younger woman simply because she flattered him. I'd met PC Vivien Morris on a few occasions and found her fatuous, almost embarrassingly eager to be liked and prone to making embarrassing gaffs in an overloud voice. She'd seemed quite charmless, but Mark had obviously responded differently. I am not a man. At some point, very gradually, through the beginning of the affair, the disintegration of our marriage and the decree nisi, the scales had dropped from my eyes. I had seen Mark for what he was and, with that and the loss of exclusivity my own love had finally died. Now the overwhelming emotion I felt for Mark was pity. I sensed that the scales had fallen from *his* eyes too, the delusions melted away so he too saw himself as he actually was. He'd been deluded about himself, about romance, sex, love, family bonds. And now he was about to become a reluctant father. I felt sad. Mark hadn't been the greatest of fathers first time around – shift work and overtime had seen to that. But he had been there for our children, Stuart and Lara. So what about this child? Where would he be for the son or daughter about to be born? Maybe – and I hoped this would be the case – he would love it. I thought back to the Facebook post and realized Vivien had not had a *gender reveal* yet. Or was that too politically incorrect these days? Did one wait until a child was old enough to announce its own gender?

I swallowed the thought, smiled and returned to Will Summers.

Did I want to pursue a relationship which might well end in tears? Mine or his? I wasn't sure. I scolded myself for being a wimp and even got as far as finding his number in my phone contacts, but I didn't press the call button. Because? I had a sudden loss of confidence. I wasn't sure I wanted to step into the unknown. So instead I dialled a friend of mine's number, Catherine Zenger, and arranged to have a drink in a wine bar after work on Monday. I liked Catherine. For the first couple of years when I had joined the practice she had been the senior nurse. From her I had learned not only all the rules about taking blood, chronic disease management and various other procedures as well as the life histories of most of the patients (she had worked in the practice for almost thirty years, right up to the moment when she had retired on a comfortable NHS pension). There was only one problem. If a story lacked drama Catherine would 'embellish' it, inventing scandal where there was probably none, bending possibilities into hard fact. And that could be unfortunate and misleading.

I might ask her questions about the Clays, but whatever she told me might not be the truth.

However, there was no one better to discuss them – if she stuck to facts.

EIGHT

Monday 25 September, 12.05 p.m.

I always kept half an hour clear at the end of morning surgery in case of 'walk-ins', as had been the case for Ryan with his knife wound. This morning Christine Clay had requested an urgent appointment and so she'd been tacked on to the end of my morning surgery. If anything worried me about her I would have to involve Jordan Bannister.

I was intrigued.

Normally Richard made appointments. This was unusual. I wondered what was disturbing her this time, what needed immediate attention. And, as always, when I saw her name tacked on to the end of my morning list, I felt my shoulders tense and my frown lines deepen.

I heard his and her footsteps outside my clinic. Again, the contrast between husband and wife was marked – hers a slow shuffle, his a brisk, decisive, almost angry step. I opened the door. She was huddled up, almost collapsed in the chair outside my door. Dressed in a flowered dress, a misshapen cardigan carelessly wrapped around her shoulders. Her legs were bare, white with blue veins and flaking skin, her feet pushed into flat black shoes, the heel trodden down. She was hyperventilating and clutching her chest, chin dropped. Her husband stood over her, making no attempt to either comfort or reassure her. I observed them both for the briefest of moments before ushering them into the clinic room. I didn't even try to suggest I see Christine on her own. He was pressed too close to her. As they entered I read the look of frustration and irritation on Richard's face and heard a sharp, *harrumph*. She dropped into the chair, exhausted and still hyperventilating. I took her pulse and blood pressure before laying her on the couch for an ECG which was normal except for a bounding tachycardia. Behind the curtain – away from her husband's angry gaze – her breathing started to slow down and her pale eyes looked pleadingly into mine, her hand reaching for mine. 'Mrs Clay,' I began. 'All seems well. All your readings are fine.'

She shook her head. 'No,' she said. 'All is not fine.' Her eyes wandered towards the shadow against the curtain where her husband stood.

'Do you have chest pain?'

She shook her head but her eyes were still fixed on the shape of her husband outside the curtain.

'How do you feel now?'

She shrugged. 'Not so bad.'

I sat with her for a while as Richard huffed and puffed on the other side of the curtain. Her eyes half closed; her breathing slowed. A panic attack, I thought. Nothing more than her emotions. It was time for me to tackle this head on and introduce the subject of our psychologist. As it had an impact on practice finances, I felt sure Jordan Bannister would have wasted no time in making the referral. At the same time, I was curious as to how Richard would respond to this suggestion – with relief, or would he erupt like a volcano? Would he turn on us? Accuse us of deciding his wife's problems were psychological? Or would his irritation be focussed on her?

I looked at her again. She was so vulnerable, her eyes frightened.

I was going to have to deal with this very sensitively.

And at the back of my mind was a warning Morris Gubb had given me in my early days at the practice. 'Even the patient who cries wolf,' he'd warned, 'dies of some pathology. However frustrated you might be at our frequent attenders, they are the ones whose diagnoses we are most likely to miss. Because'– he'd given one of his wise, sad smiles – 'at some point in the past we stopped listening to them.' The words rang in my ears right now as I sat beside Christine Clay and watched her. She needed help, but more tests and scans would not solve the underlying problem.

Maybe Ruth Carroway, our visiting clinical psychologist, would.

Outside the curtains I could still hear Richard Clay pacing, his breathing tense and angry as a dragon's breath. I half expected him to stick his head through the curtains and demand I get a bloody move on or at least tell him what was going on. On the examination couch Christine was watching the curtains for movement. The atmosphere in my small clinic was electric. As the minutes ticked by I studied her resting face as it started to relax. And I realized something surprising. She had good bone structure. Once she must have been a beautiful woman, I thought, before she had been trodden down like the old black shoes which were now standing side by side on the floor underneath the examination couch. I looked again at her and thought I'd better play safe. Sometimes ECG changes take a while to manifest following a cardiac event. Richard Clay had already decided the surgery was incompetent. I couldn't risk being wrong and so I decided to refer her to the acute cardiac clinic at the hospital where they would check her troponin levels. If the second level was raised it would indicate some cardiac damage. If both levels were normal it would rule out a cardiac event.

I had my plan, Dr Gubb's warning still echoing in my ear.

Christine got dressed and quickly returned to the chair where she waited with anxious eyes searching the floor while her husband met mine with tighter lips and an even angrier expression.

I explained my plan, the thinking, pathology and evidence behind it. Christine took her cue from her husband, looking up at him, while his face grew increasingly angry. But, in spite of himself, when I explained the rationale behind the hospital referral, he nodded, and for the first time since I'd met him I saw a touch of humanity, which was when I allowed myself a very private smile and some reflection. Maybe I'd judged him too harshly. But then, reading the tension in his face, maybe it was *his* blood pressure I should be checking (I smothered a smile), preferably before he exploded.

I noted then that his eyes looked tired, his face worn out as though he was beginning to realize he was fighting a losing battle. Convincing someone they are well is more difficult than telling someone they really are ill. But we humans are resilient creatures and the defeated expression on his face was gone almost as soon as I'd identified it. I felt some fleeting sympathy for him until I observed the interaction between them: he turning to avoid her face, while she seemed to be begging him for something. Understanding? Sympathy? For the briefest of moments the room was silent, the atmosphere calmer. I wished I could wave a magic wand and preserve this peace, convince them to appreciate their advantages. They were in their sixties, financially stable. Whatever she thought, she had no real health problems. They were all imagined. I would have bet my last dollar that both troponin levels would be stable, any cardiac event disproved. They could easily have twenty and more years of good health ahead of them. Our psychologist might have an uphill job to convince them of this, but if she succeeded the rewards would be great. If there was an underlying psychiatric problem then Ruth Carroway was better positioned to deal with it than any ECGs, blood tests, MRIs, CTs or X-rays.

Richard Clay gave me a thin smile and a nod as I typed the referral letter. I took the blood test, labelled it with my note and gave it to him. 'They'll test this and then check the second reading at the hospital.'

While she was looking at me in a way I couldn't interpret, she actually patted my hand. 'Thank you, dear Florence.'

This time it was her husband who looked confused as he pulled her cardigan back over her shoulders and I was left to puzzle out her meaning.

Having seen them on their way to the hospital I wandered into the reception area and checked out the waiting times for Ruth. As I'd thought – three months minimum.

Underneath her diary she'd scrawled: *Unless there's a cancellation or it's really, really urgent*. With a creditable emoji of *The Scream*, hands over ears, mouth open and three exclamation marks.

NINE

1 p.m.

When Jalissa came with her sandwiches at lunchtime she could tell I was distracted. She gave me a little pat on my back. 'Somethin' disturbin' you, my friend?'

'Oh – just patients,' I responded, and took my time choosing my sandwiches because I felt I needed some time to return to normality after an unsettling morning.

I often worked through my lunch break, checking up on stores, filling in details on the computer, checking the patients on the chronic disease register had had the checks they were due, making sure none of our drugs had passed their use-by date. And then I made my silly mistake – I checked up yet again on the FB entries Rowena had shared.

More images of Vivien, side view on, so her enormous belly was exposed. Lots of little bootee emojis and the rest of the baby category: dummies, bottles and a nappy, but, as before, no mention or sign of Mark. So where was he? Taking the picture? I looked again. It looked more like a selfie to me, judging by the angle. Besides, in the early days all her posts had been of them both cuddling up, gazing adoringly – pukingly – into each other's eyes. So what was going on? Had he gone AWOL? He'd never been very keen on pregnancy 'and all that stuff', he'd growled when I had complained about his lack of involvement when I'd been expecting both Stuart and Lara. That had been over twenty years ago. Now he was in his fifties and I was pretty certain he'd be even less tolerant of the changing shape and demands of a pregnant woman. Looking at Vivien's triumphant face, I wondered. When he'd left me, at a guess, he'd anticipated lazy cruises in endless sunshine, flaunting his bikini-clad, much younger mistress. Not broken nights and baby wails, bottles and engorged breasts. Stretch marks. And he'd confided in me once, before the Vivien thing, he'd thought he'd like to do some voluntary work for an environmental charity. 'Something like Woodland Trust,' he'd said gruffly, embarrassed at such sentiment.

Well, no more now, my ex, I thought, with a touch of malice. You'll be working long past your colleagues' retirement ages. Kids need money and that means an income. There's also the small matter of another mortgage when ours on Endicott Terrace has no more than a couple of years to go. Forget lazy days or voluntary work. Think broken nights instead. And those ear-piercing baby wails.

I closed the site down. Maybe I would text Rowena and see if she knew why Mark wasn't in any of the pictures.

But then Catherine Zenger's voice whispered in my ear. *Stop stalking him, Flo. Cut him free, love. Let him go. Find yourself a new love.*

I took her advice and finally texted DC William Summers, trying to keep the tone jaunty and my mind away from Mark.

About that dinner. Offer still on? Fancy Thursday? I'm free.

I saw from the double ticks that the message had gone through and waited but he didn't ring or text back. And my call to Rowena went straight through to her answerphone. So no luck there either.

However, I did have one bit of good news from the hospital. Christine's second troponin level was plumb normal, which meant my instinct had been correct. No coronary event. Tagged on to the message was another welcome bit of news. Patient informed and sent home, so there was no need for any more contact or intervention on my part, though I suspected it wouldn't be long before we met again.

TEN

'd arranged to meet Catherine Zenger after work for a drink and a bite to eat at The Wharf, a recently refurbished arty pub at the top end of the town. I called for her at her flat and we walked up together, chatting. Since retiring Catherine had tried various pursuits to fill her time: helping out in a charity shop; volunteering to be an appropriate adult for the police; even taking a post as a teaching assistant at a local school. But the truth was she hadn't really found her place. 'I'm a nurse,' she'd said to me, rather sadly. 'Cut me in half and you'll find a bandage, an Elastoplast and antiseptic.' I felt her attempt at a joke held more than a touch of pathos. She added, 'I'm just no good at being anything else, Florence. That was my place in life.' Her words acted as a warning to the rest of us. Having lived a life being useful, sitting around, lotus-eating held no pleasure. But, post-retirement, this was where she'd found herself, drifting along life's course, aimless as a stream and uninspiring as a school dinner. A contrast to the brisk, busy person she'd been when I'd joined the practice, a little over ten years ago now. Then she'd been a bright, bustling, competent member of the team only too happy to share her wealth of knowledge and experience with her juniors. Now she just looked . . . sad.

So was I.

I was a little put out that DC William Summers hadn't phoned or texted back. He'd asked me out twice now and though each time I'd refused, I hadn't actually said no, only that I'd think about it. Surely he'd realize that it hadn't been an outright refusal – just a delay? And then I had another unwelcome thought: maybe he'd met someone else. Maybe he'd never really wanted a relationship. Maybe he'd just wanted a companion every now and then. I listened out for my phone but it remained silent. There was no doubt about it. I was being ignored. Never mind the fact that I'd ignored his invitation for a few weeks.

And so, on the walk up to The Wharf, I was disconsolate.

And, intuitive as ever, Catherine picked up on it. 'What's the matter, Flo?'

I tried to slide past her intuition, keep it general. 'Oh, I don't know. You know how sometimes things just don't seem to be working out?'

She nodded solemnly then perked up. We'd arrived at the double doors of The Wharf. She pushed them open with the flourish of a Hollywood star uttering an immortal line. 'What you need is a drink.'

So we bought a bottle of house red and perched at the high wooden table. Chat had always been easy between us and I relayed the events of the last few days and my concerns about Christine Clay.

'I remember Richard Clay,' she said. 'Tall, thin guy. Bloodless.' She gave a little chuckle. 'Reminded me of Count Dracula.' Now she was making a face. 'Those thin lips. That pale complexion.' She picked up the menu. 'Looked as though he could do with a nice juicy steak.' Then her forehead puckered. 'I don't really remember much about his wife. She was sort of . . . quiet?' She bent her head and studied the menu which made me wonder. Was she hiding something?

But I ploughed on. 'He hardly lets her get a word in. Answers all the questions for her. And whenever she comes to the surgery – which is often – he always comes with her.'

I shivered. Maybe it was the combination of Catherine's Dracula reference which made Richard seem suddenly sinister.

She made a face and poured us both another glass of wine. 'There's lots of couples like that. So what's the real problem?'

'That's the trouble,' I confessed. 'She's always at the surgery. Seems convinced there's something seriously wrong with her though.' I frowned. 'I don't know what's at the heart of it. And I'm not sure he's sympathetic. In fact, I think he makes her worse. Doubt herself.'

'Do you think you could be missing something?'

I shrugged. 'No. She's had every test under the sun. Scans, MRIs, CTs, blood tests – all coming back normal. If we are missing something pathological it's hiding beneath a stone.'

She and I looked at each other.

'And you know what?' I was experiencing some enlightenment. 'I get the feeling he sort of feeds on her insecurity. It makes him feel more—'

'Manly,' she put in and I nodded.

I searched for a less histrionic explanation. 'Or at the very least,' I ventured, 'he doesn't seem to want to reassure her. He just stands by, disapproving.'

'Hmm.' Her face took on the firm expression I remembered well before she proffered her opinion.

'It suits some guys to have a wife who's constantly ailing. Makes them feel good. They like the'– she scratched speech marks into the air – 'little wifey at home who does as she's told and sits in humble adoration of her man.'

I thought about this and it didn't fit. 'But she doesn't,' I observed.

'Doesn't what?'

'Look at him with adoration. She hardly looks at him at all.' And maybe I'd found the source of my unease. I realized Richard was impatient with his wife. But Christine? Submissive, yes. Beyond that I couldn't decipher her feelings. How did she feel about her husband? Was she intimidated by him? I wasn't sure. So I remained silent.

While Catherine watched me, her eyebrows raised in silent question, waiting for me to come to some conclusion.

'His dominance is almost pathological.'

She waited. 'He's denying her a voice.'

'Why would he?'

She stopped in her tracks. 'Frightened of what she might say?'

I remembered those words which had made me uneasy. *To be expected.* It had slipped out.

I felt thoughts dragging out of me and stared around the bar with its congenial atmosphere, people sharing jokes and conversations, eating, drinking. Friends, family. 'I think . . . I think . . .' My thoughts had seemed to catch on something I couldn't put into words.

And so I sidetracked. 'I guess that's the relationship they've sort of fallen into,' I said, and she looked a bit sad. Catherine's marriage had ended long ago. I'd never even known Mr Zenger; she never talked about him. The name, I knew, was German, but there are some things you don't ask. Sometimes it's better to bury the past deep and not dig it up. Let grass and flowers grow over it.

We looked at each other. The conversation seemed to have stalled and so I returned to the subject of the Clays and their uneven marriage.

'Jordan Bannister is referring Christine to a psychologist.'

'Hmm.' She tossed her head dismissively. 'Nice way to put her on the back burner. She'll wait for ever.'

'Minimum three months.'

'And what good will that do?' She took a large swig from her wine glass then continued with a wry look. 'Get her off his back. That's what. So how are you getting on with Dr Gubb's replacement?'

We descended to our common ground – the GP practice.

I looked around me. The Wharf was a comfortable hotch-potch of random, almost hippy taste and avant-garde design, bits acquired from a reclamation centre, all pieced together to provide a unique, comfortable atmosphere. There were doors reclaimed from men's toilets, bits of an old theatre, stained-glass windows from pubs, pointing the way to long gone smoking rooms and pool bars juxtaposed with arched windows depicting saints. Built on the site of the old Joule's brewery, whoever had finally put it together was either a genius or slightly mad according to your point of view. Certainly the effect was bohemian. In the centre was a huge log burner, not lit at the moment but wonderfully warm and cosy in the winter, heating both sides, front and back. And, judging by the filled benches and queue at the bar, it was popular. The place to be if you found yourself near Junction 14 of the M6. It even had a terrace which bordered the canal – much to the annoyance of the folk who had bought expensive properties across the water.

Catherine had picked up on my reluctance. 'You don't like Dr Bannister, do you?'

I confided in her my feeling that he was more involved in the business side of things than the health of his patients. She listened then pressed her lips together in a flat, prissy line. 'It didn't used to be the way,' she said. 'In my day doctors stuck to their medicine. Their role wasn't to balance the books. That's what a practice manager's for.'

I made a weak defence. 'You can't blame them for wanting to watch where the money's going.'

'Ah,' she said, and with that unhelpful comment I changed the subject.

ELEVEN

10 p.m.

One drink had led to two and two to three. It was getting late by the time I was walking home. I'd gone to Catherine's flat and waited while she'd let herself in. She was nervous about being out in the evenings alone and as she'd had a few drinks I thought I'd better do the right thing. Chivalrous or what? I was smirking as I retraced my steps and headed back up the High Street towards home.

Outside The Crown there was a huddle of young guys but they were too engrossed in what looked like a heated argument to take any notice of me. They were shoving each other in the chest in the way that easily escalates into a fight. Without turning my head I gave a surreptitious glance at them, checking whether Ryan was somewhere in the group but, without prolonging my stare and drawing attention to myself, I couldn't be sure. Even though they didn't seem to have noticed me I quickened my step and was glad to reach home.

Living in a cul-de-sac someone always notices your comings and goings. You can do nothing without being observed. Tonight it was Marianne Winters, the sixty-something-year-old lady who still blamed me for failing to resuscitate her husband after a heart attack that proved fatal. She managed to give me a disapproving look, pulling her top lip down, as though she knew I'd been drinking, before snapping the curtains shut. I felt like sticking two fingers up at her and exaggerating a stagger, but I restrained myself. I remembered one of the introductory talks from my student-nurse years: a nurse should always keep her composure. Through fatalities, haemorrhages, sudden death and . . . disapproval, I'd tacked on the end.

I felt like patting myself on the back for my restraint when I finally let myself in and flopped on to the sofa. That was when I pulled out my phone, realizing out of politeness to Catherine (who was no great fan of conversations interrupted by pinging texts) I'd set it on silent. I'd missed three calls – two from DC Summers and one from PC Rowena Bartlett, no doubt responding to my call and bringing me up to date on the Mark/Vivien latest. Neither of them had left a message and it was too late to ring back now, so I was left to use my imagination. I felt deflated as well as curious. By not responding again to his texts William Summers would think I was playing a childish game of hard-to-get or rather push-me-pull-you. I kicked my shoes off and stared at my phone, realizing there were too many pitfalls in this middle-aged/social media dating game. And I wasn't absolutely sure I was up to it. I'd have to square things up with William Summers. I'd ring him back in the morning, maybe during my coffee break.

TWELVE

Tuesday 26 September, midday

The first part of the morning had dragged even though Sebastian Timor, the surgery pin-up, asked me (very nicely) if I could possibly squeeze in a couple of extra patients who needed urgent blood tests to save them having to make a double journey. *Pretty please?* Who could resist that charm? I batted my eyelashes at him and he gave me one of his dazzling Hollywood smiles. I felt reimbursed even though one of the patients had invisible and impalpable veins! However, by being patient and asking her to hold her arm down, I struck enough red gold to fill a couple of sample bottles. So I had had a busy morning but eventually twelve o'clock crawled around when, without any idea what I was going to say, I summoned up the courage to call William Summers back.

He responded straight away which set me off babbling, apologizing first for not having picked up his call yesterday, spending too much time explaining I'd been out with a friend and had left the phone on silent. When I'd finished there was a brief, awkward silence between us until he prompted me gently in a voice that I was sure harboured a smile. 'So? Dinner, Florence?'

I felt immediately calmed and responded with dignity but not too much enthusiasm. 'That would be really nice, Will.'

'Good. Tomorrow? There's a nice Thai at the bottom of the High Street.' I picked up on the warmth and enthusiasm in his voice. 'We can probably walk it from your place.'

Immediately I had the picture of us walking together down the High Street, hand in hand, pushing open the door of the restaurant to the sound and smells of Thai cooking, replacing the ghost of my last visit there, when Mark had broken the news of his affair. It was a nice image but, without recognizing the reason, I substituted, 'I'll meet you there.'

'OK,' he said slowly, but I'd heard an edge of disappointment. Maybe he had shared that very same hand-in-hand vision. I even felt a moment's regret, particularly when he said, 'Eight o'clock all right for you?' And it registered that a little coldness had crept into his voice, like a draught under the door. We hadn't even met up and already I was spoiling things.

When Jalissa came, she could see I was down in the mouth, doubting myself. And in her warm-hearted way, without asking what was wrong, she put her arm around me.

I looked into her dark eyes with their pretty, curling lashes and shook my head. 'This dating game is a tricky one,' I said, and she nodded in sympathy.

'I know. The marriage one not too simple either.'

'Don't tell me you and Brett are having problems?'

At which she threw back her head and gave one of her great belly laughs, mouth so wide I could see a pair of healthy tonsils. 'No,' she roared. 'But I missin' the kids.'

I tried to console her. 'They're only at school for a few hours on weekdays,' I said, and she nodded before her face grew grave. 'But the lonely day, it seems twice as long.'

And now it was she who needed consoling.

'I think I need somethin' more to fill up my time, Florence.'

'Good idea.' I was pleased she was tackling this in a positive way.

I had a couple of visits that afternoon and when I put my radio on I caught the lunchtime news. The lead story was about a woman whose abusive partner had finally murdered her. The details were chilling enough; the recriminations would be picked over right up until another sad story replaced it. There were criticisms of the way the police had handled the multiple callouts; a psychiatrist gave his opinion on abusive marriages, controlling partners – both male and female – and the failure of the general public, family and in particular health professionals to either pick up on the gravity of the problem and protect a vulnerable person. Which brought me straight back to the Clays and my assessment of the pathology in their relationship as well as my own responsibility, as a health care professional, for a woman I perceived as being vulnerable.

Which pulled me up short. Was Christine Clay vulnerable? Was her husband's controlling behaviour just the tip of the iceberg? Was she being abused at home, mentally or even physically? Or was I reading too much into this? Searching for a hidden drama?

And there my prosaic, rational mind started going round in circles. Richard Clay was domineering and controlling. He wasn't a killer or a psychopath. His wife was not in any danger.

Surely?

All the same, when I left the surgery for my visits, I found myself driving along the Newcastle Road, slowing down as I passed the Clays' house. It was a lovely house, one of those big, Victorian semis which have huge numbers of bedrooms, cellars and spacious attics, high ceilings and are endowed with so many of the features one doesn't get in a modern house – or in a 1940s semi, as mine was. The Clays' house looked well kept with a shiny old black Mercedes standing in the gravelled drive, at the end of which was a brick garage (obviously a later addition). I stopped for a moment. The trees partly hid the front door from view but I still slowed down which was when I saw Richard Clay emerge. He stood on the front doorstep before walking towards the road and looking up and down, as though he was waiting for someone. I shrank into my driving seat trusting he wouldn't recognize my car. I watched him for a moment and wondered. What are you up to, Mr Clay? Who are you waiting

for? After standing there for a little while he turned on his heel
and went back into the house. Even from the other side of the
road I could sense the vibrations when he slammed the door with
a force that would have provoked a comment from my mother:
Temper Temper. I added this physicality to my opinion of him.
It hadn't been simple anger that had been behind the door slam.
It had been fury. And now that the door was closed and the house
again presented its elegant exterior to the world I drove off with
a greater understanding of why Christine seemed so cowed by
her husband.

One of my visits that afternoon was to Sophie Ward, who had
multiple sclerosis. Her whole house (bungalow actually) had been
transformed into a sort of spaceship with a track for the hoist
leading almost everywhere, from bathroom to kitchen, sitting
room to conservatory. Sophie Ward had full-time carers and was
heartbreakingly only in her early fifties. She was a pale lady with
thick, dark hair. How she remained cheerful I had absolutely no
idea. Her husband had abandoned her soon after her diagnosis
and had gone on to have a family with his new wife, something
which, she'd confided in me, had broken her heart even more
than her diagnosis and his abandonment. 'It is my greatest regret,'
she'd said, tears forming in her eyes, 'that I have no children.
They would have eased my burden, you see, Florence.'
    I'd nodded and kept private the details of my own unsatisfac-
tory marital state and parenthood. Sophie had two consolations
and one dread. Her consolations were, firstly, her books. She
loved reading, audio versions and downloads as well as paper
books which had to be held up by a stand and the pages flipped
automatically by a blink. Through books, she'd confided in me
more than once, she escaped to lands where she was young and
healthy, beautiful and desired, was surrounded by quiverful of
beautiful children and, deep into the pages she grew wings and
flew to far-off countries, both real and imagined, and faced all
sorts of situations over which she almost always triumphed. I
knew lots of people who enjoyed books, attended book clubs,
author sessions and library events. But I had never known any
of these people to fold themselves so absolutely between the
pages of a book.

Her second consolation was a Siamese cat she'd named Tuptim after a character in *The King & I* and who spent her days either purring, curled up on her lap, or else prowling around the garden as though on guard for her mistress. Tuptim was a fussy feline, as haughty, dignified and pugnacious as a Korean bodyguard. It had taken her a while to tolerate me. For my first few visits, her back had arched and her eyes, as bright and blue as Burmese sapphires, had glared at me with unmistakable hostility. These days she usually gave a dismissive flick of her tail and turned her back on me, which I interpreted as showing indifference. Simple toleration. I usually visited Sophie on a Wednesday afternoon, ostensibly to check up on her pressure areas. But I didn't want too much work tomorrow. I had a date, I thought excitedly, and so I wanted to get home in time to wash my hair and have a shower. I'd changed my visiting day to today. I had a cup of tea with her and we exchanged gossip, largely innocuous chat about the practice and various businesses in the town while she shared some sad details of her latest book, *A Fine Balance*. 'The tragedy of some really poor folk in India, when Indira Gandhi introduced her Special Measures,' she said, her eyes filling with tears. 'Sometimes my life seems comfortable.' She gave a brave smile. 'It depends who you compare your lot to.'

Which set me thinking. She was right and, considering her actual circumstances, I usually left her bungalow feeling uplifted and strangely happy. She was an inspiration. But occasionally her inner sadness mingled with the fiction. I'd caught a glimpse of it before she smothered it with one of her signature smiles. Not before I'd seen it in her eyes, a slight droop of the lids, as though it was an effort to hold her eyes open, a quick couple of blinks to disperse a tear and a brief break in eye contact as though she didn't want me to read her inner self. 'Not today' her physiognomy told me, and I respected that. But the pall of sadness had surrounded me too, so I also felt bleak. Right up until I reached my car and remembered. I had a date tomorrow night.

Suddenly I felt like skipping.

THIRTEEN

Wednesday 27 September, 3 p.m.

Surgery seemed tedious that afternoon, each patient's problems mundane. My mind was fixed on my date tonight and the banishment of the ghost Mark had left when he'd used our favourite restaurant to confess his affair with the buck-toothed harpy aka Vivien Morris.

In the end it was Ryan – his usual swagger slightly less showy – who made the day marginally more interesting.

He'd turned up late for his two thirty appointment but made no apology for keeping me waiting, simply sliding into the chair. He tried one of his signature grins but it lacked depth and there was no corresponding cockiness in his eyes. Only a faint anxiety illustrated by the frown that lay between his eyebrows and a certain thoughtfulness.

He pulled up his sleeve displaying the wound which he'd covered with a grubby Elastoplast. I peeled it off gently. I've never been in favour of ripping dressings off. Anyone else would have acquired an infection with such poor hygiene but Ryan Wood must have had a robust immune system. It had healed perfectly and I couldn't help a small twinge of pride when I noted my neat little stitches. I looked up to smile at him, quite expecting him to agree with my comment of 'nice work'. But he was twitching, staring at the opposite wall, and he looked like the frightened little boy he really was. I often forgot how very young he was – early twenties – but with his life experiences it didn't count for much. He was streetwise but didn't really have the resilience, the intelligence, or the family support he'd have needed to survive on his own. He lived intermittently with his alcoholic mother, Celine, who had a succession of boyfriends – all of whom took her for a ride, squeezing money and favours out of her before dumping her. While Ryan looked young and innocent for his age, his mother looked what she was – a world weary alcoholic of the indeterminate age of the heavy smoker with poor nutrition, a bit of a drug habit and a daily alcohol intake measured in bottles rather than glasses. And yet, buried deep underneath, Celine Wood was someone quite different. On the rare occasions when she had, with professional help, temporarily dried out, she displayed a rather sweet, kind, naive nature not unlike her son. But then she always fell back into the bad, unhealthy, life-limiting habits too deeply ingrained to escape from. One day, I feared, she would be found dead at the bottom of the canal or in some city or town street. Somewhere insalubrious. Possibly with a knife sticking out of her. Celine was a woman who attracted the worst responses.

As I removed the stitches, Ryan didn't flinch but kept his eyes fixed on me rather than his arm. When I'd finished and put a dry dressing over it, I was about to advise him to keep it covered for a day or two when, hesitatingly, he started to speak. 'Nurse Florence,' he said, 'your husband's a policeman, isn't he?'

'Ex-husband,' I responded automatically, without really thinking. I was clearing away the debris: stitch cutter into the sharps box and the other dressings bagged and into the bin.

'Ex?' he queried, sounding disappointed. 'So you aren't in touch then . . .?' His voice dwindled away.

That was when I finally looked at him. 'Ryan,' I said, 'what's up?'

He took a long deep breath and was about to speak when there was a sharp knock on the door and Jordan Bannister poked his head round. 'Got a minute, Flo?'

And the moment melted away. Ryan was already shrugging his jacket back on. He gave me a hesitant, apologetic glance, then left.

I gave Jordan my full attention. 'So what is it?' I could have added 'that's so important you have to interrupt a consultation?' but I didn't.

'Flu vaccines,' he said, his voice tense and focussed. 'How many have we ordered?'

It was hardly an urgent matter though I realized to him it was. We order and pay for flu vaccines and, provided we use them *all* on the eligible patients, we make a hefty profit.

However, if some slip through the guidelines or are not used at all, those profits quickly dwindle. And Dr Jordan Bannister, with his business brain ever active, would not like that.

As usual, it was a financial concern.

FOURTEEN

7 p.m.

I had an hour to prepare for my 'date'. Even using the word made me nervous even when I scolded myself. 'You're not fourteen, Florence. You're middle-aged and any illusions you might have had about romance turned out to be proved fairy tales, didn't they? All froth and no cappuccino. So just enjoy the evening but don't get your hopes up.'

I'd already decided what I'd wear. Nothing too smart. After all, this was a meal in a local restaurant. Not a night out in Sloane Square. But I still wanted to look my best. And so I kept my make-up subtle, spent some time tidying my bob and slipped on a pair of black Moschino trousers I'd splashed out on when we'd had a backdated pay rise last year and which were *very* flattering, particularly in the waist and bottom area. I twirled around in front of my full cheval mirror and was glad I'd foregone my lunchtime cake for almost a week. I wouldn't exactly class myself as svelte but neither could I describe myself as podgy middle-aged. I teamed the trousers up with a blue silk blouse with a pussy bow at the neck and black ankle boots with thick, black, high heels which would just about support the walk to and from the restaurant. Over that I wore a red jacket and was ready in plenty of time. A brisk walk would see me arrive bang on time. Even in heels I can move fast when I want to.

7.45 p.m.

I walked down through the town, stepping past the shops I knew so well; the same shops which line every High Street in almost every town: B&M, Superdrug, Boots the Chemist. Hairdressers, barbers and a few other individual shops which seemed to change hands every couple of years as though they'd tried – hard – and then, slowly realizing there *was* no passing custom, they yawned their way into a Closing Soon sale and then the To Let signs went back up. It was that quiet time in the evening. Workers gone home, pub drinkers not out yet, the streets empty as people had headed homeward for their tea. My steps echoed on the pavement, my reflection the only movement as I passed darkened shop windows. Stone's High Street felt more like a ghost town, the opening credits of a spooky film scrolling up, I the sole actress in the drama. An evening breeze swept up the pedestrianized area, keeping me cool in spite of my brisk pace. As I passed Joule's clock its hands moved towards eight. I managed to arrive at the Thai restaurant just as it chimed and felt a ridiculous pride in my punctuality(I have a sad obsession with time-keeping). Will was already there, standing outside the restaurant, somehow managing to look as though he wasn't waiting for anyone in particular but was simply loitering. He gave me a wide grin as I approached and to my relief didn't fall back on any cliché, like 'you look nice'. The grin was enough. It contained warmth and a certain sincerity which no words could supply and I wondered why I'd hesitated at sharing an evening with him. He had followed the same dress rule as I: smart casual in navy chinos, leather loafers and a dark green sweatshirt. Hmm, I thought, sweeping my gaze from head to foot before returning his smile with a grin of my own.

'Hi,' he said, and I felt the warmth of his greeting as he kissed me very gently on the cheek. It marked the beginning of an evening which promised, for the first time, to live up to my fantasy, at the same time setting a stamp on the evening. This. Was. A. Date.

I felt unaccountably happy and contented, suddenly realizing how different the rules were for middle-aged 'dating'. It felt comfortable with none of the affectations that can mar evenings shared when you're younger. I took a deep breath in as I felt any awkwardness melting away. I was going to enjoy the evening. It felt like a new start.

He kissed my cheek again, gave me an even broader grin and held the door open. 'Hungry?'

I understood then that his emotions were mirroring mine.
I nodded.

He'd booked a table which proved unnecessary as few people were eating out midweek and we sat down and pretended to study the menu rather than each other. When I looked up from the menu he was looking at me, his eyes bright with fun. 'Sorry,' he said. 'I am so unused to this, errm, dating thing.'

'Me too,' I confessed. 'It's been a while.' I gave one of those mock laughs, the sound you make when you don't know what to say and the humour hasn't quite hit.

He was still watching me. 'I've hardly seen you out of uniform and never looking so . . . .' He was searching for the word. 'Glamorous.'

'Glamorous?' I queried.

He nodded, repeating the word firmly, 'Yes, glamorous.'

I was narrowing my eyes as I regarded him, but he met my suspicions with a smile which looked genuine.

We chose our food, a selection of dishes to taste and dipped into them, commenting as we sampled them, balancing each mouthful with chopsticks. He chose a Thai beer while I had a glass of something less exotic, a Spanish Rioja. And gradually I felt myself relax as he asked me about my job which I fended off with some surgery anecdotes (anonymous, of course) while he talked about his role in the police, currently car parts stolen to order and various other traffic related offences. To be honest it sounded a bit boring to me, but then Mark used to say that police work was that: ninety-nine per cent boring; one per cent Action Man. And after the Action Man back to ninety-nine per cent filling out forms, justifying your actions and answering question after question after question . . .

We skirted around our personal histories although I knew he already knew about Mark and me. Gossip would have been rife around the station. I even confided in him a little of the hurt I had felt when Mark had finally confessed, on the verge of telling him we were at the very site of his confession. The same Thai restaurant, though a different table.

We turned to *his* past. '*You* haven't been snatched up by a fellow officer?' I'd tried to make it sound like a tease but it didn't. It sounded exactly what it was – a probing question made by someone who was wondering just how far this 'friendship' might go.

Luckily for me and my integrity William Summers treated it as a casual enquiry, without any hidden agenda, shaking his head without regret. 'No,' he said. 'I've escaped the noose.' It was the first misstep of the evening. I felt my face darkening. I don't like men who describe marriage as a noose.

Perhaps sensing my reaction to his comment, he retrieved it. 'Not that I think of marriage as a noose,' he said quickly, 'at least not when it's to the right person.' He took a big swig of beer and frowned into the neck of the bottle, speaking into it. 'I was in a long-term relationship,' he said before taking another swig and sighing. 'I have no idea how or why it lasted so long.' He was looking past me now, studying the gaudy pictures of scarlet and gold dragons and tigers that festooned the walls. 'She kept nagging me to do something else, something other than policing. More money, regular hours, something more glamorous. And I always felt' – another swig – 'inadequate.'

I couldn't stop myself. 'That's horrible. I think I'd almost rather go through what Mark and I had. At least we had *some* happy years before it all sprung apart. And we did have two children.'

'Oh yes.' He brightened up. 'Children. Tell me about them.'

I smiled. 'Stuart and Lara. Not exactly children anymore and they have their own lives.'

'And that's a bad thing?' He looked curious, interested in my response without being judgmental. His face was bright, engaged.

'No. No. Of course not.' Now it was I who was retrieving a hidden meaning. 'It's a good thing.'

'But?'

That one syllable forced me out in the open. 'I don't see much of them.'

Those toffee brown eyes were looking straight into mine and I knew he read it all, the phone calls that never came, the birthday cards that arrived a few days late, if at all, the drop-by visits or lack of invitations to spend a weekend with them. 'And that's something you regret.' It was a statement not an interrogation. And it deserved an honest answer.

I nodded. 'I wish . . .' I began but couldn't finish. I suddenly felt choked up, a little over emotional, strange and off-kilter. We'd finished our food and reached an odd sort of hiatus in the evening where we looked at each other and didn't quite know how to end the night. I stood up and made the suggestion. 'It would be nice to walk back through the town.'

He nodded and I sensed his relief joining my own.

He paid the bill (no going Dutch for him), and as we emerged out on to the street I slipped my hand into his. It felt natural. Together we headed back up the deserted High Street.

Not quite deserted. There was the same bunch of guys gathered in the market square halfway up the High Street. I sensed William's (I still hadn't worked out what to call him) tension. His hand gripped mine and, looking at him, I saw his eyes, but not his head, slide left. I'd seen Mark do the same when he'd noted something: a girl alone, a guy following too closely; a group of potential troublemakers; a loiterer whose eyes seemed to be searching for easy prey; a drug taker out of control; a child too young to wander far from an adult; the sound of a car alarm. It was as though his, and now William's, antennae went up and quivered in the proximity of anticipated crime. I said nothing but stored it away because I *had* turned my head and seen, at the centre of the pushing, shoving, snarling group of men whose body language indicated pure aggression, Ryan Wood.

Neither Will nor I mentioned it though I knew we had both noticed the same thing. William walked me all the way home with no mention of where he'd left his car or where he actually lived. I didn't invite him in. Too soon for that and we parted with another chaste kiss – again on my cheek, a simple brush of his lips against my skin.

As he turned to walk away (watched by neighbour Penny, who was staring anxiously out of the window – probably having thrown Darryl out yet again), William said, 'Shall we do this again?'

I nodded and the date was sealed.

FIFTEEN

M y next encounter with Christine Clay was the oddest of all. In fact, it was probably the strangest encounter I have ever had with a patient. It was as though there was a disconnect between us. It came on the back of a quiet and contemplative lunch break. Maybe sparked by William's question about my children, I'd spent time thinking about my family. In particular, remembering how I'd felt when Lara, then Stuart, had finally left home. The memories had been further stirred by Jalissa's disconsolate face when she'd brought in her basket of sandwiches and flopped into the chair at the side of my desk.

'Still missing the children?'

She nodded, two fat tears rolling down her cheeks. 'I just wait for home time, Florence. House is so quiet I can hardly bear to be inside.'

'But surely you're busy making sandwiches all day and then out delivering them?'

'Yeah.' She lifted a mournful face to mine. 'But Charles, he pass me the containers from the fridge and Petronella she dance and sing to me when she home. House is too quiet,' she said again.

All I could do was nod in sympathy.

We were interrupted by a knock on the door and a face peered round. 'Florence.' It was Darcey. Darcey was one of our newer receptionists. She was around sixty and hadn't really settled into her role as doctors' receptionist. She simply didn't know what to do when confronted with almost any situation. At times she booked in patients, adding them into already overbooked surgeries. At others she was aggressive, inviting complaints from the other side of the hatch. She'd previously worked in a bank where, possibly, her attitude was appropriate or at least in proportion to customers' requests. But the High Street bank had closed and she had been left jobless and couldn't afford to coast her way to retirement. 'Not if I want to eat,' she'd said to me on one occasion when I'd witnessed her dealing with a stroppy, distraught mother who was furious she'd had to bring her two-year-old to the surgery rather than have the doctor visit.

I'd watched her face up to the young mum, crushed by the amount of aggression that was being directed at her. I did feel sorry for her. Life had kicked sand in her face when she'd been unable to change course. It wasn't her fault she'd lost her job. She'd had the choice of redundancy pay or switch to the Stafford branch but she didn't drive; her husband was on long-term sick leave following a Covid infection and her pay grade had been such that her redundancy pay wouldn't exactly fund a pleasant lifestyle. They'd have to watch every penny. And so she had taken the job at the surgery where her manner wasn't helped by a thin, reedy voice that bleated of inadequacy. Maybe that had held her back in her bank career too.

Jalissa stood up. 'Best be goin',' she said. She picked up her lunch basket and shot out through the door. Gone inside of a second.

'So?' I said pleasantly to Darcey. 'What's the problem?' Because it always was a problem.

'It's Mrs Clay.'

At which my ears pricked up. 'What about Mrs Clay?'

'She's come to the front desk and is asking to see you.' She corrected the statement resentfully. '*Demanding* to see you. Now.'

'With her husband?'

Darcey shook her head. 'On her own.'

That was when my pulse quickened. 'Did she say what it was about?'

'No.'

'OK,' I responded. 'I'll see her.'

One never knew about these walk-ins. Most of the time they were nothing that couldn't have waited – and waited – but just occasionally people arrived with a serious condition. Christine Clay had a long history of spurious consultations but Dr Gubb's words of advice rang in my ears. One could never afford to stop listening, particularly with patients already classed as frequent attenders. And if she was alone it might be the perfect opportunity to unravel some of my curiosity about the relationship with her husband which I'd already judged toxic.

Maybe without her husband answering my questions I would learn something of the real Christine Clay. But even I couldn't have foreseen the flavour of our encounter.

'But first, get her old notes out, will you, Darcey?'

These days most of our consultations were detailed on the computer using the classifications of the Read Code symptom followed by free text. But sometimes, buried deep in a patient's past medical history, was something that defied the straightjacket of a Read Code and had slipped through the records' transfer on to a computer without being detailed. Computers work in algorithms and logical straight lines but there are times when human thought bends round corners. Sometimes significant secrets lay hidden behind these sharp corners – a clue as to why the patient you saw before you was as they were.

Moments later there was another knock on the door and Darcey handed me a thick Lloyd George envelope. I didn't have time to study them now. That would have to wait till later. I asked Darcey to call Christine Clay in.

The first thing that struck me was the fact that her knock was hard, decisive, a quick staccato knuckle rap.

I stood up and opened the door and immediately sensed something else different about her. Not something else. Everything else. She even smelt different, not of old clothes long hung in a wardrobe but of perfume.

She was standing tall, not folded over. Dressed tidily in a red jacket over a loose, dark dress and leather loafers; her face in minimal make-up looked alert. She followed me into the clinic room, seeming to appraise me, before she apologized and sat down. 'I'm sorry to bother you.'

I simply nodded and waited and she corrected the sentence to: 'I'm sorry to *keep* bothering you but . . .'

I waited, saying nothing, but she didn't complete the sentence so it was left to me.

'It seems to me, Mrs Clay, we're not quite getting to the bottom of your problems.'

It was a good opening comment, leaving opportunity wide open.

She opened her eyes wide, put her head on one side. 'But you are. You have.'

She was watching me. And for once I didn't know what to say.

'You've all been so kind,' she said. 'I wanted to thank you.'

That was where the disconnect began. 'But . . .' It was unusual for me to flounder. I wanted to ask her, *We have?*

'I don't sleep too well but' – again her expression changed and she repeated the phrase that had jarred previously – 'only to be expected, I suppose.' Her face assumed a jolly look.

I tried to make a connection. 'Well, if you're worried it can often have that effect. Trouble sleeping, I mean.'

'Exactly. But in a way wakefulness gives us a time to reflect.'

I was thinking, *What's brought you here today?* I tried to steer the consultation round. 'So is it sleeping pills you're asking for because—' I was about to say, because I'm unable to prescribe sleeping tablets but can put in a request to your doctor if you like, but she forestalled me with another odd phrase.

'Sleeping tablets won't really help, will they, in my condition?'

Now I was truly confounded. *What condition?* Instead I found myself in the odd position of defending hypnotics.

'They can be really useful. A decent night's sleep can be restorative.'

But in my eyes she looked alert rather than tired. Almost keyed up. To hide my confusion I studied her list of medication on the computer – past as well as current. She'd *never* been prescribed anxiolytics, sedatives or hypnotics so I tried a spot of therapy instead.

'Is anything specific preying on your mind?'

She stared at me, eyes open wide. 'Of course there is.' She actually had a soft, pleasant voice but now she sounded exasperated.

'May I ask what?'

She gave a huff of a disbelieving laugh and shook her head. 'Look,' she said, 'you're very kind. Really kind. I knew you'd see me today because . . .' She didn't finish the sentence but patted my hand. 'But really, Florence. You don't have to pretend.'

I was at a loss now. 'Mrs Clay. Pretend what?'

Something inside her seemed to snap. She sucked in an angry breath, glaring at me at the same time as her face screwed up, her cheeks reddening. She stood up. 'I can't play this any longer,' she said, visibly angry now. '*You* know and *I* know.'

I was at a complete loss but, feeling anything I said would further inflame her, I said nothing and waited, simply watching her.

'If you can't prescribe me something to make things easier . . .'

I picked up the thread. 'What things?'

She stared at me, hostility beaming out of her. 'I can't play these games,' she said.

'Mrs Clay,' I responded realizing now was the perfect time to introduce the subject. 'I'm not authorized to prescribe anything to help you sleep. I did discuss your problems with your doctor, Dr Bannister. He wondered if some therapy with a clinical psychologist might help. Has he contacted you about this?'

She didn't answer my question and was positively incensed now, breathing hard. 'And that'll cure me?'

I was confused, unable to understand the phrase. Cure her of what?

But I knew I had to tread carefully. Christine Clay was angry. And I had no doubt that her husband was perfectly capable of picking up the cudgel. So this was where the consultation finally dissolved. I made one more futile attempt to regain balance.

'Ruth Carroway is an experienced clinical psychologist who holds counselling sessions here once a month. She's helped lots of our patients who have had long-term problems. I really think she might be able to help,' I said gently.

But she was leaning over me, her hand gripping my arm. 'You really believe that?' There was pure hostility beaming out of her now. I was so taken aback I couldn't respond. And I still had no idea why she'd insisted on seeing me today.

But I backed down. 'I'll have a word with your doctor,' I said weakly. 'See if he has any other suggestions.'

'Thank you.' Her voice was back to normal now: polite, soft, quiet, almost submissive. She dropped her head while I stared at her, trying to get a fix on this woman who morphed from victim to bully and back to victim again. Somehow I'd lost the sense that I knew this woman. Or rather these two women. I studied her, disorientated.

I thought I'd had a handle on her but I understood now that I hadn't. Underneath that quiet woman, dominated by a controlling husband, was someone who fizzed full of misconceptions, resentment and a lack of understanding. I now realized I'd been fumbling all along. I didn't know this patient at all.

She gave me a strange smile, almost condescending, putting her face close to mine. 'My husband,' she said, giving another of those strange, disconnected, floating smiles. 'He's quite a dominating presence.'

'A strong personality,' I agreed, tiptoeing along the tightrope.

'Yes,' she said. 'You could call it that. Goodbye.' Her voice now was light and airy.

I decided then that I would speak to Ruth Carroway myself and try and expedite Jordan Bannister's referral. I felt we could not afford to waste any time. Something strange was going on and that same instinct urged me to hurry things along. Something was buried deep in this woman's mind and it was causing a troubling conviction. If Ruth could unearth it maybe Christine Clay and her husband could mend.

Or at least reach a detente.

After she'd left I sat, motionless for a few moments, trying to make sense of one of the strangest consultations I had ever experienced. Somewhere, I felt I'd missed something vital. She'd been trying to tell me something but I hadn't understood. The way I interpreted it then was this. She believed she had some serious pathology that we were either failing to unearth or alternatively were refusing to be open with her. These convictions, however bizarre and unfounded, can be deep-seated and gnaw away at a person's health and psyche until the patient can be disabused. But . . . normal tests and results have no impact. The patient can never trust them because they have an explanation that prevents them from trusting the health professionals. We hadn't requested the right tests, they weren't detailed enough, they had been performed wrongly – the wrong solution of dye in contrast media, the wrong setting on the X-ray machine, insufficient detail on the request form. The list was endless.

They knew; everyone else was wrong.

It's unusual but I have met this situation before. Ruth Carroway was the perfect response. The only possible response.

What puzzled me was trying to work out what role her husband played in this complicated and unsatisfactory game. His anger and irritation had registered. And now it was Richard I was curious about. He was an intelligent man. What was his take on his wife's condition? What was he trying to achieve by taking over her responses? Was this his way of trying to convince his wife she was well – or was he contributing to her misplaced conviction? Feeding her belief that she was in fact ill and we were failing to be honest with her?

I wished I could ask him.

Straight.

I was listless for the rest of the afternoon, unable to properly focus on anything. I realized I'd jumped from one conclusion to another. Initially I'd pitied poor downtrodden Mrs Clay, this silent victim. But now I didn't know whether her husband had in fact been shielding her. I did wonder whether she might be an atypical case of Alzheimer's, displaying symptoms not primarily of memory loss, but neuroticism. Had he been accompanying her to the surgery in the hope that we would identify her mental state and treat it? Was his overbearing intervention really a mark of desperation?

How the pendulum swings. To and fro. Now it was Richard Clay I was feeling sorry for.

At three o'clock I had a break in my clinic which gave a chance to read through her last few consultations on the computer before delving deeper into her paper notes, trying to find a clue. But her past seemed pretty normal. There were scattered consultations with Dr Gubb. Nothing excessive. The usual complaints: a sprained ankle, persistent headaches, a tetanus shot after she'd pricked her finger on a well-manured rose bush. It wasn't until I searched right back into her childhood that I found anything remotely unusual. At the age of ten, in the 1960s, Christine Pastor (as she had been then) had moved to Staffordshire following the death of her father. There was no mention of how he'd died. The original address on her notes was a street in one of the South Wales mining valleys. The move to Staffordshire had been when she was ten, so she had lost a parent and moved location. Double disruption. There was no mention of any siblings. However, Pastor was an unusual surname, presumably once indicating a connection with the church. Her mother's name had been Melody. Melody Pastor, I mused. What a pretty, resonant name. And unusual. I typed the name Melody Pastor into a search engine. But it was the same problem. Someone has to have fed the information online in the first place. Nothing came up. Wondering if something dark lay in my patient's past which would explain her strange mental state, I tapped in the name Christine Pastor, adding the area in South Wales where she had lived as a child. But there was nothing there either. And yet, like a dog who smells a bone, I sensed there was something. Some reason why Richard Clay formed a fence of thorns around his wife. And again, I came full circle. Had I misunderstood the whole drama? The pendulum swung once more. Rather than bullying her, had he been protecting her?

From . . . ? And here I completely ran out of ideas.

Because that last, strange consultation had turned everything on its head. I'd judged him controlling but Christine, without her husband speaking up for her, had seemed, if anything, even more damaged. Had I done *him* a disservice?

Not for the first time, I wished Dr Gubb had not retired.

I wandered into the reception area and found Ann Barnett, one of the receptionists who had been with the practice almost since its inception. 'Do you have a telephone number for Dr Gubb?'

She smirked – not quite the response I'd expected. 'You'd need his mobile.'

'He's not at home?'

'No,' she said meaningfully. *Wink, wink.* 'He's on holiday?'

I was glad to think of the elderly, retired, lonely widower having some fun and sunshine. 'Oh, good.'

She had more. 'On a cruise.'

I felt my mouth drop open. 'I wouldn't have thought that was exactly his cup of tea.'

She pointed to a postcard pinned to the noticeboard which featured a huge, white ship. 'Well, from what I see,' she added with a wink, 'he's having a very – good – time.'

SIXTEEN

5 p.m.

With five partners, two nurses, a bank of receptionists, plus cleaners, at a doctors' surgery there is nearly always some drama happening behind the scenes as well as the births, deaths, accidents, ill health and crises of our eight thousand (give or take a few) patients.

This time it was one of the 'girls', as I called our two female GPs. Dr Gillian Angelo had arrived late for her surgery and was in a filthy mood. 'Some bastard,' she fumed, 'has nicked the friggin' catalytic converter from my car. In broad daylight.'

While we all sympathized my mind flicked over to DC William Summers and the attention he'd given to the bunch of guys standing along the High Street, combined with his description of his current priority: thefts *from cars targeting specific parts to order.* His eyes, ears and instincts had been fine-tuned to the group on the High Street. I was sure of it. I'd seen that slide of his eyes while appearing to look ahead. But my concern, as always, had been the person at the centre of the group, Ryan. While I recalled that knife wound, I saw its significance now. Rather than a fight it had been a warning. But if these guys were herding together, openly, in the centre of town, they were being rather blatant, almost challenging the law, drawing attention to themselves rather than staying hidden.

But then I remembered one of Mark's comments. 'They think they're Teflon-coated, that they'll never be caught. That they're immune, somehow, that the police will never catch them. And so they swagger around, drawing attention to themselves with their fast cars and designer trainers. Loud and over-confident, while we watch and take notes, gather our prosecution cases. They think that by intimidating a few witnesses, and hiring expensive lawyers, they will get off.' He'd given one of those sad, sweet smiles, lopsided and regretful as though he regretted having to pull them in to face the consequences of their actions. 'We're the ones who sweat and check, comb through every tiny detail, trying to find the loopholes, before the lawyers do. But we have one hand tied behind our backs as we're forced to expose every single shred of evidence.'

He'd touched my hand then, searching for an ally.

I blinked the memory away.

'Have you called the police?' Sebastian had wandered in and, automatically, all eyes turned to him. The proverbial tall, dark and handsome, added to a naturally optimistic nature and sense of fun, he would have been hard to ignore.

'Yes,' she said irritably, 'though much bloody good it does. This gang have been targeting our part of the town. Going for bits off high-end vehicles.' Gillian drove a practically new Mercedes V Class convertible – a flashy and no doubt expensive car. 'But have I seen any arrests? No. I haven't. All that happens is you get a crime number.' She scratched speech marks into the air. 'For the insurance.' She picked up the printout of her surgery list and groaned.

Immediately Sebastian and I exchanged glances. I nodded. 'We'll do your surgery for you.'

Sebastian chimed in. 'Yeah. Take the evening off, Gill. Go home and arrange for your car to be mended.'

Her gratitude was off the scale. She looked at me first. 'But what if . . .' She stopped right there.

'If there's anything serious I'll pass it through to Sebastian,' I said, having picked up on his nod. She was in no fit state to manage a busy surgery. The patients who particularly wanted to see her would be disappointed but it was a small price to pay. 'Don't worry,' I said. 'No one will die because you're not there.' It was meant to comfort her but actually it seemed to do the opposite. She paled before thanking us yet again and disappearing through the door.

Her surgery was actually a doddle with nothing very serious turning up apart from one elderly gentleman who seemed to have all the signs of prostate cancer and had hesitated too long before consulting. I took some blood and sent him through to Sebastian. The PR (per rectum examination) was not a job for me.

By seven o'clock we were both through.

SEVENTEEN

7.45 p.m.

I'd dawdled on the way home; after the dramas of the day I wasn't anxious to arrive at an empty house with a desert of an evening stretching before me. However, the evening was not to be without its own little dramas.

Two messages blinked on the answering machine of my land-line. First of all – surprise, surprise – one from my daughter, Lara. After years of anxiety, a dangerous eating disorder and a couple of messy relationship bust-ups, she sounded so happy, I hardly recognized her voice.

'Hi, Mum.' Even in the greeting to an anonymous answerphone I recognized her buoyancy. 'Just wondered how you are.' My heart leapt. 'And Mum, I have some really happy news. Hope we can share it and that I can get up to see you soon. Anyway, ring me back when you've time. Bye for now.' My heart soared.

I played it twice, just to drink in the happiness in her voice, before I moved on to the second message.

Which was, surprisingly, from Mark. 'Hi, Florrie.' If my daughter's voice had sounded happy, his was tense. 'Just checking you're all right.' It annoyed me that he still called me Florrie – the pet name he'd used in the past.

I made a goofy face at myself. Checking I was all right? What was that all about? What right did he have to even worry whether I was or wasn't all right?

Maybe I'd take a sneaky look on Facebook later on and see if he'd reappeared on Vivien's home page. The tightness in his voice seemed to confirm my suspicions that all was still not well in the nursery of my ex and his lover. I recognized that tone. Desperate.

But having had two phone calls I checked my mobile and smiled at a text from William Summers. It said just one word: *Again?*

You bet, I thought, and texted him right back with that very same message. And then I poured myself a glass of wine, kicked my shoes off, lay back on my sofa and allowed myself to sit back and reflect on my day. And from where I was sitting, apart from that weird consultation with Mrs Clay, it looked like a win-win. I felt good because I'd helped Gillian out by seeing her patients. She'd helped *me* out in the past, given me a lift when my car had been incapacitated, and teamed that with some helpful advice to stop blaming myself when a patient ran into trouble. It could be applied to so many circumstances – even Christine Clay. Fair and quits, I thought, while wondering exactly what Ryan Wood and his seedy gang of mates had to do with nicking catalytic convertors. It wasn't a big step to take. I had a feeling William Summers might be threading the same little beads together to make a necklace. I smiled as I recognized that I just might have the beginnings, the embryonic stage, of a relationship?

My first since Mark.

I leaned into the back of the sofa, closed my eyes and pictured him. He wasn't the pin-up that Sebastian Timor was, but then neither did I fit the image of arm candy. Me? Wrong age, wrong shape, wrong personality. And DC Will Summers was stocky rather than tall, but muscular, not podgy and unfit. I suspected he did some exercise to maintain his shape. I tried holding my stomach in, giving up after a millisecond. It was too uncomfortable. I touched my hair, chestnut thanks to Boots the Chemist while his was au naturel, brown with streaks of grey. His eyes, as I have already mentioned, were a warm brown, flecked with amber, and his mouth smiled rather than sulked. So far so good. All in all he was Mr Nicely Average. My mouth curved into a secretive smile. Well, I could match up to that.

Next, I dialled my daughter's mobile and knew she'd been waiting for my callback when she responded on the first buzz. 'Mum.' Again, I heard that lightness in her tone. 'I wondered if you're busy this weekend?'

'This weekend?' I sensed she was waiting for my response. 'Not especially.'

'Is it OK . . .' She changed that to: 'I wondered about popping over to see you?'

'That'd be lovely.' She lived less than three hours away but 'popping over' had never been on the agenda before. I waited for the subtext. The happy news.

It came. 'Is it OK if I bring a . . .' Some hesitation there. 'A friend?'

'Of course.'

Another pause before adding, 'I thought we might go out somewhere tomorrow night.'

'Great. I'll book somewhere.'

No details about the friend and no mention of her dad or the impending half sibling, I noticed.

'See you tomorrow then.' The phone was put down before I could pin her down to a time or ask where she wanted me to book.

Now I had a full weekend ahead and plenty to think about, and so I forgot about my ruminations over Ryan Wood and the company he was keeping, and I didn't give the Clays and their confusing marriage another thought.

Until . . .

EIGHTEEN

Thursday 5 October, 11 a.m.

It was almost a week later; the weather had turned golden and I was still in a fizz of romance. Not only had I watched my daughter gazing adoringly into the eyes of a thirty-something Lloyd's Insurance underwriter, David – a blond-haired Adonis, shy and attractive with impeccable manners – but I had also had two further texts from PC Will Summers suggesting we 'try out' the Chinese in Eccleshall which had a banqueting night (all you could eat) on a Thursday. I put aside concerns about my waistline (I'd ask Jalissa which were the lowest calorie sandwiches she provided and pass on the cake) and accepted. And this time he would pick me up from home. Having seen my daughter soften and melt when David put his arm around her, I was in the mood for love and a second date felt a confirmation.

Of something anyway.

Vivien was still posting update after update on Facebook – some of which Rowena shared with me – using every single baby emoji in existence: bootees, babygrows, a tiny Moses basket, a feeding bottle. I hadn't realized there were so many. I was tempted to ask Rowena to comment on at least one by adding a poo emoji and a few more nappies underneath, but I didn't want Rowena to take the blame and, naturally, I wasn't one of Vivien's Facebook friends. The posts came thick and fast – four or five a day, according to Rowena, since she'd taken maternity leave. I could sense her coyly puffing up her not inconsiderable chest as she posted that *they* hadn't asked the sex of *their* baby. 'We'll love it to bits whatever it is,' she'd said, making a sly dig tinged with criticism against those who couldn't wait to know whether their *little treasure* would be pink or blue. Or maybe, in these days of gender neutrality, lemon. The more I learned about Vivien the more I realized she and Mark were completely incompatible. After a lifetime's work and bringing up his family, he'd wanted some fun in his life. And talking of Mark – he really had vanished. There was no sign of him. Not one single picture and my sense that all was not well in the Vivien camp was on high alert. But as they'd wisely trans-ferred jobs from Stone to the Potteries I didn't know anyone who still kept in touch with them physically rather than through media posts, apart from Rowena, who'd once claimed to be her best friend. In response to my gentle probing Rowena had texted me that she didn't have a clue what had happened to him and Vivien wasn't saying, so I couldn't explore my ex's absence.

The police force can be surprisingly disapproving of extra-marital affairs and many of the local force had known me ever since we'd moved here over twenty years ago with two small children.

So I didn't know why Mark had appeared to vanish. And now, I thought smugly, I didn't care.

Work seemed lighter these days now the pandemic was fading into the rear-view mirror. We were back to the routine mundanity of flu clinics and the usual chronic disease check-ups. The autumn colours were slowly appearing; the leaves were starting to fall and I dug out one of my lighter winter coats in preparation.

So Thursday came around and at seven thirty I heard a car outside. Tonight I was wearing a skirt and cardigan. And although the skirt was fitted, I hadn't had to breathe in when I'd pulled the zip up and fastened the button at the top. Cake avoidance was working. I pulled the jacket around my shoulders and opened the door. But instead of my date for the night Mark was standing there, hair dishevelled, eyes bloodshot. It didn't take a detective to know he'd been drinking. I could smell it at arm's length. He held a bottle of wine out to me. 'You look nishe.'

His voice was thick with alcohol which took up my first concern. 'You haven't driven here in this state, have you?'

His answer was a hiccup and he held the bottle out again, a stupid grin smothering his face.

I was truly horrified. 'Mark,' I said sharply. Not only because he'd driven here roaring drunk which could mean a suspension from driving as well as cost him his job. As I've said the police force can be moralistic as well as unforgiving. And since the Sarah Everard case they took a hard line on any misdemeanours. Plus I was acutely aware that I was fairly obviously dressed up to go out. And call me a complete and utter marshmallow of a person but I felt guilty about that.

Mark was propping himself up against the doorpost. 'You look nishe,' he said again.

I pulled him inside, holding up my index finger like a strict teacher. 'You can't drive like that.' I had to quickly think what to do.

Option One: call Vivien to come and fetch him.

Option Two: call a taxi to take him home.

Option Three: let him stay here.

Before I'd reached a decision another car pulled on to my drive. And this time it was more welcome. DC Summers with a wide, friendly grin – until he saw who had collapsed against me. As he climbed out of the car he gave me a long, searching look. 'Florence?'

I propped Mark up in the doorway and stepped towards him. 'I don't know what to do with him,' I said. 'He just turned up here.' I moved in closer. 'He's pissed as a—'

Will Summers looked past me. And that was when I caught a glimpse of his true character. He looked back at me to study me thoughtfully.

'You can't let him drive,' he said, and I shook my head, agreeing.

'So, a taxi?' He gave a mischievous smile and touched my cheek. 'You could get your own back,' he said. 'Give PC Vivien Morris a call and put the ball in her court. Or . . .'

I waited.

'You could let him sleep it off here while we go out.' He waited while I ruminated but I'd already come to a decision. 'I'll put him in the spare room,' I said. 'I couldn't be that cruel even to PC Vivien Morris. She's pregnant.'

'Ah,' he said. A neutral comment so I wasn't sure whether he already knew that fact or not. 'Do you need a hand?'

'Best not.'

'OK. I'll wait for you in the car.' His face was still soft. 'Bit of an unpleasant surprise, eh?'

It was not to be my only surprise of the night.

NINETEEN

8.30 p.m.

We were settling into a feast of prawn crackers, seaweed and Peking duck before moving on to the main course. This time round the chat was easy – and became easier – as the evening wore on. Will had a beer while I, not driving, indulged in half a bottle of rosé which seemed to go nicely with the food. Will kept off the subject of Mark until he put his fork down (we'd given up on the chopsticks). 'Does that happen often?'

'No.'

He waited and I tried to make a joke out of it. 'I'm a hard habit to break.'

'Thanks for the warning.' But he accompanied that with a warm flash of a smile before looking very hard at me. 'It's not really fair,' he said, and then he made an attempt to turn the situation into a joke. 'A relationship isn't the okey-kokey, you know, left leg in, left leg out.'

It felt like he was giving me a gentle nudge, trying to protect me. It could have felt controlling, intrusive, an echo of Richard Clay. In fact, it felt rather nice. I smiled at him.

'Let's change the subject.'

A mistake. Because inadvertently I'd avoided one pitfall only to fall straight into another.

'Awful tragedy. Always makes me feel sad for them.'

I didn't have a clue what he was talking about. 'What?'

'Nice couple, I understand.'

I was bemused. 'Who were?'

'Couple. Only in their early sixties. Lived in those lovely big Victorian semis.' Without realizing he'd just set off a firework, he forked some chicken and rice into his mouth and chewed it slowly. 'Love those houses. Loads of room. Big gardens too,' he added, without understanding.

I was suddenly ice-cold.

'What's their name?'

'Clay,' he said, still blissfully unaware. 'Looks like a suicide pact. Or rather *attempted* suicide pact. Being bigger, fitter and a bloke, he survived. She didn't.'

That was when the chill reached my toes.

He continued before I'd had a chance to comment. 'Apparently she was convinced she had cancer.'

'What?'

Finally he'd picked up on my response and gave me a questioning look.

'I know them,' I said quietly, as I was realizing I'd been dreading something happening. Something bad. Some tragedy I might have played my own part in.

Just not this.

He put his fork down to study me. 'You know them?'

I nodded, still frightened to learn the truth, where I might have made the mistake.

He reached out and touched my hand and I sensed the empathy behind the gesture. 'Are they your patients?'

I nodded. The restaurant was quiet this evening, with few diners taking advantage of even the eat-all-you-can offer but I still leaned towards him, keeping my voice low. 'And she hasn't got cancer.'

Those brown eyes looked deep into mine with sensitivity but

behind that was a policeman's interrogation. 'Then why . . .?' His voice tailed off as I absorbed another piece of his information.

'You say he's survived?'

'Yeah. Looks like they both took a hefty dose of barbiturates.' His face changed as maybe he considered an alternative line. 'We haven't got the tox report yet.'

I realized he didn't know where to go with this.

I cut him off anyway. 'When did this happen?'

'Some time last night. They were found by their next-door neighbour. She called an ambulance.'

Only afterwards did I realize I had skated over the most important fact. *He survived.* But then I was focussed on the tingling in my toes, a warning I recognized and never ignored. 'Where is he now?'

'He *was* at the Royal Stoke,' he said, 'in the medical admissions unit. I'm not sure if he's still there now.'

'Will he be charged?'

He was watching me very intently. 'You knew them *that* well?'

'I did,' I said. 'I do.' I wondered how much I could confide in him. He was, I reminded myself, a police officer first. And then my concern turned inwards as I wondered whether I would be called to give evidence in the coroner's inquest. After all, I had seen her less than a week ago while she hadn't seen a doctor for months – possibly more than a year. *I* was the one who'd initiated a referral to the psychiatric team. Jordan Bannister referred her on *my* recommendation. I stared into my dish of Peking duck, feeling slightly sick now; the food looked unappetizing. I was already constructing an excuse, running backwards in my thoughts, defending myself. I'd discussed Christine Clay's case with her GP; I had suggested referring her to the psychologist because all the tests for physical illness had proved negative. I hadn't expedited the appointment to the psychologist because there were no red flags. No planned suicide, or so I'd thought. *He* had denied it. But I saw now where I might be subject to criticism. I hadn't booked a consultation for Christine with Dr Bannister. I could hear the coroner's comment, pinning me with one of those accusatory stares. I realized now I might be held to account over these omissions.

But one thing I was sure of: Christine Clay had not had cancer.

I had picked up that there was something strange in her condition but neither of them had confided this particular fear, although some of the phrases she and he had used now struck me as strange.

Maybe I was focussing harder, but I found myself asking questions I could have but hadn't at the time.

Only to be expected. What was to be expected?

Her insistence that sleeping tablets wouldn't really help.

Her comment that I didn't have to pretend.

Phrases you might use if you thought we were concealing a diagnosis from her.

I hadn't picked up on a cancer phobia. But now I realized how it might look. A puzzling feature was her husband joining her in a suicide pact. Really? And that I couldn't swallow – like the Peking duck which was staring miserably at me from the plate, congealing as it cooled.

William Summers was watching me with concern as he tracked each emotion across my face. Again, he reached out and touched my hand. 'I'm sorry, Florence. I've just ruined the entire evening, haven't I?'

I shrugged, thinking, yes, but it's hardly your fault. You couldn't have known the bit part I played in this drama. He waited for a moment then continued speaking slowly, testing the water as he inched forwards, watching my face for signs he should stop. 'As for whether Mr Clay will face a charge . . .' He was still being very careful, checking around him in case anyone in the sparsely populated restaurant might listen in. 'It depends on his statement when he is well enough to be questioned. He *may*'– he was giving the word more gravitas than it warranted, as though suggesting this version – 'testify that he found his wife in a comatose state and decided to join her.' His toffee-coloured eyes looked straight into mine. 'It depends whether there was any coercion and what corroborative evidence exists. Probably not,' he finished.

At which point I felt an icy finger touch my neck now. I know the way a coroner investigates, searching for answers to the circumstances surrounding an unexplained death. At some point they *would* turn their attention to me, as the health professional most frequently involved. I would be questioned and while I believed I had done nothing wrong there is always something, some tiny needle, the court can insert. I felt despair, trying to reassure myself that I had acted professionally at all times. I was running through words and phrases in my head, running through them so fast they were bumping into one another and making no coherent sense. I wished I had the computer screen in front of me so I could read what I'd actually typed.

Will picked up. 'We'll have to wait for his formal statement.'

I felt anxious now. 'Will he be taken into custody? Charged?'

'Oh, I very much doubt it.' His tone was casual. 'He'll probably be asked to make a statement under caution.' He was still watching me very intently. He would have picked up on the tiniest twitch. 'In cases like this—' he began.

'Cases like this?'

He looked awkward. 'Frail, elderly couple.'

Again, I interrupted. 'They weren't frail, Will, and they weren't that elderly either. They were in their early sixties and, apart from a few minor problems – nothing more than most people of that age have – they were healthy. I think Christine was a year or two older than her husband but no more.'

He smothered a smile, which I didn't return. Because I was picturing Christine when I'd last seen her. She *had* appeared frail except that strange last time, when she'd arrived at the surgery and demanded to see me. On her own. Maybe frail wasn't really the word. I frowned as I pictured her. Downtrodden like those cheap plastic shoes she'd worn. And Richard? No way. He had looked robust physically and mentally. I couldn't imagine *him* swallowing a load of tranquilizers to join his wife in Nirvana or wherever they believed in.

'How is he?'

'He *was* in a coma but last I heard he'd come round and there was no real concern for his condition.' Sensing something more, he stopped speaking. 'You seem very interested in this.'

I couldn't tell him the whole story mostly because I didn't understand it myself. Something I could hardly share with him. But as the facts were slowly sinking in I was even more convinced that none of this was making sense. I knew this couple and while I could imagine Christine taking her own life in a fog of belief that she had some incurable disease, I couldn't fit Richard into the picture. But, as I met Will's concerned eyes, regretfully I knew I couldn't share my misgivings with him. However much I liked and trusted him he was still a police officer who had, I sensed, a strong moral compass. Once I'd shared my impressions with him he wouldn't be able to erase his bias. And anyway, anything I was thinking was based on confusion and an instinct, nothing more. But then I'd known the Clays whereas, in all probability, Will Summers had never even met them.

Alive.

He'd been observing the emotions rippling across my face.

'This seems to be bothering you more than just a casual tragedy to one of your patients.'

He was still searching my face. I knew what this was. It was a tentative probe.

But I was revisiting the encounters I'd had with the Clays, in particular the way Richard had stood over his wife during the consultations, answering for her, supplying her responses, becoming her voice. It was obvious she was the frail, weaker person in their marriage. Yet I couldn't quite fit a narrative into the facts. Had *she* been the one to suggest they die together? Had *he* used her misconception to persuade her that her life would not be worth living, taking a token dose himself – just enough to convince the police that this was a suicide pact rather than murder?

I looked up. 'What evidence have you got?'

Will looked startled. 'I'm not the investigating officer on the case. I'm not sure what evidence one would expect.' His mouth straightened. 'What is it?'

Almost without realizing it I was shaking my head. 'Not in a million years,' I said.

Will leaned back in his seat, appraising me while I was wondering. How had Richard Clay engineered this? And was he was going to get away with it?

I had to get it off my chest.

'Will,' I began.

He lifted his eyes lazily but I could see the light burning in them. However, he didn't prompt me but sat, watching me, as alert and tense as a tiger ready to spring. I knew anything I said would translate into action.

Then he sat back, took a mouthful of the mild Chinese curry

we'd ordered as a side dish, and regarded me calmly. 'Come on, Florence,' he said finally. 'Spit it out.'

I fell back on a limp offering. 'You're convinced this *was* a suicide pact?'

He shrugged. 'That's what it looks like.' He waited for a moment before following that up with: 'Why?' And when I simply watched him, making no attempt to respond, he continued. 'The man was in a coma, Florence. And he's just lost his wife. We can't exactly subject him to the third degree.'

I searched for clues. 'Was he on a ventilator?'

He shook his head. 'Why are you asking all these questions?'

'He didn't seem the type.' It was a limp comment at best and Will's response measured up to that.

'What is the type? We never really know someone's inner self.' Although he was now forking in some fragrant rice, I sensed his simmering interest as he pondered my words. Then he put his fork down and looked straight at me. 'What exactly are you trying to say?'

I had to back off then. 'Just that it seems unlikely.' But I knew from his sceptical face that he knew exactly what I was up to.

The next moment he leant across the table. 'Be honest with me, Florence. You think he somehow persuaded his wife to take a lethal dose and then swallowed a lesser dose himself?'

I stared at the tablecloth, resisting the compulsion to confirm his assessment and get it off my chest. He leaned back, half closing his eyes, abstracting himself from the quiet, almost empty restaurant, speaking quietly, almost to himself, finally shaking his head and spreading his hands flat on the table. 'I can't see any way we could possibly prove it. *She's* dead and there won't have been witnesses to any coercion.'

Except me, I thought, while knowing I could never testify. 'Life insurance?'

He was still shaking his head. 'We haven't got that far yet.'

We'd finished our meal, realizing the evening had been spoilt, the romantic date turned into something damaged and distasteful.

And I still had a drunken ex at home probably snoring his head off.

Never make plans.

TWENTY

We were both quiet during the twenty-minute drive back to Stone. The diversion to the Clays' tragedy had formed a distance between us as we each saw this from a different perspective. As we passed the top of the pedestrianized High Street the lights turned red. I glanced down to see if the group of men were still there, in particular Ryan. My scrutiny must have registered with Will because he looked at me and smiled. Which broke the ice. And then, as the lights turned green and Will started to move forward a man raced across the road desperate to escape a pursuer who was hurling threats after him. The atmosphere felt electric with imminent violence.

'Shit. I could have—'

The second man was close behind him. Both were so fast had Will been more anxious to speed off once the lights changed he could hardly have avoided hitting one of them.

As it was, he drew in a long, shocked breath. Sensing a drama unfolding we waited and watched while the two men raced up Station Road and out of sight.

I wondered for a moment whether Will would follow them. He seemed to hesitate but he carried on into the left hand lane in the direction of Endicott Terrace.

I broke the silence. 'That felt . . . dangerous.'

'Yeah. Trouble in the camp.'

'Are they the—?'

He nodded. 'At least part of the local contingency.' He gave a wry smile. 'Foot soldiers rather than the generals.'

I started thinking about the damage done to Gillian Angelo's car. Her fury, the expense of it all, and I felt angry. If the police knew who was responsible, surely they should be arresting these guys and putting a stop to it? But I felt a hand grasp my arm. Will was shaking his head. 'There's a right time and place,' he said gently.

The incident had felt shocking but at least it had diverted my mind from the uncomfortable thoughts I'd been having about Richard and Christine Clay.

I slid my gaze to study Will's face and felt calmed. I could trust him to keep tabs on the street gang, leaving me to fret about my patients and my own role in this tragedy. Mark would have done the very same thing, storing mental notes, remembering numbers, descriptions, details he could regurgitate later in court. They had the same sliding, sideways look, their antennae quivering with awareness, while they faced forwards.

Will stopped outside home and turned to me. 'Hearing about your patient tonight – it really upset you, didn't it?'

I couldn't deny it; instead, I tried to apply his question to a general meaning. 'Whatever you think,' I said, 'nurses do form attachments to their patients.'

'I think I've realized that,' he responded, equally quietly, and I gave him a sharp look.

'I could see it in your face,' he said, smiling. 'You looked sad. But worried too.'

Another observation I could hardly deny. 'We feel responsible when something goes wrong.'

He gripped my hand. 'Yeah,' he said. 'I realized that too.'

'And something has gone very wrong.'

'Mmm.' I could tell that his mind now had reverted to that hot pursuit which had burst out in front of the car. There had been real terror in that first man, menace in the second. A situation that had felt edgy and dangerous that could erupt into violence with a tiniest spark. It was as though I was seeing a re-run of the night Ryan had his arm slashed. I glanced across at Will. He had his concerns. I had mine. I also suspected that he didn't share my suspicion that Christine Clay's death was anything but a tragedy.

And so the evening ended, both of us distracted by our own problems. While he was shadowing those two men up the road I was trying to work through the events that had led to Christine's death. Was it possible she persuaded him to take a near fatal dose of, presumably, a barbiturate? I shook my head unable to see any way that could have worked. More likely he had engineered her poisoning while taking a token, decoy dose himself.

A dangerous move.

All would be revealed, I thought, when he was questioned. If he remembered.

Another puzzle. Where had this spurious cancer diagnosis originated? I could hazard a guess as to when it had emerged. Around two years ago the frequent surgery attendances had started, so it was a safe bet that something must have triggered her fear about that time.

The rogue idea that entered my head was: had it come from him? Gaslighting? Had this been a carefully laid plan all along, maturing over the two years? I realized then that I would back it up. I was the one who had made a psychiatric referral, sanctioned by her doctor. I felt myself start to shake. I was part of his plan.

So was he one of the cleverest of tricksters? Setting me up, playing that part in front of me, pooh pooh-ing any idea that her symptoms were due to organic illness while feeding her fear?

I was going round and round, trying to make sense of each and every phrase.

I think I must have given a sigh of exasperation because Will gave me a sharp look followed by a brief silence. And then he spoke, as softly as he had in the restaurant, although here, in the darkening street lit by small pools of light from the lampposts, there was no one around to eavesdrop.

'Florence,' he said, 'will it help if I keep you up to date on the investigation into the Clay case?'

I wished I could say yes, but our relationship could only be built on the solid foundation of truth. And so my answer was less positive but more honest.

'It might,' I said. 'I'm just worried about my part in things.' I didn't say my active part; neither did I say that I feared it was a part that had been cleverly scripted for me. I could see from the orange streetlight that he was anxious. I watched his brow furrow while I wished I could have reassured him that he could help. That maybe he could even solve my problem. But when or if the truth came out I did not know where I would stand.

He couldn't know that in my mind I was seeing not just a tragic murder and suicide or a suicide pact but something much more subtle. Murder by stealth. Maybe Richard Clay had planted the seed of a cancer diagnosis and fed it.

But that didn't explain that last strange consultation I had had with a Christine Clay I hardly recognized.

I tucked my hand in his and gave him a warm smile while he responded with a hug and a light kiss. Then we both pulled away, laughing.

We felt like a couple of teenagers.

I might have my own concerns but Will Summers had his own problems too.

'You were miles away,' he said.

I nodded. And then he changed the subject – or appeared to.

'You know Ryan Wood,' he said. It sounded like an accusation, as though I was an accomplice.

I was smiling now, my mood lightening. 'I think everyone in Stone knows Ryan Wood.'

'I mean he's a patient of yours.'

'Yes.' I was wondering where this was going.

'What's your opinion of him?'

'There's no real harm in him,' I began but he cut me off.

'That's what I *used* to think.'

I waited.

'I don't like the company he's keeping these days, Florence.'

It was the memory of the eight stitches it had taken to close the wound on Ryan's arm that persuaded me to nod.

I gave him a sharp look and he looked awkward. I recognized that look. Mark had worn it when he was about to say something he shouldn't, leak details of an impending sting. I made no comment, didn't let on that I could read between the lines. But I knew exactly what Will was doing, just as I knew why he'd mentioned it. He wanted me to warn Ryan to stay away without realizing I already had – and with very good reason.

I wondered what my neighbours were making of the pair of us sitting in the car, talking. No doubt at least one of them would be watching and passing judgement – ex-husband arrived drunk as a skunk to stay the night and she's bringing another guy home? Shameless! I smiled, rather enjoying the description.

At the front door Will hesitated. 'You want me to . . .?' He left the sentence creaking in the breeze like a rusty pub sign.

Reluctantly I shook my head. 'No thanks, Will. Mark'll have passed out and tomorrow will have the mother and father of all hangovers.' He searched my face for a clue to the subtext, then smiled as though happy with what he read. I brushed his cheek with the palm of my hand and felt our relationship had progressed to step two: sharing some confidences. I left it there a little longer.

'Thanks for tonight,' I said. 'I know it ended up not being quite as planned but life is life.'

He just grinned and nodded before adding, 'Again?'

'For sure.' I liked the pace we were moving at – slowly.

TWENTY-ONE

11.15 p.m.

My prediction about Mark proved correct. He was stretched out in the guest room; still in his clothes (I hadn't been able to face undressing him!). He was lying inelegantly on his back, snoring heavily. I challenge any man to look attractive in that position. I watched his chest heaving up and down for a while, feeling some affection for what we'd once had, but no regrets for what was now completely gone.

I went downstairs. It was only just past eleven. And now I had a decision to make. Should I call Vivien and tell her he was here, safe, but too drunk to drive? I smothered a grin. That would put her mind at rest that we were hammering at it for old times' sake as well as putting me in the pound seats. Both for possession and virtue. But I knew how hard it would be for me to make that call without gloating. And so I went back upstairs, fished Mark's phone out of his jacket pocket, kept my fingers crossed that his code was still Lara's birthday and texted her.

Sorry love, had a shedful, staying with a mate. See you tomorrow. I finished with an X. Just one. No point overdoing it. And if my observations on Facebook were correct about their current distance, she'd be suspicious at too overwhelming an expression of love. The message landed and I switched the phone off. I was hardly going to start a dialogue.

Friday 6 October, 7.20 a.m.

The next morning began, predictably, with the usual apology and visible hangover. Mark looked awful, his skin a greenish colour, and he couldn't meet my eyes but kept his head in his hands, a penitent gaze on the kitchen floor, while I sat at my breakfast bar having my first meal of the day, granola with coffee. After a moment or two he started a slurred apology, something about his life having taken a terrible turn, something else about being manipulated, but I didn't want an explanation. I just wanted him gone. I felt no anger towards him but was veering towards pity mixed with exasperation. 'I sent Vivien a text last night,' I said coldly. And to respond to his horrified expression, added, 'I sent it as you, saying you were OK and staying with a friend. You can check it if you like.' I wanted him to be prepared for the inevitable grilling.

But Mark looked alarmed. 'Christ,' he said. 'You didn't?'

'I thought she might just wonder where you were.'

He managed to look even more sheepish. 'What did she say?'

'I don't know because I switched it off.' I waited. Suddenly, unexpectedly, Mark began to laugh. And having started he couldn't seem to stop. Maybe it was the alcohol still in his blood but the tears streamed down his face.

'The tables have turned, Florrie,' he said. 'You're the one with a date. He's a nice guy, by the way, while I have to reassure *Vivien* where I am.' That started him laughing again and even I managed a snigger and a shrug before he took in my uniform. 'You have to go to work? I thought—'

I had no idea what he might have thought.

I nodded, biting back any retort that some people had to work. I made us both another coffee, finished my bowl of cereal, then went upstairs to clean my teeth. I peeped round the door of the guest room when I passed and had a surprise. He'd made the bed. All was neat and tidy, even the window ajar to let out the noxious fumes of a drunken stupor. I smothered a smile. When we'd been married I don't think he'd even realized beds were meant to be made. Perhaps Vivien had schooled him into good habits.

He was even loading the dishwasher when I re-entered the

kitchen! He looked up and managed a grin. His colour was slowly coming back. I smiled back at him and unhooked my car keys. 'Just close the door behind you,' I said, and he gave another sheepish grin.

I couldn't think what else to say so I simply left and drove in to work.

8.45 a.m.

In our surgery we have a death board. It had been suggested by a patient when we hadn't realized his baby son had died. 'Share the information,' he'd said, fury compounding his grief. As many of our staff worked part-time, making it easy to miss out on events, it had been voted a good idea as long as it was out of sight of the waiting room. After the person's name and age, we also filled in any pertinent details: cot death, road traffic incident, suicide, etc, so our responses could be appropriate.

The first person to learn of the death could write it on.

Christine Clay's name was already up with 'suicide' written by it. I stood in front of the board and stared. The judgement felt premature. I felt like reaching up and erasing the word, feeling strongly that it was wrong. It shouldn't be there. Not yet at least. Not until the coroner, aided by police investigations, had formed a verdict. I resented the fact that someone had written the word as though it was a given fact. But I left it even though it felt disloyal.

I reached my clinic room and closed the door behind me, feeling I'd failed her.

Then I rang the hospital switchboard, explaining that I was Mr Clay's practice nurse, to be told that he would be discharged later that day, providing his blood results were back to normal. They were currently waiting for those before the consultant discharged him. I thanked them and ended the call, while wondering how long the police would leave him before the inevitable interview. A day? Two days? And then I started wondering about the funeral arrangements once the coroner had released the body for burial. As far as I remembered they had a daughter, Harriet, who had been a couple of years older than

Lara. She must be in her early thirties now. I remembered her
as a skinny, ginger-haired teenager with a truculent manner. One
of those youngsters who looks at you with disdain when you
check their immunization status or start to advise on safe sex. I
had no clue what had happened to her. Like most of the offspring
from Stone, they went to university and disappeared.

Morning surgery was uneventful, like so many mornings. There
was no word from Will Summers but I was not troubled by this.
I was starting to have confidence that he just might be a keeper.
Straight, reliable, slow, steady and honest. When he was ready
I trusted I would hear from him again.

To my relief I also heard nothing from either Mark or Vivien.

When I came to the end of my day – and my week – I decided
I would leave it until Monday before visiting Richard Clay at
home, assuming he had been discharged. Give him time to settle
down. Whatever the truth behind this 'suicide pact', Christine's
funeral probably wouldn't take place for a week or two. There
would have to be a post-mortem, after which it would be up to
the coroner to release the body for burial and hold an inquest.
Richard Clay would be expected to give evidence – when he'd
recovered fully. The police would interview him and whatever
story he'd cooked up would, I suspected, be believed.

It's easier that way.

But whatever fable he gave would probably be accepted by
coroner and police.

Not by me.

When I faced him I trusted I would divine the truth, understand
how and why my patient had died. But paying a home visit was
a risky strategy which could easily land me in hot water because
I wasn't sure I would be able to bury my suspicions deep enough
for Richard Clay not to sense them. He was too intelligent and
perceptive enough to sniff out my doubts, pick up on my
attitude.

Besides, nurses aren't supposed to suspect their patients of
murder.

TWENTY-TWO

I arrived home late that afternoon to a nice surprise. On the doorstep lay a huge bouquet of flowers. I could smell the roses, lilies and peppery night-scented stock even as I opened my car door. I could guess who they were from. Mark had always been good at extravagant gestures of apology when he knew he was in the wrong. And he knew my love of flowers. I stood still for a moment breathing in the stock, the sprays of lilac, the riot of roses, lilies, carnations, lavender and freesias. He must have emptied the shop. I picked them up and buried my face in them, immediately sneezing hard. As expected, the card was a 'Sorry' without the unnecessary name.

Well, I love flowers anyway. My arms full, I let myself in.

Apology accepted.

I spent ages arranging and rearranging the flowers into my largest vase before finally putting them on the shelf in the lounge where I could look at them as I ate my tea on my lap and watched television, a smug feeling blotting out many of my recent concerns and anxieties.

My weekend was blissfully quiet. Lara rang to ask what I'd thought of her beau and I responded with warmth that he was delightful. I listened to her extolling all his virtues while what I remembered was a pair of calm blue eyes, lines of kindness around his mouth, plus a thick head of mussed-up blond hair. I was smiling right up until she said in a tentative tone, 'I suppose I'd better introduce him to Dad.' She paused. 'And *her.*'

That stopped my reflection with a bump.

But she was right and there was no alternative. I didn't want to expose my social media stalking or her father's brief stay last night but the fact was my daughter was in for a shock. Just when she was possibly contemplating a stable relationship for herself, maybe even future motherhood, she was about to have a half-sister or brother – courtesy of Dad.

TWENTY-THREE

Monday 9 October, 4 p.m.

'd rung the hospital first thing and confirmed that Richard Clay had been discharged late on the Friday. So, as I worked my way through my surgeries, I laid my plan. I would call round to his house, in the afternoon, without warning. I wanted to catch him on the hop. Off guard. He'd spent just a couple of days in hospital which could, arguably, justify a 'post discharge' visit, which would be a golden opportunity for me to start probing. I was determined to find out the truth behind this facade of 'suicide pact' which I didn't believe for a minute. I wondered whether the police had asked the same questions I was planning.

How had this come about – really?

Who had suggested they die together?

Exactly what had they taken? What dose? The same? He was a male and getting on for twice the size of his diminutive wife. What would kill her might well have just put him to sleep for a day and a half if they'd had the same amount. He would have survived while she would not.

Was there a significant life insurance? Was financial benefit a factor as well as his possible dislike or irritation with her?

Where had this cancer story originated? How long had she had this conviction?

Had the couple taken the same drug, and if they had, what drug, and how had they obtained it? I'd checked the computer. Neither of them was prescribed anything that could potentially be lethal. Certainly not an opioid which would be the most likely drug. He had acquired a hypnotic from somewhere. And there lay his weakest point. The story of the agreement they may or may not have made relied purely on his testimony now. But the lab results of his and her blood tests would not lie. That was where the proof might be. How had he obtained it? If I could track down the source of poor Christine's fatal dose I could at least testify to coercion. She was vulnerable; he was not. So, within my role of practice nurse, what could I do about it without losing my job? Well, I thought, sitting in my surgery room, waiting for my next patient – I hadn't worked that one out yet. I would have to tread carefully. But I had an advantage. I knew them both and I had access to their full medical files. Plus I had seen them fairly regularly over the past year or two.

And so I resolved I would gain access to his statement, possibly through Will, and pick holes in it until I could see right through, straight into the whole picture.

What evidence did I have? None yet except a gut feeling and insight into the power balance inside the Clay's marriage.

Oh, I had a hundred questions, but I would have to ask them with care. An investigation was not part of my remit.

But I knew the truth as clearly as if I had been there, watching.

He'd set his wife up, gaslighting her, so she believed she had cancer and a slow, painful death staring at her from her future. I laid the scenario out before me, working it out step by step, thinking it through.

He'd convinced her that the kindest thing to do to herself was to swallow a couple of pills and go to sleep. Oh yes, I thought, I could just see him standing over her, having described the extended painful future that stared back at her, holding out a couple of white pills with that icy stare and, probably, a glass of water with which to swallow them. And so poor, bullied, vulnerable Christine had obediently swallowed the pills while he had taken a token one, the dose having been carefully worked out beforehand. And so, they had both swallowed. Maybe even doing that 'thing' – holding hands while lying side by side like a couple of medieval effigies lying together in a crypt. My mind pictured Christine's final minutes – sleep overtaking her – while he watched and played his part. Just enough to feed out the story that this had been a suicide pact. Convince the coroner and the police of this fictional narrative. A story I didn't believe for a minute. What I couldn't understand was *why*? Why on earth had he taken this risk? Why had he needed to tease out *this* narrative? He hadn't needed to take anything at all. And drugs are notoriously difficult to titrate exactly. He could have died himself, not even necessarily from the actual dose. A response to opioids is varied and unpredictable. Opioids make many people sick. Inhalation of vomit is a not uncommon cause of death. The entire plan might have gone wrong, his plans misfired. And Christine had been so pliant she would probably have agreed to anything he'd suggested.

Except that last time, that discordant consultation which had seemed so out of tune, as though she was a different person. Was that why he'd decided on his plan? Because she was starting to reassert herself?

I continued with my musings, trying to burrow into his motives for taking this risk. One answer could have been life insurance. But many life insurance policies refuse to pay up in cases of suicide. Anyway, the Clays were hardly short of money. They had that lovely house on the Newcastle Road. I leafed through his notes, focussing on him this time rather than her. He'd been CEO of his own company in the Potteries. I'd read in the local paper that he'd sold it for a hefty amount when he'd retired. So, no money worries, although I qualified that. One never quite knows. There are plenty of folk who appear wealthy but struggle to retain that image. Was he possibly a gambler? Again, I pictured his granite face and shook my head. No. Richard Clay liked control. Not weakness.

I moved on to another theory. Another woman? I did give that theory some thought before throwing this one out too. He didn't strike me as a highly sexed man who would risk all for lust, although again, one never really knows. Sometimes it is the most tightly wound men who need an outlet in sexual deviancy. But if he had a lover he and Christine could have divorced. It would have cost him money but this plan had been a risky strategy. Besides, someone must have planted the cancer theory in her mind. And the only real possibility had to be him. I leafed through her notes again looking for evidence that he had sown the cancer seed and waited for his chance to use it. But I couldn't find any hint of that so was it a lie to the police? I stared at the walls of my clinic room searching for answers and wondering.

I set off for Newcastle Road.

TWENTY-FOUR

T
he first thing I noticed was that in the drive, standing beside the Clays' elderly black Mercedes, was a silver Audi TT. A swift, flashy car. At a guess it belonged to one of their friends – or maybe Harriet, their daughter, had surfaced.

My second guess was the right one. She answered the door. The intervening years had done nothing for Harriet Clay's looks, which I'd remembered as plain. Dressed in jeans and a dark sweater, she was skinny, like her father, with a pale, freckly complexion and blue eyes as cold as stones, a narrow nose and a thin, disapproving mouth. Her ginger hair was tied back in an untidy loose ponytail. And it was obvious from her glare that she didn't have a clue who I was.

I gave the nearest I could manage to a winning smile. 'I'm Florence Shaw,' I said briskly, smile broadening as I sensed it needed to override her hostility. 'I'm the nurse from the surgery. This is just a courtesy call following your dad's discharge from hospital.' I made no mention of her mother.

She looked me up and down, disdain oozing out of her response. She looked as though she was considering whether to tell me to bugger off, but apparently, thinking the better of it, she stood back against the door and allowed me to pass.

I'd only been in the house once before when Christine had been in bed with flu, but it had been years ago. Looking around nothing had changed. There was a stale, neglected air as though it too had died. Harriet was right behind me, almost pushing me forward now. 'In the sitting room,' she said curtly. 'On the right.'

I entered a large, square room with a high ceiling, dark furniture, a coffee table in front of a red sofa, a piano standing at the opposite side, next to a modest-sized TV. The atmosphere was damp and cold reflecting the general ambience of the house.

He was sitting in a chair, muffled up in a grey blanket, his head dropped on to his chest. He could have been sleeping but he wasn't. With an effort he raised his head, looked straight at me and said, 'Nurse Shaw.'

I was taken aback, quickly revising my take on the situation. He actually looked terrible – tired, defeated and depressed, hunched over as once his wife had been as though he'd adopted her characteristics. Instinct took over and I dropped into the sofa, confused thoughts tumbling into one another. 'I am so sorry,' I said genuinely.

He nodded, avoiding my gaze but accepting my offering. And then he was shaking his head. 'I couldn't,' he said, then substituted with, 'she wouldn't.' And then he broke down completely and filled in the missing words. 'Stop,' he said. 'She wouldn't stop. I couldn't persuade her.'

I was shocked, starting to wind in all my assumptions. I must have misread the situation, was my initial thought. I couldn't mistake the genuine grief, heartbreak in his voice. Harriet was watching from the doorway but I couldn't interpret her expression. Cynicism? Pity? I couldn't detect grief in her manner. Even when she spoke.

'Cup of tea?'

I realized then she was having trouble dealing with this – and him – as well. I looked from one to the other, father to daughter, and accepted the offer, confused.

He was shaking his head and staring intently at the carpet (an unpleasant shade of green decorated in an abstract, swirling pattern) as though it held an answer. I watched him carefully, wanting to embark on my list of questions. But observing his fragile state, I knew I couldn't ask a single one. I'd come here as an envoy from the surgery ostensibly to offer my condolences and check whether he needed any support – physical or mental.

I kept my mouth shut and focussed on him.

Richard Clay looked like a man broken. This happens when you have two people in a relationship, a 'strong' one and a 'weak' one. I'd seen it many times before. Sometimes the truth is, in a long marriage, that each props the other up. Remove the 'weak' one and the 'strong' one suffers as though at the last moment they switched places. Or maybe, I thought, as I recalled that last consultation with his wife, I'd misread the roles. So strong was really weak and vice versa.

I sat still, both of us silent, as I threaded thoughts through my mind, trying to put them in order. And then I realized Harriet was still standing at the door, making eyebrow signals at me which, combined with a jerk of her head, were obviously meant to direct me towards the kitchen. I gave a swift glance at Richard; he would neither notice my exit nor would he care. I made a quick comment about giving his daughter a hand with the tea. I suspected he knew it was a ploy and didn't respond except with a shallow twitch of his shoulders. Otherwise, he continued to stare at the floor. I shot a glance at him just before I left the room and was convinced. This was no act. And it was turning all my theories upside down, spinning them around, so I couldn't make sense of any of it.

The kitchen was at the back of the house and from the dark wood units it too could have done with a makeover. Harriet closed the door behind us before she launched into the attack. 'What on earth,' she said, 'was the surgery doing for my poor mother?'

I stared at her. 'Sorry?'

'Daddy's told me. Nothing he could say would convince her.'

I was even more mystified. 'I'm sorry,' I said. 'I really don't—'

She hadn't finished. 'What on earth were you playing at?'

'Harriet,' I said, really concerned now. 'We saw your mother regularly. We did test after test.'

'She was convinced she had cancer. It was all she thought about.' It burst out of her. 'Why didn't you get her some coun- selling – or something,' she finished lamely.

'She was on the waiting list for counselling,' I said quietly, realizing it did not mollify this angry daughter. So I continued, 'We were unaware of your mother's erroneous belief.' I was trying to retrieve my dignity. 'All we saw was a plethora of random symptoms, each one of which was investigated thoroughly with scans and various tests. What were we supposed to do? She never said she believed she had cancer, and her scans showed nothing untoward.' I decided to toss a pebble into the water and see where the ripples reached. 'Where did this conviction come from?'

She stared at me, still hostile, but starting to ask the same questions that I was.

Which neither of us made any attempt at answering.

I paused to catch my breath before launching back into the

attack. 'Your father was present at all consultations' – honesty compelled me to add – 'except the last one. No . . .' I repeated the word to give it emphasis and maintain control of the narrative, '. . . *no* mention was ever made of cancer.' I realized then I was missing something – the result of the post-mortem – and felt the ice crack beneath my feet, felt my balance shift and my feet slide from beneath me. 'None of the tests showed anything serious. Your mother had pernicious anaemia, sure. And her blood pressure was a little high but there was nothing, *nothing*,' I repeated, 'to suggest your mother had cancer. However,' I was forced to add, 'we were concerned at her frequent attendances at the surgery and she *had* been referred to a psychologist to see if it might help her persistent fears.'

'And how long until she reached the top of the list?' Harriet spoke to herself as she turned away from me, then stared out over the garden, a square lawn surrounded by still-colourful flower beds.

'What are you talking about?' Richard Clay was standing in the doorway and I was struck at the change in him. He was watching us both with a gleam in his eye. The very quietness of his voice sounded menacing.

I eyed Harriet, even took a step towards her, in the unexpected position of being her ally.

Then I took the bull by the horns. 'Harriet was just telling me your wife feared she had cancer.'

He dropped his head again and nodded and I caught the hint of a smile. 'Nothing I could do would convince her otherwise.'

Oh, you clever man, I thought. Such an act.

His eyes were firmly on me now, sounding me out, and I felt uncomfortable, veering on threatened. He was reading my mind, sucking out my thoughts and slowly chewing on them, always with that smile. Harriet had her back to me, busying herself making the tea which now, feeling so uncomfortable, I wished I'd refused. I wanted out.

Harriet bustled back into the sitting room, her father and myself trailing behind her like recalcitrant schoolkids. I drank my tea as quickly as I could without burning my tongue, made my apologies and prepared to leave after repeating my sympathies to the bereaved widower.

Harriet followed me to the door. It was obvious she wanted to say something more. 'I wondered,' she began. She seemed to have lost some of her confidence. 'Would you be able to see me?' She gave a quick look back into the house and changed the request to a rather desperate: 'Can I come and see you at the surgery? On my own. Please?'

'Yes, of course.' She had every right to come and talk to us if she had questions about her mother. And even if she hadn't, she could register as a temporary resident.

I did try to sidestep. 'Is it me you want to see or her GP?'

She stopped and thought about that for a moment. 'Who saw Mum most?'

'Probably me.'

'Then I'd like to speak to you.' Another swift glance behind her and she repeated, 'On my own.' And, reinforcing for clarity, she added, 'Without Dad.'

TWENTY-FIVE

5.15 p.m.

As though designing to satisfy at least some of my curiosity, Will Summers rang just as I was reaching home. Seeing his caller ID on my screen, I felt that warm feeling one has when a woollen blanket wraps around you against the chill. Comfortable.

I felt that even more when he greeted me with a simple, 'Hi,' not having to explain who he was. That is the sign of a close and exclusive relationship, I decided.

'Hi,' I returned.

'You managed to ditch the ex then?'

I laughed because there was no undertone in the question. No jealousy, interrogation or spite. It was a merry mockery. 'I did.' I laughed again. 'I'd like to say I sent him away with a flea in his ear but, to be honest, I suspect he got enough earache when he reached home.'

Will laughed too and there was a brief pause. I wanted so much to ask him how the investigation into Christine Clay's death was proceeding but I was worried he'd think that was the only reason our friendship was blossoming. I'd picked his brains before and didn't want him to think I was using him and our friendship simply to get an inside story on an investigation. There were borders I would be unwise to cross.

Instead, I invited him over for dinner.

'What?' He sounded astonished.

'I can cook, you know.' I was only slightly insulted.

He tried to rescue the situation with a hasty: 'I'm sure. I'm sure.'

Which made me laugh again. 'I suppose I'd better check on allergies?'

'None,' he responded quickly.

'Or anything you simply can't eat for love or money.'

'Not that I can think of,' he said brightly.

And I thought how simple, how pleasant, and how uncomplicated this relationship was – so far.

'Tomorrow night then? Around seven. I don't like eating late,' I added.

'I'll see you then.' I was already planning what to cook. Nothing too heavy, plenty of veg. Something healthy but massively tasty. I wanted to impress.

But first I would have to deal with Harriet Clay who had booked into my surgery tomorrow. Darcey had rung to ask if she could add her on to the end of my morning surgery and I'd agreed. Tackle her sooner rather than later, I thought, because for sure I'd sensed she was going to be full of complaints. I was starting to doubt my original theory about the Clays' supposed suicide pact. What I'd witnessed from Richard had been genuine grief. I was sure of it. But I wasn't confident the police would conduct anything but a superficial investigation. Maybe make a casual enquiry into the source of the drugs, but I suspected they would not dig deep. Perhaps even if the source could be traced back to him he might claim Christine had pressured him into buying them because she had trouble sleeping. Which I'd documented in her notes – if they looked that far.

And there was no way I could see of proving he'd manipulated his wife.

I felt my face crumple into a frown. My conviction, which had been so strong, had melted when I'd seen his wrecked unhappiness. However he had appeared when she had been at the surgery, he now seemed distant and I was doubting my own observation. I tried to think back, to resurrect my memory of the consultations we had had. I tried to picture her vulnerability, hunched up in her chair, the dowdy clothes she had worn, her quiet submission and something in me shifted.

I tried to find a narrative.

Maybe he had planted the cancer story. Possibly he'd even encouraged it? If so, why hadn't he confronted us with a direct question? That was in his nature after all. Maybe they had both been waiting for one of her numerous tests to confirm it.

Perhaps his impatience had been with us rather than her.

In my eyes Richard had always held the upper hand. Dogmatic, intelligent, coercive. I simply hadn't found the reason why. Simple dominance? And now I struggled with another image of him – as a victim. Also, seeing him as a victim, the likelihood was that the police and coroner would agree not to press charges unless some hard evidence turned up.

Coercion is notoriously hard to prove in a court of law. Particularly with the main witness dead.

Perhaps having done his worst, Richard was now regretting the murder of his wife.

Or maybe his grief was a clever mask.

No one but I would have watched his behaviour. They lived alone. I hadn't seen their daughter for years. There would be no witnesses.

Unless I could find some hard evidence.

Such as?

It would have to be watertight. Sympathy for the grieving widower would tilt the balance towards him. But testifying against one of my patients was not part of my job description.

I tumbled around this moral conundrum.

The rights of patients.

For now I spent the evening tidying up the house, cleaning the kitchen and planning a menu. I wanted DC Will Summers to see me as an efficient housewife, my home sparkling with cleanliness.

TWENTY-SIX

Tuesday 10 October, 12.15 p.m.

I was nervous when I saw that Harriet Clay had booked in for midday. I didn't know what she wanted from me and I couldn't think how best to respond to any interrogation she might subject me to about her mother and father, their relationship and the tragic events that followed. I could hardly be honest or share my suspicions that her dad had had a hand in her mother's erroneous belief that she had had cancer, let alone my fear that he had actually orchestrated the suicide pact scenario.

However, she had already indicated she was after blood and blame so I should be wary.

Both her parents were protected by a confidentiality clause as they were patients of the practice so my options were limited, even to their daughter, unless Richard gave his permission for his information to be shared. After checking the screen I flicked it over to blank as my finger hovered over the bell to summon her.

Maybe she had something she wanted to pass on to me or else she wanted something from me – some small detail or opinion. I could hardly share that when my opinion pointed a finger at her dad. What would she ask? I wondered. My finger shook as I pressed the buzzer and moments later heard her footsteps, crisp and determined, step towards my room.

Even her knock felt a threat, an assertion.

I stood up and opened the door.

Today her hair was scraped back which emphasized her pointed, witchy features: sharp nose, thin mouth, narrow eyes, and she didn't look as angry as I'd expected, but . . . the only word I could use was grief-struck. I'd expected confrontation. Not defeat. For a moment I was taken aback feeling primarily sympathy for her. She had lost her mother in terrible circumstances. Illness happens but in a suicide those near to the deceased feel guilty, convinced their neglect played some part in the tragedy. Ultimately they believe they failed them. And, if the accepted version was to be believed, almost her father too. She must be feeling a terrible daughter. But what could *I* do to alleviate her guilt?

She sat down and looked me straight in the eye. And her opening gambit was unexpected. 'How much do you know about me?'

I was taken aback. That was not what I'd expected. 'Not a lot.' I tried out a smile, 'Which is to say nothing except . . .' I was about to say, 'your parents', but I stopped myself just in time, the words almost colliding into each another.

'I make documentaries,' she said, 'about wrongs that need to be righted.'

It sounded like something out of fiction, a child's version of Robin Hood, or *The Three Musketeers*. I almost smiled. But her next sentence sucked any humour out of me.

'You could say I'm an investigative reporter.' Her pale eyes were focussed on me, watching for my reaction.

I couldn't think of a suitable response so said nothing while I wondered where this was leading, why she was here. What she wanted from me. I felt the tiniest frisson of concern when she added, one elbow on my desk, chin resting on her knuckles so her eyes were level with mine, 'In fact, Nurse Shaw, I've done a couple of programmes on health matters.'

That was when my heart started pounding and instead of feeling sorry for her I felt intimidated. And angry. I'd thought she'd wanted to talk about her parents, in particular about her mother. Not chase up some story about NHS failings. If there is one thing that worries health professionals it is that two-word phrase, investigative reporter, because however well we feel we have performed they will always find something, a weak link, a failure to provide . . . and so on.

Now she worried me, not as a recently bereaved daughter of one of my patients, but as a combatant. The press don't do good stories about the health service. And this one wasn't good anyway. Someone had died so how was that not a failing? Only bad stories make headlines. What was she going to focus on? What failures in my part had robbed her of a parent – almost two parents?

I met her eyes now, as cold and flat as an ice floe, and challenged her. 'So am I talking to you as an investigative journalist?

In which case I should have my union representative present –
possibly a lawyer too.'

She took her elbow off the desk and sat back, thinking. I
caught the whiff of trouble, meeting her eyes and clamping my
mouth tight shut.

I had colleagues who had had a rough time on the other end of
an investigation and they hadn't gone well. One, whom I had
considered beyond reproach, had subsequently left the profession.
Demoralized and depressed, she had rung me late one night, admit-
tedly when she'd had a couple of drinks. 'Nursing's changed,'
she'd said sadly. 'Once we were loved and trusted. Heroines. Now
we're constantly questioned. Suspected. People are looking out for
our mistakes.'

'But surely—' I'd begun.

She'd cut me off. 'Don't you believe it. The public want blood
or else they want money. They're baying for it and they want
someone to take the blame for any ill health.' She'd given a
high-pitched, almost hysterical laugh. 'And as most of them are
atheists, they can't blame God any more, can they, Florence?'
Chuckle, chuckle. 'People feel they are entitled to health, happiness, a long life and designer handbags, so these days they can't
accept illness and its consequences. Or the results of poor lifestyle
choices,' she'd added with a huff.

I hadn't known what to say and there had been a brief silence
between us before my friend had turned into a Cassandra. 'You
wait,' she'd said and, even on the end of a phone, I'd felt her
index finger jabbing into me. 'You just wait. One day it'll happen
to you. You'll get blamed for something that isn't your fault.
You'll feel the injustice, Florence. And you'll want to hang up
your nurse's uniform and never see a patient again.'

But I couldn't, I thought now. I couldn't afford to hang up my
uniform. I had a mortgage and no other source of income. No
one to help me out. I didn't have a husband who might step in
with bills if I was struggling. I was on my own. There was no
backup.

And now, as I met Harriet Clay's frozen face, I recognized I
was faced with just the situation that 'Cassandra' had predicted.
And, I confess, I felt shaken.

I tried to read the motive in Harriet Clay's hard, unforgiving eyes. Why had she really booked in to see me today? What did she want from me? To see me strung up for her mother's death? At the same time I recognized I had two choices now – refuse to speak to her without a legal representative or else try and find out what she was after. Cautious curiosity won as I sat and faced her. 'So what do you want?'

The full-frontal assault, or rather capitulation, took her aback. She hesitated then spoke in a low voice that felt as threatening as a shout. 'I want the truth, Nurse Florence.' I could hear the derision in her voice and the heightened threat it held. Her sharp little chin jutted out like a stroppy eight-year-old's. 'Someone cocked up here, didn't they?' She leaned back in her chair, bony knees pressed together. 'She *believed* she had cancer and that she was dying. If she *didn't* have cancer, she should have had some counselling, shouldn't she?'

I could have prompted her into asking where that belief had originated but I was silent for a moment, gathering my thoughts, before I finally found my voice. 'Your mum never questioned anyone directly on that subject, neither did your dad.'

Her pale eyes met mine and her response was quiet. 'Maybe she was frightened to.'

I absorbed this sad little statement for a moment until I realized her eyes were still fixed on me. But her head had shifted to one side as though she was appraising me. 'Harriet,' I said, falling backwards into the cliché, 'I'm sorry for your loss. I really am, but I think you're barking up the wrong tree.' I didn't dare point her towards the right tree. 'Your mum didn't have cancer. All her symptoms were investigated thoroughly.'

'I know,' she admitted quietly. 'The post-mortem showed there was no evidence of cancer.'

To say I felt relief would have been an understatement. I let out my breath. I wanted to say, *See, told you.* I also wanted to ask her what the drug they had taken was. But I found I couldn't say anything.

For a moment anger took over. Her hands gripped the arms of the chair and she stared at me, lips pressed together. I sensed a gathering storm but she hadn't left her seat and she was shaking her head like some sage of old, shaking her head in incredulity. 'You don't understand,' she said. 'I don't want confrontation,

Florence. I don't want trouble. I just want to find out why my mother killed herself.'

I said nothing for a moment, though the words 'I think I know' hovered dangerously near my lips. But I wanted her to see this from my perspective, so I sat back and folded my arms. 'You're a journalist, Harriet,' I said. Fragments of a documentary I'd watched were swimming through my memory. I saw the rocky journey of a bodycam secretly recording patients in distress, hands reaching out for help that never came. Brusque responses from unseen members of staff. Undercover work in somewhere advertised as a luxury nursing home with eye-watering fees. I'd switched off five minutes into the programme, unable to watch any more of this pathetic sight. But, I reflected now, as the silence between us thickened, the programme had been fair, without obvious bias. I didn't know who had produced it or gathered the information, but it had got a point over articulately.

But journalists don't make programmes about the success of the NHS, only its failures.

'I'm sorry,' I said.

She still didn't budge. Her face crumpled and her shoulders bowed. 'I was fond of my mother,' she said.

I could have thrown back at her all the stones in my armoury. Like if you were so close how come you hadn't picked up on her vulnerable mental or physical state? Her weight loss? How often did you visit? You never accompanied your mother to the surgery, did you? When did you last see her – alive? Or were you too busy chasing up your stories? Cruel, I know, but true. However, judging by the firm set around her mouth, Harriet Clay was quite capable of returning the favour and accusing me of missing something important. She got to her feet, smart and quick as a soldier, and was almost out of the door before she added a phrase that at the time I took as a threat. 'I'm very like my mother,' she said, with dignity, 'in that I can harbour a grudge for an inordinately long time.'

Well, that was unexpected.

But I read the threat only too clearly, even though it didn't quite match my opinion of Christine. I didn't respond but stood up and held the door open so she had no option but to thread past me and leave, almost managing a smile with her Parthian shot. 'So because I'm a journalist that cancels out the fact that I'm also a bereaved daughter?'

I wanted so hard to shrug and say, 'Whatever', that I had to force my shoulders downwards and press my lips together.

'If you want to speak to one of the doctors,' I said carefully, 'I think you should give them fair warning.' I meant of her profession. 'Her registered GP is Dr Bannister.'

I could have added, 'And good luck with that one.' But of course I didn't.

TWENTY-SEVEN

5 p.m.

As the weather had turned cool I had decided to cook a chicken katzu curry with Thai rice. It was one of my favourites, a nice warming dish, sweet and spicy. (Just like me, I thought, smiling as I cut the chicken breasts into smaller pieces.) There was the added bonus that I could put it in my slow cooker while I had a shower and tarted myself up. I'd shopped for the ingredients on the way home.

As I added the mango chutney I reflected how much I was looking forward to this evening. I felt warmth rather than apprehension. Will was such comfortable company and as well as my anticipated pleasure at his company was the added bonus that I might hear some added facts about Christine's death, maybe a detail from Richard Clay's statement which would confirm or refute my suspicions. I was curious to hear what limp explanation he'd come up with for his wife's sorry death and his survival. He'd need a bloody good story to convince *me* he was a victim. Actually I felt I could have written his statement myself. In my version he'd claim he'd been coerced into swallowing a dose of whatever by his wife and had merely complied 'distressed by her fragile mental state'. I only hoped he hadn't added he 'wanted to join her'. That would have been a step too far. Even the police might have been sceptical at that. But then I visualized him sitting in his chair when I'd visited, shrunken and crushed. And I wondered. Where was the truth?

I wondered if he had his fake facts lined up – like which of them had obtained the lethal drugs and how. I couldn't exactly see Christine fishing around on the dark web for illicit substances, researching what would work best at which dose. And they certainly hadn't obtained them legally from the surgery. I'd checked both Christine's and Richard's prescriptions and there was nothing there that could possibly have proved lethal. Which left street vendors. Which, in turn, brought me back to Ryan who, with his newfound friends, might be able to answer that one. Which one of them had approached the seedy bunch that hung around the High Street? Would they not have realized this would put them in a vulnerable position, open even to blackmail? In my mind here was possibly the threadbare area in Richard Clay's narrative. If only I could subtly introduce that angle to Will the police might have a case they could prove in a court of law.

Intent. Procurement. Planning.

The questions stayed with me as I carried on cooking. If the police couldn't produce a case – and I feared their resolve would be weak – they'd let it slide and Richard Clay would get away with murder, whatever angle his investigative journalist daughter might decide to take. We weren't at fault. It was her father.

But introducing the subject to Will might jeopardize our relationship. He might jump to the conclusion that I'd invited him round just to squeeze information on the Clay case out of him. And it wasn't that. I really liked him.

And so cooking done, chicken katzu in the slow cooker, bubbling away nicely, rice at the ready, it was time to get ready. In his honour I was wearing a dress. Nothing too formal, a short grey dress over which I'd put a bright red cardigan. I pushed my slippers under the bed and fished out a pair of black leather wedges. I straightened my fringe and put my make-up on, grinning to check I hadn't smeared the lipstick over my teeth.

I was ready – ten minutes too early.

I poured myself a thimbleful of white wine. I wanted my wits about me and so I sat, in readiness, at the kitchen counter while idly scrolling through my phone. I'd heard nothing from Mark since the flowers which I had acknowledged by text. A quick:

Thanks – all my favourites. I'd seen from the double ticks that the message had been picked up. If it was picked up by Vivien sneaking a look at his phone I really didn't care. She, in the meantime, had gone ominously quiet on social media posts. I checked to see if PC Rowena Barrett had reposted anything. But there was nothing, which made me curious. Vivien should have been boasting about the impending birth by now, leaking little pink or blue hints, expectant father stuff – or else, if she'd already had the baby, pictures of two – yes, *two* – adoring parents peering into a tiny pink, wrinkled face. I was finding this silence a bit creepy.

And even though you might think my attitude strange, I actually hoped all was well, that some tragedy hadn't befallen either mother or baby because, as a midwife myself – or at least with the SCM qualification tucked in my belt – I knew obstetrics could be a risky business for both mother and child. There is no entitlement or guarantee that there will be a healthy mum or healthy, perfect infant. For some what could have been the happiest of events can turn tragic. I stared across the kitchen and hoped sincerely that this was not the case. I actually felt worried for all three – mother, father, baby – and took a larger sip of wine, my mind spinning around with possibilities.

Why wasn't goofy Vivien posting the happy news? Because it wasn't happy? Because a tragedy had taken place? Something wrong with the baby? Had the baby died? Or was it something to do with Mark? For a moment I'd forgotten about the Clays; my mind was focussed on my ex and his family. I almost went so far as to text Rowena and check whether she knew anything.

And then the doorbell went.

And DC Will Summers was standing on my *Welcome* doormat. For once I hoped the neighbours were all looking because this was so obviously a date standing there. Wine in one hand, flowers in the other, big, big smile plastered across his face. In fact, as I looked past him, I did see a few faces peering through their windows – a couple of the Indian children and Robert Ford. Mr Ford even gave me a bit of a wave, a sly grin and a discreet thumbs up. He and I had become allies over a previous case.

And just for show before ushering him in I gave Will a peck on the cheek which widened his grin to XL.

I waited until we'd put the flowers in the sink and the bottle of wine, de-corked, was standing on the kitchen counter, before I gave him a really tight hug, which led to him regarding me with that warm grin on his face. 'That's nice,' he said. I liked his response. It sounded sincere, genuine, nothing too over the top.

As I served the meal and poured us both a decent glass of wine I spent some moments reflecting, taking stock of where we were. DC Will Summers and I seemed to have settled into a comfortable relationship where we could share conversation or silences. I felt we were edging forward at the same pace, hand in hand, side by side, our minds attuned. Something warmer waited in the wings; we were inching towards it but slowly. The pace suited me fine. The last thing I wanted was to leap into bed, have mad passionate sex a few times before we both leapt out again because we'd moved too fast, tripped over the sex before really evaluating our feelings for one another. I was happy for the relationship to move at a more realistic and sustainable snail's pace. In fact, what I really treasured, as I met his eyes across the table, those calm, honest eyes, was exactly that – the honesty that was growing between us. Although I did feel a sudden snag. That wasn't quite true. I hadn't revealed my suspicions or intense interest in the Clays' suicide pact. And now I knew that however subtly I introduced the subject it would sound clumsy, misplaced and destroy that trust that a millisecond ago I had valued so high.

But it was soon obvious that Will had his own agenda.

TWENTY-EIGHT

He introduced the subjects one by one, as though he'd lined them up beforehand, beginning with one of the topics that had occupied my mind before he'd arrived.

'Florence,' he began, putting his fork down and looking me straight in the eye, 'do you think you'll ever take Mark back?'

He'd obviously been giving this matter a deal of thought and was watching me for my response. I was flattered – but cautious too. I shook my head. 'No,' I said. 'It's done. No going back.'

'Ever?'

He really was forcing the pace now, running, when I'd been simply strolling.

I shook my head, looking straight into those warm brown eyes, reading nothing but blunt honesty while noting the way his eyelashes flickered as I spoke. He hadn't struck me as a man who'd needed reassurance but I knew he wanted more and so I said what had been running through my mind but leaving out my concern for Vivien – and the baby. When I thought about Mark, he was, in my mind, now sidelined, displaced by other issues. I too put my fork down and faced him. 'The way I feel about him, Will, is pity. He's not a bad bloke, but he's made some bad choices.' He was still watching me, guarded and sensitive to any misstep I might make. He said nothing and so I continued, 'He'll always be dad to Lara and Stuart.' I shrugged. 'And that's it.'

He was watching me, his face relaxed – and curious. I took a sip of warm red wine, tasting it on my tongue. 'Affairs are good fun while they last, I guess. Everything's exciting.' Even I was smiling. 'Steamy little trysts, cloak and dagger stuff, giggling when someone spots them together and starts to string the beads into a necklace. But the consequences are all too real and quite ugly.' My mind had reverted to Vivien and the invisible baby and maybe Will read something in my face because he reached across the table and took my hand.

I turned the conversation around. 'What about you and Lydia?'

He shook his head. 'It was never right, but we were both so busy in our jobs, the cracks took a long time to become fissures. We should have ended it at least five years before we did. In fact,' he added, 'she became a problem. At times a big problem.'

'As in . . .?'

'Not quite stalking but pretty near. In fact, that's why I gave up on the sergeant's exams. I was too distracted.' He stopped abruptly. 'Florence.'

I was alert to a change in his tone.

'Ryan Wood.' He paused before continuing, 'He's bitten off more than he can chew.'

I nodded, waiting for him to enlarge.

But he didn't. He was thoughtful. It was on the tip of my tongue to tell Will about the knife wound. I could tell he was watchful, sensing there was something I was keeping back, but he didn't pursue it. Instead, his mouth twisted and he frowned. 'If you get a chance, Flo,' he said, and there was an earnestness in his voice that made me study his face. 'If you do get a chance, warn him off. Some of the guys he's mixing with have histories of extreme violence. They won't go easy on him. Get him away from them.' There was urgency in both his face and his voice. 'He's not their sort. He doesn't understand what these guys are like.'

His fear communicated itself to me. 'I think he might already be in too deep.'

Will gave me a sharp look but didn't pursue my statement. Instead, he continued, 'We have our eye on them.' His voice was very low now. 'At some point we'll be sweeping them all up. And soon. If he's part of the haul he'll get sent down with them. Under the law of joint enterprise he can be convicted of all their offences. Some of them we'll be deporting. Others will go to prison.'

He was shaking his head now. 'Ryan won't do well in prison, Florence. He needs to put some distance between himself and them.'

He couldn't know he was compounding my concern. I was silent for a moment, silently agreeing with him. Then I said innocently, 'Car parts?'

I'd realized Will had a list of subjects he'd intended sharing with me. I was hoping he'd move along to the subject of the Clays' suicide pact. But he was looking very hard at me and his response was quick. 'What do you know about car parts?'

I told him about Gillian Angelo's catalytic convertor and it seemed to damp down his suspicion.

'If it was just that,' he said, bothered about something else now, 'we'd have banged them up months ago. It's bigger than that and well organized. Centrally. Internationally.'

He'd lost me now, speaking to himself and frowning.

'I don't know why they came here of all places where, quite honestly, they stick out like a sore thumb. They could have disappeared in any of the larger conurbations: Manchester, Birmingham, Rochdale. Take your pick. Even Stoke. But they chose here. And we want to know why, what their connections are, who their connections are. Why here, Florence?'

Needless to say, I had no answer. And he patently hadn't expected one because he continued, speaking to himself rather than to me. 'That's just one of the reasons why we're holding back. We need to know more.'

I was aware that he was being unusually frank and wanted him to keep going.

He was still musing, half to himself, almost as though he'd forgotten I was even there. I wanted to prompt him – to move him on to being this frank about the Clays but I didn't want to break the spell. 'This is no place for them,' he repeated. 'Why . . .?'

He was patently preoccupied. I sensed I'd get nothing out of him tonight about the Clays, where the investigation was, or any detail. I clenched my teeth in disappointment, but I'd met this with Mark. He would worry at a case, trying to make sense of events that were, in themselves, senseless. But until he'd found a thread he could pull he would stick to that subject, impossible to divert to any other topic – sometimes for days and nights at a time. Until he'd finished with that one question his mind was stuck in the groove. Round and round and round and round.

Will gave me an apologetic smile. 'I'm sorry,' he said, again reaching across for my hand. 'I haven't been great company this evening, have I?'

I wanted to tell him that he was more than entertainment to me, but the only words I could find were a sort of milk sop, bland and meaningless. 'It's OK.' We both stood up, sensing the evening was nearly over. I moved forward, kissed him on the cheek and stepped away, but he caught my arm, gripping it hard and pulling me towards him. 'Florence,' he said and covered my mouth with his own. It was a passionate kiss with some heat behind it, but we both knew the evening had been spoiled, polluted by his current case and my preoccupation with the Clays.

He left and I decided I had to put my concerns about Christine Clay on the backburner and would try and speak to Ryan.

TWENTY-NINE

10.30 p.m.

T he house felt empty after I'd heard Will back down the drive. This time I hoped none of my neighbours was watching as I waved him off. No passionate kisses on the doorstep this time. After watching his taillights disappear down the road I returned to the empty room, cleared away the dishes and sat down fingering my phone. But this time I was not thinking about Mark, Vivien or the baby – born or unborn.

My mind had turned to Ryan. I agreed with Will. He was out of his depth, almost a child, in a forest of hardened criminals who would not hesitate to turn cruel if they doubted his loyalty. It was OK Will suggesting I have a word with Ryan, but there was a practical issue. I did have his mobile phone number, but what could I say in a text message? What if one of his villainous cronies picked up a message from me and, knowing my links with the police, past and present, they made a dangerous connection?

In the end my conscience forced me to act. If I didn't and something happened to the boy I'd watched grow up with all the disadvantages a lack of family support can cause, I would always feel guilty, that I should have done something however empty and powerless.

So I typed out a bland message. *Florence Shaw here, the nurse from the surgery. How is the giving up smoking going?*

Sending it this late at night would be unwise. The time itself would cause suspicion so I didn't send it. First thing in the morning would do. I put my phone away.

He probably wouldn't respond. But bumping into him in the town would be a chance affair. Besides, every time I'd seen him in the town recently he'd been surrounded by his new 'mates'. So I felt a bit scuppered. I liked Ryan and I did want to help but, apart from this one message, I couldn't see how I could contact him without inviting suspicion.

And I had my own concerns. Frankly? I was worried. Yet again Mark and Vivien had receded and the Clays had moved to the fore. I felt agitated. I'd relied on finding something out from Will but I'd found out nothing.

I was too twitchy to go to bed. I had to do right by my patient but I didn't know how to find out any facts. Will would know instinctively that I was fishing. So my list of questions remained. What line were the police taking? How would Richard Clay's role in this tragedy be viewed? Would they ultimately blame him? Would he face any charges? Much depended on the result of the inquest.

And now I had the added complication of their nosey daughter whose real role I still hadn't figured out. But her aggression combined with her profession cast a shadow over me. I would have to watch my step because she would be there, peering over my shoulder. But surely her profession would lead her to wonder about her father's role?

Or was it too close to home?

I opened up my iPad, where I soon realized that Harriet Clay was, like most investigative reporters, tenacious, cynical and prone to winkling out secrets folk thought had been hidden forever. She was a wolf who would drain the blood out of any story. And it was obvious from her backlist that one of her abiding missions was to 'expose' any failings of the NHS, its staff, premises, anything. There was story after story of various failings: treatment delays, appointments cancelled, results of tests which had never been acted on. It was all there. I could see some of the failures had led to prolonged ill health and, in at least one case, untimely death articulated by a grieving widow who described her husband's illness in graphic details. A death which even I could see had been preventable. Sepsis – every single symptom ignored. She seemed to cover every speciality – mental health, maternity services, so on and on. The public might adore their NHS but because they feel they own it they also take negative stories about it personally.

And some journalists seem to believe it's their duty to expose these stories to the harshest daylight.

Worried at her sheer tenacity and pounding negativity, I snapped my iPad shut. I had had enough of Harriet Clay and her stories. But I couldn't help wondering how she'd feel about investigating her own father.

THIRTY

There followed a couple of days' quiet and, as expected, Ryan didn't respond to my text message; neither did I see him around the town. Which could be a good thing – or not. I did get a message from Will thanking me for the dinner but it was brief, seemingly detached, almost cold, even though it ended in a kiss and I noticed he hadn't suggested another date. I wondered if, somehow, I'd misread the signs, dreamed up this 'closeness' – in other words blown it. Or maybe my original guess was nearer the truth – that he was wrapped up in his case and not the problems my mind was tussling with.

But there was an upside to my phone silence. I heard nothing from Harriet Clay either, though she was still staying with her dad. When I drove up the Newcastle Road and passed number fifty-two, her Audi TT was still sitting on the drive. So she hadn't gone home. Was that because she was being a dutiful daughter and wanted to comfort her dad, arrange her mother's funeral, or was she planning a personal approach to her next programme, the poor treatment her mother had received from her local GP practice?

Allegedly.

I could only guess at which of those three was the right version.

But there was another possibility. Unlikely but still possible. Did she have a suspicion that the true version differed from the accepted narrative of her parents' tragedy? Maybe living with her father had she noticed something that made her wonder?

And then, worryingly, ominously, on Friday the thirteenth I saw from my patient list that Richard Clay had booked into see me. By the side of his name there was none of the traditional explanations for the request – no 'health check due' or 'blood test wanted'. It was left blank. He was due in at eleven o'clock, and as I pressed the buzzer to summon him my mouth felt dry.

Even my imagination was failing to provide an answer. I just knew it spelled trouble.

You can learn many things about a patient if you listen to their footsteps as they approach your door, as well as the sound and rate of their knock on the door. Demanding, tentative, angry, reluctant.

Richard's footsteps were dragging, soft and sneaky, his knock on the door quiet, as though he wanted to test me, make me wonder whether I'd heard it or not.

I had to hold the facts fast in the back of my mind: the pathological dominance he'd held over his deceased wife plus his daughter's profession and the harm she could potentially do to me as well as the surgery. I couldn't even begin to imagine where we had slipped up so badly, particularly as the post-mortem had proved beyond doubt that she hadn't had cancer.

I didn't really cast Harriet as a dutiful daughter, but the fact remained she was still there.

What other motive for prolonging her visit could she have other than to unearth some failing on our part and translate that into lurid, accusatory headlines.

His footsteps dragged to a stop right outside my door. I could hear his breathing through the wooden panel, raspy and anxious. There was a pause, a wheezy deep breath and then the door handle was pressed down.

Immediately he entered my doubts about him surged back. He stood in the doorway – not quite entering but standing on the threshold. Eyes, like his daughter's, cold as an Arctic ice floe, scanned the room before resting back on me. He said nothing; neither did I. I couldn't even seem to find my usual greeting,

The words were lodged in my throat. I fiddled with the notepad on my desk, picked up a pen, turned my head as though reading the notes on my screen. But really my heart was pounding. Was I looking into the face of a cruel man who had murdered his wife, swallowing enough pills to disguise it as a suicide pact? And at the back of my mind was still the dangerous fact of his daughter's profession. Finally, when he entered, closing the door so carefully behind him, there was no click. He sat down in the chair his wife had inhabited so often and now I looked straight at him. And had the odd impression he too was wondering something: at a guess whether he could trust me.

No.

I cleared my throat and managed, 'Mr Clay,' the words rasping in my throat which was as dry as a riverbed in a drought.

'Good morning.'

'What can I do for you today, Mr Clay?'

He licked dry lips and stared at me with those polar eyes. 'I wanted to talk to you, Florence,' he said, his voice soft. I leaned forward and I picked up his scent: coal tar soap, E45, antiseptic.

I pasted on my interested, interrogating face.

'I want to talk to you,' he repeated.

'About?'

'My wife,' he said, keeping a steady eye on me.

My heart started yammering now. However, I managed, 'In regard to . . .?'

'You know what she was like.'

I looked blank, not sure what he was getting at.

'Her depression,' he said earnestly, a note of desperation making him sound almost shrill.

I stared at him, puzzled.

'Her erroneous belief that she was terminally ill.' His voice was now haughty and I had the sense this was not what he'd planned to say.

'Don't you think you should be discussing this with a counsellor?'

'No,' he said. 'I can only discuss this with you, Florence. *You're* the one who saw her most regularly.'

I couldn't argue with that so simply nodded. He put his face close to mine while I shrank from his antiseptic smell, seeing too clearly that thin face, the narrow bridge to his nose, the unemotional eyes. Possibly primed by his daughter, he was out for blood. I could sense it. There was no real question. Only antagonism. He was out for blood.

'Where did that conviction come from?'

Had it been anyone else asking the same question I might have shrugged and responded with a rhetorical question of my own. *Who knows?*

'It was real,' he insisted.

I stared at him stupidly, fearing that any response I made would be a misstep.

'Let me clarify,' he continued. 'My wife was under a misapprehension that she was suffering from a terminal illness which would prove painful and drawn out.'

I wanted to say, 'And who planted that seed in her vulnerable brain?'

I felt an urge to defend myself. 'At no time,' I said firmly, 'was I made aware of this erroneous belief.' It was the best and safest I could do – under the circumstances.

He was still fighting. 'Had she act-u-ally' – he was drawing out the word to maximum effect – 'had the pleasure of a consultation with a psychiatrist I am certain he would have disabused her of the conviction that was slowly destroying her and led ultimately . . .' That was when his face changed. 'Ultimately led to her taking her own life.'

That was the moment I could have adopted a police role, asked him about events on the night of the fourth of October. But one question would lead to another – and that to a further question – and so on. And I didn't have the right.

But I couldn't suppress my instinctive responses, the questions that were stacking up in my mind.

Who suggested this suicide pact?

Who acquired the drugs?

Who swallowed first – or was it a simultaneous act?

Why didn't you tell us Christine was convinced she had cancer?

What really happened that night?

How was the alarm raised – in time for you but too late for her?

But I was more aware than ever that I had to be very careful. The world saw him as a damaged, bereaved widower.

Even if I didn't.

I was selective in the words I chose. Speaking carefully, as though crossing a river on stepping stones, hopping from one rock to another, only too aware of what would happen if I slipped.

I'd decided on a risky venture, turning the accusations on to himself. 'Had *you* confided in us about your wife's' – I rejected the word delusion as being too close to psychosis, choosing instead – 'misconception, we could have done something about it.'

And for a moment he was stumped. I realized he hadn't

prepared a response to this. He'd expected me to be too crushed and guilty to fight back.

His mouth was open ready to speak but he'd lost his thread, while I was just finding mine.

We both waited and it was he who broke the silence.

'What choice did I have? I couldn't have broken her trust . . .' He paused. 'However much it annoyed me. I kept myself in check worrying what if you *did* find something? I would have felt awful.'

It might not be the truth, but his version did make sense.

'What else could I have *done*?' he asked. 'I tried everything.'

He was shouldering the guilt himself now? Shaking his head while asking the questions, not to me but internally, to himself, while I searched his face for clues that would explain this apparent revelation. I was back to thinking had I been wrong all along? Misread him and his motives? Honestly I was more confused than ever.

But Mark's words rang in my mind, tolling as solemn as a funeral bell. *Look at the facts, Florrie.*

And what were the facts?

He was alive and she was dead. Those were the hard facts.

Eventually he looked across at me and now his eyes were very hard and cold. 'I intend suing the practice,' he said, 'for dereliction of duty. I feel you and your colleagues are ultimately responsible for my wife's death because you failed to convince my wife she was in good health.'

As did you, I thought, and my mouth dropped open. It was a new one on me.

In my dreams I am able to cook a snook at a complaining patient with a cheeky 'suit yourself' or 'whatever'. But I never had in real life. Instead, I was recalling the sour, unhappy words of my retired colleague and hoped I was up to date with my subs to the Royal College of Nursing.

But his threat did give me the perfect excuse for standing up. 'Then in that case, Mr Clay, I feel it better if we don't continue with this conversation.'

The look he gave me was pure poison and he stayed sitting. I would have to manually evict him, I thought, without a clue how I would do that. We had no security staff.

He was biting his lip now while I watched him and read something unexpected. His eyes were flickering towards the floor as though he'd delivered his line and was now waiting for my response. His daughter had fed him the lines and he had delivered them. But he was uncomfortable and unhappy. And something else struck me. That man with the iron will and the dominant personality had, himself, been superseded by his own daughter's dominance. Interesting but it didn't actually change anything. Whichever of them had delivered the line the threat was the same and I didn't doubt one, or maybe both, would drag this issue through the courts. I was in for months, possibly years, of torture and heartbreak. Christine Clay's tragic suicide would be placed at the wrong door – not the door of number 52 Newcastle Road, that large and lovely house – but at the door of the medical practice.

It had fallen to him to deliver her message. I was surprised she'd been able to exert such an influence over her father when he'd always struck me as a person who would not easily be manipulated into doing something that went against the grain.

But recognizing his daughter's strength, my thought now was if only I could harness that strength, get her on my side, maybe ask her father a few of the right questions, perhaps as a tribute to her mother, she would unearth the truth.

It would be a dangerous strategy.

There was a stiff silence between us. After a few tense moments he stood up, straightened to a military upright stance; I half expected a salute before, with some dignity, he walked out.

THIRTY-ONE

11.20 a.m.

When one is burning to discover a truth a solution can sometimes come from an unexpected source.

To me Jalissa O'Sullivan was the supplier of Stone's most excellent sandwiches which she brought round to the practice every day, without fail, in a wicker basket which she carried over her forearm. In fact, she supplied many businesses around the town but always assured me that her trip into the doctors' practice was her favourite because she and I had developed quite a close friendship. I know it's a rather meaningless, overused cliché, but her sandwiches were not only made with the very best of ingredients but they were also handled with love. They seemed to contain the sweetest of tomatoes, the crispiest of salad ingredients and there would often be an added sprig of fresh parsley or a slice of lemon if one chose the smoked salmon. Her talents were as artistic as one of the best celebrity chef's.

And since Petronella, and now Charles, had started school, my champion sandwich supplier had some spare time on her hands. And so she had found a way to fill it. What I hadn't known until that day was how.

As I heard Richard Clay's footsteps heading away from my room and down the corridor, I heard him stop and then voices. Moments later Jalissa was waltzing into my room and I quizzed her.

'You met Mr Clay in the corridor?'

'Yes, the poor man.' And then she said something that really surprised me. 'He my employer now.'

'What?'

'Yeah, since his wife die his daughter suggest poor Mr Clay have a lady in to help clean up the house. So, knowing I was after a way to fill up my time now my two small angels have to attend school, someone suggest me. He interview me on Wednesday and . . .' She looked justifiably pleased with herself. 'He hire me.'

I contained my amazement, which was quickly followed by pleasure. Serendipitous, I thought, even though I hadn't quite filled in the small detail: how? I clung to the conviction that handled carefully, sensitively, maybe Jalissa could find something out. I felt my eyes narrow. Possibly the bottle of fatal pills? I guessed the police would have searched for them but Jalissa's idea of cleaning would be every bit as thorough as a forensic search if not more so. But Jalissa was both honest and loyal. And as an employee to Richard Clay, she would not betray his trust. Which meant that unless I handled her very delicately she wouldn't 'spy' for me at 'poor Mr Clay's house'. And there was no way I was going to share my suspicions with anyone just yet.

She would be horrified. Obviously unable to read my mind, she held her basket of sandwiches out in front of her, chuckling. 'You lose your appetite today, Florence?' Her chuckle grew louder. 'You in love or somethin', girl?'

I reached out and helped myself but maybe I hadn't spent enough time choosing because she followed that up with: 'It that policeman fella?'

My mind was still tussling with a means of using Jalissa's new job though I hadn't quite worked out how. But I was realizing one can approach a problem from many different angles.

From our talk the other evening I'd realized that Will's mind was focussed on the car parts investigation. Which meant he wasn't focussing on the Clay case. Which meant it really was up to me to find the truth. The Clay suicide pact would soon fade into the police's rear-view mirror, which would give time for any evidence, such as a packet of drugs, to be destroyed. Time was of the essence.

The trouble was nobody really cared. A suicide seemed to answer any questions. Richard would want the whole episode buried deep. And Harriet? Simply wanted our blood to flow. I'd thought she would want to learn the truth about her mother's death and the role her father had played. But she seemed to have found her own version.

And Jalissa's sympathy lay with her employer.

I had no idea what my next step should be without stepping not simply into the lion's den but right between its jaws.

Something must have been triggered in my mind as I bit into my sandwich – egg mayo. I made a face. It was my least favourite. No wonder Jalissa had picked up that I was distracted.

At the same time a misfit of a memory had swum into my mind which seemed, in some way, to tie in (I had no idea how) to that last, strange consultation.

It had been a few months ago, during one of Christine's many frustrating consultations, which had been heading into another blind corner. I must have said something – I can't remember what – but as the words left my mouth I intercepted a long look between husband and wife. A sort of challenging stare between them. But it was Christine who was holding her own with her husband and, as I'd watched, it was he who dropped his eyes first. I couldn't read what it meant or what particular statement had triggered the exchange, but it appeared meaningful. And now I was wondering. Why had that singular moment stuck in my mind?

I ate half the sandwich and threw the rest away. Suddenly I wasn't hungry.

THIRTY-TWO

6 p.m.

What I really needed were the hard facts in the possession of the police. First of all, the drugs used and their source; second, who had acquired them? Third, I needed a picture. Exactly how had Christine's body been lying and where had her husband been found? Who had actually raised the alarm? Not Richard, because he'd been described as being in a coma. And not Harriet who lived in London. I lacked specific detail. And now I didn't have Mark's brains to pick (he'd gone ominously silent since the drunken night and the flowers-on-the-doorstep incident), I had no option but to sugarcoat DC Will Summers who, car parts apart, might be persuaded to take an interest in the case of the Clays' suicide pact.

The next part of my plan was hardly subtle. It was, I acknowledge, a blunt instrument, but time was marching on. Memories quickly fade, evidence degrades or is deliberately destroyed, and I was becoming anxious that Richard Clay would get away with it. I didn't dare even mention my suspicions to Harriet because without some hard facts to support my theory, she would literally tear me to pieces. I hadn't forgotten her threat. Almost daily I expected a lawyer's letter to arrive at the surgery detailing her legal action. But I had to do something.

I did, however, have one tiny consolation. Ryan Wood had not attended the surgery with any more injuries. As expected, neither had he turned up for his next Give Up Smoking appointment, but on my drive home I'd passed him crossing the road in the direction of Morrison's, nonchalantly and unapologetically smoking a cigarette. He'd been alone, sauntering along, and as far as I could tell he'd looked OK.

So that evening on the unlucky date of Friday the thirteenth, I risked it, pressing Will's number and asking him, in a slightly suggestive voice, whether he fancied another home-cooked meal the following night. Luckily for me and my self-esteem, he took the bait.

'I'll bring the wine,' he said, 'if you tell me what's on the menu.'

Which led me to confess I hadn't actually decided.

'I'll bring rosè then,' he said jauntily. In fact, as I put the phone down, I reflected he'd sounded gratifyingly chirpy. Suspecting nothing. I reminded myself he was a police officer. Maybe his buoyant mood was because he was close to concluding his other case and banging up the undesirables who'd been haunting our streets.

After my bait had hauled in a success it was only fair to make a special effort with the edibles, and so on Saturday morning I got up early enough to catch the fish van that drove down from the north-east, having met the fishermen off the boats. I bought two generous portions of monkfish which cost as much as fillet steak. But I needed good bait. The fish van stopped off in the market square every Saturday morning and there was always a queue, which I was happy to join. Next, I raided the fruit and veg shop and bought a couple of unwaxed lemons as well as asparagus, Little Fingers baby carrots which were, it was proclaimed, grown locally on the allotments and picked fresh. For dessert I had late raspberries from Scotland and Cornish cream. I walked home convinced my line would soon be ready to haul in with such quality, sustainable bait. I felt a bit guilty making all this effort, candles as well, knowing I wanted something in return. Verbatim preferably. Something I could use to convince Harriet to work *with* me rather than *against* me.

Saturday 14 October, 7 p.m.

He turned up promptly, looking rather fetching in a pair of dark blue chinos and an open-necked cream shirt, his face bright with that all-encompassing, genuinely warm grin. He seemed relaxed as he handed me a bouquet of yellow roses which could replace

Mark's lavish bunch, just beginning to droop. He also kissed my cheek before giving me a searching look as though asking questions. Then he produced a bottle of rosé from under his arm. 'Vintner said it goes with anything.' Another jaunty grin. 'But then they always say that, don't they?' He paused, eyebrows poised for my response, which gave me time to look suspiciously at him. I had the sneaky feeling he knew he was being set up and would spend at least part of the evening being milked for details. I needed to play this more skilfully and, as I arranged the flowers, I tried to work out the best way to achieve maximum result. While I brought the lemon butter sauce *almost* to the boil he peered over my shoulder and made appreciative noises. I nearly leaned back into him. He'd *looked* so good with that friendly grin and now he *felt* good too, a pair of solid arms cradling me against his chest.

I savoured the moment.

I'd practised a nonchalant expression in front of the mirror, focussing on a neutral face, but it was no use. As we ate, once we'd got through the obligatory appreciative lip-smacking, every time I looked up he was watching me with a sort of knowing smile and now I was certain he knew *exactly* what I was up to and was prepared to play along. Finally he put his fork down with a smile that was both warm and wide. 'You may as well come out with it, Florence.'

I'd been rumbled. And I felt relieved rather than abashed. 'Is it that obvious?'

His eyes were bright and warm as he nodded.

So I put my fork down while he cued me in. 'It's the Clays, isn't it?'

I nodded.

He took a sip of wine and topped up my glass before taking a long slow breath in. 'So what exactly is it?'

'He's made a statement – under oath?' I was aware I was testing his trust of me.

'Of course.'

He skewered me with a hard stare. 'I hardly need to tell you this is strictly *entre nous*.' I moved my head up and down like an obedient schoolgirl.

'His story is—'

My ears had already pricked up at his choice of word. 'He

says his wife was convinced she had cancer and didn't want to go through all the treatment options.'

I interrupted him. 'We never discussed treatment options because she never mentioned this cancer phobia to us. Her symptoms were fully investigated and no cancer was found. The post-mortem further proved she didn't have it.'

He shifted in his seat, uncomfortable. 'But people *can* have an unfounded cancer phobia, Florence, can't they?'

'Then why didn't he speak to us about her fear? He had plenty of opportunity. We could have got her psychiatric help earlier. Will, in my opinion this was a lie fed to her by her husband.'

'Florence,' he said, his voice kind, but firm, 'there was a letter.'

That knocked me off balance. 'A letter?'

He nodded. 'Whether she had an erroneous belief that she had cancer or not the letter means that the coroner will have no option but to return a verdict of suicide.'

I was appalled. 'And her husband?'

'Freely offered that he was unable to dissuade his wife that she did not have a terminal illness and so he—'

'Took a token dose knowing hers was lethal but he would wake up,' I supplied. 'If he'd known about her phobia surely we would have been the best people to explain to Christine that she didn't have a terminal illness?' My voice was razor sharp.

'Apparently she was convinced you – and the other members of staff,' he added hastily, 'were shielding her from the truth.'

Oh, clever, clever Richard, I thought, to supply an answer for everything.

Will was watching me carefully. 'And so he attended every consultation in the hope that something would be said or suggested to disabuse her of her conviction.'

He attended every consultation except the last, I was thinking. Except that strange, final meeting when she dropped little hints, confirming my impression that her husband was a dominating presence. And a few days later she was dead.

'Why didn't he confide in us? Use *us* to convince her?' I appealed. 'He had plenty of chances to bring up the subject. Will, we could have tackled it.'

'That's true, Florence, but it was hardly my place to ask that sort of question.'

'So you simply took his statement at face value?' I had a sudden vision of Christine's bent shoulders and frightened expression and now I felt angry. But at the same time I felt unsettled. But a suicide note put paid to my theory. I only wished I could see it.

'Any chance . . .?' I began, but the words were hardly out of my mouth before Will was shaking his head. 'The coroner has seen it and doesn't need it as evidence. He gave it to the daughter who was anxious to have it.'

I'll bet, I thought, feeling vindictiveness bubble up inside me like methane.

He hadn't finished. 'She sees it as tangible evidence of her mother's state of mind.'

'You know she's an investigative journalist with a particular interest in the failures of the NHS?'

'I didn't.' But I noticed it hadn't seemed to faze him.

'So when is the inquest?'

'End of the month,' he said, watching for my reaction. 'Twenty-third, I think.'

'Will I be called as a witness?'

'Possibly. It's up to the coroner, Florence.'

And now I was so troubled I'd lost my appetite for the fresh raspberries sitting in the fridge.

Will regarded me for a moment, then said quietly, 'You have your own version of events, don't you?'

I didn't respond straight away. I knew if I gave vent to my true feelings this was the moment when our relationship could sour. I also recognized that if I wasn't completely honest with him our relationship would never last anyway.

And so I plunged in with my version.

'First of all, she didn't have cancer and never mentioned that fear to us.' I carried on, 'So where did the idea come from?' I answered my own question. 'It has to be Richard.'

'No, it doesn't. I consulted a psychiatrist.'

'Who?'

'A forensic psychiatrist from the Potteries. I just asked her a few questions.' He grinned. 'Got a bit of background knowledge. She did say that suicide pacts are actually very rare. There were only two cases last year. I looked them up. She also said people can be convinced they have cancer or some other terminal disease when there is no real evidence. They can have test after test – all negative – and it can be impossible to dissuade them. Florence,' he finished gently as though he was sorry for having to disappoint me, 'it happens. And,' he added, 'if your theory is true, that her husband put the idea in her head – however cleverly – there is no way we can prove it.'

Now I was absolutely crestfallen because I knew he was right. Then I picked up.

'The drugs,' I said. 'What about the drugs?' I was clutching at a single straw now. 'What drugs did they use?'

'OxyContin,' he said, almost sadly. 'Responsible, it seems, for millions of deaths.'

'And where did they get it?'

'He says one of your doctors prescribed it.'

I was triumphant. 'Except we didn't. Not one of our doctors would have prescribed such an addictive and dangerous drug. OxyContin? It's a potent opioid. It's only prescribed for severe, intractable pain and in terminal illness. Not in a million years would it have been prescribed for her. She had *no* history of pain. And even if she did, any doctor would go through the gamut of everything in the pharmacopeia before possibly encouraging an addiction.'

'We did speak to her doctor,' he said sniffily, 'who told us almost word for word exactly what you said. I was just telling you what *Mr Clay* said.'

'So did you go back and tax him with that?'

'He said he didn't have a clue when or how she'd accessed the drugs. He'd just assumed they'd come from the surgery. He couldn't think where else she might have obtained them.'

'He didn't ask her,' I asked sharply, 'before he swallowed his non-fatal dose?'

'He says he can't remember.'

'How convenient.'

'So where *did* she get it from?' He was musing rather than inviting my opinion, but I had the stirrings of an idea.

I sat back and poured us both another glass of wine. 'Is it on the streets here, in Stone?'

'It's everywhere,' he said.

THIRTY-THREE

9 p.m.

The conversation seemed to be stalling but my mind was busy. OxyContin? A villain of a drug responsible for so much misery. But Ryan, or his newfound friends, might have some idea of who supplied it. And if he knew that he might even know who had bought it. It was my chance. An opportunity as perfect as the apples of Hesperides.

Will had read my mind. 'If you're thinking about Ryan,' he said, smiling, 'we're keeping an eye on him. But he's not trading in OxyContin, Florence. It's out of his league.'

I curbed my optimism, consoling myself that Ryan might not be involved in the illegal trade but he might have information about its source and buyers. I was thoughtful now, knowing the way the police worked. They would wait. More than once, Mark had described arresting the lowest in the structure as simply cutting off the head of the Hydra. There were always plenty lining up to take their place, earn the easy money. The ones nearer to the top they could put away the better their chance of having a real impact. Will was watching me, an impish smile on his face as he turned his head to regard the dish of plump raspberries sitting on the side next to two dishes and a jug of cream. I moved across and put them in the centre of the table.

We hadn't explored Christine's death and her husband's survival as much as I would have liked. But I had learned something. I knew now which drug had been used. And it could provide an explanation of sorts. Its effects could be unpredictable. So was my assumption that Richard had deliberately taken a lesser dose wrong?

There was only one way to find out. Ask him. But not me. Jalissa?

However, I was not going to let the Clays spoil my evening when I was just beginning to realize how much I liked William

Summers. I liked his sense of humour, his self-deprecation. But most of all I liked the way his eyes radiated warmth, honesty and kindness.

I realized I was smiling stupidly at him.

But I couldn't suppress that one last question. 'Are you charging him?'

He swallowed a mouthful of raspberries. 'I take it you mean Richard Clay?'

I was only slightly embarrassed. 'Yeah.'

'It's with the CPS at the moment but I think they'll consider the tragedy he's been through and advise us not to press charges of assisting a suicide. We haven't got enough evidence to convict him. And the letter clearly implies that it was Mrs Clay who initiated the suicides.'

'Suicide,' I corrected sharply.

It was as I'd expected but I was still disappointed.

'So he'll get away with it?'

Will looked weary now. 'Get away with what exactly, Florence?'

I held back my accusation, instead focussing on spooning out a second generous portion of raspberries and pouring out the cream, but they didn't taste as sweet as they'd promised; the flavour seemed to have gone out of them.

We loaded the dishwasher before going to sit in the sitting room. He settled next to me but my mind was still focussing one way while I sensed his attention headed off in a different direction. I was fixed on the letter – if only I could read it. Was it a complete fake or had he coerced her into writing it? I was sure I'd be able to tell.

'That letter,' I said. 'I take it, it *was* her writing?'

'Yeah. Their daughter confirmed it.'

And this time it was he who decided to continue with the subject. 'Charging a newly bereaved widower with aiding and abetting his wife's death will do us no good, particularly when it *appears* that he suffered from the consequences.'

I was glad he'd put emphasis on the word 'appears' even if it was only a slight inflection.

'He'll engender nothing but sympathy and if, as you say, his daughter is an investigative journalist, with a particular beef against the NHS, you can be sure the headlines will be savage.'

He waited before continuing. 'Any charges brought to court would soon be dropped. It won't benefit anyone, Florence, least of all you as the health professional most involved with her case.' He followed that up with an observation. 'You've gone quiet.'

I was just beginning to realize how much was stacked against me. Added to that was my own guilt that I had failed this vulnerable woman. Yes, I'd sensed her vulnerability, but what had I done apart from persuading her doctor to make a referral I'd always known would take months? The sad picture returned to me as vividly as though she was in the room, downtrodden, round-shouldered, unhappy. And she *had* been deeply unhappy. Harriet might have seen me as an uncaring, hard-nosed professional, but that couldn't have been farther from the truth. In reality I lived, breathed and suffered alongside my patients. And if I felt I'd let them down my guilt was tougher than the punishment any disciplinary hearing could have inflicted.

Possibly sensing the pull on my emotions Will moved towards me, putting his arm around me. 'Florence.'

I dropped my head on to his shoulder.

THIRTY-FOUR

Sunday 15 October, 8 a.m.

After that the evening had ended quite predictably with Will staying the night. We'd slept with our arms around each other, both comforting the other, but we didn't make love. Something was holding both of us back. Maybe the feeling we'd jumped into bed a bit quickly or perhaps it was the scars of previous relationships that hadn't quite healed over. Whatever it was I was contented as I dropped off to sleep, waking sometime during the night with that same feeling of comfort and safety. I woke in the morning and we stared at each other, trying to read the other's thoughts. I made some coffee and we sat up in bed, initially awkward, until I was flooded with a feeling that he was my friend and we grinned at each other, recognizing that our relationship had taken a turn. Will was smiling, eyes warm. He touched my hand. 'It's OK,' he said. 'I'm guessing we both want to take baby steps.'

I nodded, feeling a weight drop from me.

He hopped out of bed, slid into his trousers and put a shirt on. 'Fancy another coffee?'

I nodded and he disappeared for a few minutes. I heard the sound of him bustling around in the kitchen, reappearing in the doorway, a mug in each hand.

'Thank you.' I couldn't remember the last time someone had brought me coffee in bed.

It wasn't long after that that he put his mug down on the bedside table. 'I have to go into work,' he said, while I felt smug and hugged my knees.

'And I don't.'

Twenty minutes later I heard his car reverse out of my drive and head off into a misty, October morning. And so the inevitable had happened. And I felt content. I began to plan the day – tidy up the house and perhaps walk down the canal to the Aston Marina. It looked cold out there. The walk would do me good, blow away the cobwebs, and give me time to think through things. Not only my conviction that Richard Clay had engineered both his wife's death and, somehow, his own survival, but try to find a way of proving it. Even if it might not lead to a conviction, I needed to know it for myself. And now there was this evidence of a suicide note. How convenient. I wanted to see that letter. I felt I would be able to pick up on understanding Christine's damaged mind and her mental state when she had written it. If she really had written it.

I moved on. And now I had another thing to ponder. This new relationship. Where would it lead? I wondered. Will had been to my house a few times. But I'd never been to his home. I had no idea what his home circumstances were. Was he being secretive? Hiding something from me? I realized how little I really knew about him – apart from that one admission: the long-term relationship with a woman called Lydia. A relationship which after ten years together had led nowhere. Poof – disappeared into nothing. In ten years' time I would be sixty. I know relationships can start at any age but surely chances diminish as one gets older?

I worried. Was I being misled – again?

11 a.m.

As I strode along the towpath the rain drizzled down, making it even colder, and cutting my visibility down to a yard or two. The day lacked colour, seemingly producing only different shades of grey. There were none of the canal barges with their brightly coloured decorations of roses and castles. Where did that tradition originate? I wondered, and quickened my step, looking forward to a cup of hot chocolate at the marina.

To add to the grey blanket of fog that was wrapping itself around me, I now worried how to read that letter. I hardly wanted to provoke Harriet by asking to see it, but I couldn't see another way.

Even after a large mug of hot chocolate complete with whipped cream and marshmallow scatters, I was still troubled. I desperately wanted to read that letter which I was certain would hold some clues about Christine's 'suicide', but Harriet had it. And she was hardly going to show it to me unless I asked.

However, Will texted me to say the coroner had released Christine Clay's body for burial and her funeral was arranged for Tuesday. I intended being there. Partly to pay my respects to my dead patient but also it would give me a chance to observe the Clays, father and daughter. Maybe at the funeral the contents of Christine's final letter would be shared.

Monday 16 October, 8.45 a.m.

I was at the surgery bright and early, untroubled by the fact that I had heard nothing more from Will. Rightly or wrongly, I felt our relationship had climbed towards a new level. I trusted him, even if I didn't know much about him. I felt comfortable and didn't need constant contact or reassurance. He was there for me. Although, I reminded myself, I'd once believed that about Mark. And thinking about Mark: where the hell was he? Why the social media silence from Vivien when she should be shouting happy news from the rooftops? What was going on? My 'mole', PC Rowena Barrett, had messaged me telling me that she was off on holiday – in Peru of all places – and would be 'off the radar' for a couple of weeks. So that source was temporarily suspended!

The first thing I did that morning was to arrange to have two hours off for Christine's funeral. The receptionists grumbled a bit as they had to rearrange my clinic times, phoning every patient who'd been booked in between eleven and one in the afternoon and offering them alternative times or appointments. But as I'd offered to see patients through my lunch hour no one was really inconvenienced. And when I'd mentioned it to Dr Bhatt he'd nodded his approval. Even praising me for my thoughtfulness. Which, knowing my motive was less pure than investigative, actually made me feel slightly guilty. However, I believed a result would justify my nosey interest.

My asthma clinic was busy that morning because the children had gone back to school after the October half term and that meant the usual virus swap. Because each child was wheezing and coughing I told most of them to double up on their inhalers. None of them was raising alarm bells for me.

I spoke to a couple of the parents about the effect of passive smoking on their wheezy kids, which reminded me of Will's interest in Ryan. Truth? Rogue though he might be, I knew better than many that he was a decent person at heart who'd had a very messy childhood. The usual recipe of violent dad, mum with more partners than the king of Siam, mix in some hefty alcohol consumption and you had the perfect recipe for yet another villain – which, somehow, with so much stacked against him, Ryan was not. And, for all their inherent cynicism, I knew the local police shared my view.

As well as finding out what he knew about the supply of OxyContin in Stone I should warn him to steer clear of his new 'friends'. The police were closing in and if he was caught in the crossfire who knew where he'd end up. Probably in prison. I tried his mobile number again but it didn't even ring. It had been switched off – which was another cause for alarm. No one switches their mobile off these days. You put it on silent or vibrate but not off. Never off. And while most of us leave it on because we have children, Ryan had to leave it on in case his mother, Celine, who was prone to getting roaring drunk, needed her boy to come and get her. He was basically his mother's carer and

had been since he was a child. Without her son Celine would
fall apart. But that closeness could also be used. If Celine felt
her beloved son was in real danger of being harmed or imprisoned
she would panic and work on him. Ryan would listen to her, I
believed. So I rang her during my coffee break and realized from
Celine's slurred voice that she had already had a 'couple of
ciders'. Why cider? Ask one of my many alcoholics for a defini-
tive answer. It is the cheapest form of alcohol. Nineteen units
for three pounds forty-nine?

'Celine.'

She recognized my voice straight away. 'Hello Florence, love.'

At least alcohol made her affectionate rather than aggressive.

'What can I do for you, darlin'?'

'Celine, you need to keep an eye on your boy.'

'My Ryan? What's he gone and done now?' Hiccup and a
giggle.

'Celine . . .' I was struggling to penetrate that alcoholic
bonhomie. 'He needs to watch the dudes he's mixing with.'

'Who? Them foreign guys? They's dead nice, duck. I wouldn't
worry about them.'

I swear if Celine Wood had met Hannibal Lecter she would
have judged him 'a nice guy' but with 'peculiar eating habits'.
She didn't have much insight into character.

'Yes. He needs to stop home for a bit.'

'With his ma.' Another hiccup and a giggle, silence while she
swigged from the bottle. 'I'll tell him, Florence, love.'

I wanted to say they were about to be rumbled but I didn't
dare.

I couldn't trust her. Even without the booze she was loose
lipped. And with a bellyful of cider who knew.

'You might take a holiday.'

She hiccupped again. 'And where would we be heading off to,
love?' There was a pause. Something was penetrating? 'Maybe
we will,' she said. 'Maybe we . . .' She lost her thread. 'Maybe we
will go see my sister. She's always askin' me. Lives in a thatched
cottage in a loverly village.' I suspected her mind was wandering
into fantasy land. I'd never heard of this 'sister' who lived in a
'loverly village'.

'You do that,' I said.

I put the phone down knowing it would take nothing for Ryan's new 'friends' to turn on him. I suspected they would be typical villains, paranoid, ready to turn on 'friends' whom they suspected of betraying them whether true or not. They might sense the police net closing in on them and turn in an instant. Honour amongst thieves? Really? A tempting fable. I'd seen the fear in Ryan's eyes when he'd unwrapped the grubby wad of tissues and seen the extent of the slash himself. If he was harmed or sent to prison, where would that leave Celine? Since he'd been a child, Ryan, battered by a different 'uncle' every week, had somehow kept his mother alive. The bond between mother and son was almost visible, like a rainbow arched between the two. She, stumbling, vulnerable and unsure, he the stronger, steadier one of the two. I'd watched the way he'd guided his mother into the surgery, hair bedraggled, almost unable to walk, and sat her down, explaining what her problem was. It had led me more than once to wonder at another of nature's great mysteries. Where on earth did Ryan's lovely, good nature come from? Not from his father who, by all accounts, had been a violent, drunken lout. Could it be from Celine? Buried beneath her poor life choices, was there a decent woman?

What would happen to the pair of them, I wondered, long term?

I wanted to warn him as much as I wanted to find out if he knew anything about the OxyContin, either its source or the supplier. I wasn't interested in a general way, only in that one specific case.

When Jalissa came with the sandwiches (minus the children), she sat down, her food basket on her lap and gave me a very straight look. 'What's really botherin' you, Florence? You so not yourself lately.'

What I really wanted to do was ask her about her new employer, see if she'd noticed a bottle of pills – maybe in the bathroom cabinet?

But I was still wary of Harriet, hovering somewhere in the background and almost certainly still staying with her dad at least until after the funeral, maybe she'd even hang around for the inquest. If she learned that their new cleaning lady also distributed lunch to the very GP practice she was threatening to expose she would soon put two and two together and make what she could from any breaches of confidence. Focussing on Jalissa's dark eyes I heaved out a great big sigh and she guessed.

'It's that business of Mrs Clay committin' suicide, innit?'

'And if it was?' I responded, testing the waters.

She gave me a severe look accompanied by a wagging index finger. 'Now don't you go gettin' fanciful ideas, Nurse Florence Shaw. You'll get yourself into trouble. That poor lady, she leave a letter sayin' she believe she have cancer.'

It struck me then. I hadn't realized how important a part this letter was playing. I was suddenly alert. I hadn't realized this fact had been released to the general public. 'Where did you hear that?'

'He tell me hisself. He so sad he couldn't persuade her she was wrong so he decide to join her.'

And if you believe that . . . I thought.

Her face was sorrowful – mournful even. I paused out of respect but still had to ask. 'Have you noticed any medicine bottles lying around?' I'd asked the question as casually as I could but Jalissa gave me a sharp look.

'The police, they take them all away.'

And I was heartened. So they were doing something after all. It wouldn't take much effort to dust them with fingerprint powder. I smothered a grin. Perhaps my persistence had resulted in some action.

Maybe I'd prompted them into at least checking up on the source of the fatal drug as well as the fatal dose.

I swallowed a smile of self-congratulation.

But I was still intrigued to learn more about the Clay household. And Jalissa was my ideal source. 'So is their daughter still staying?'

She was easier with this. 'Oh yes,' she said, sounding vaguely shocked. 'Course she is. She family. She stay with her father until after the funeral.' And then she abruptly changed the subject. 'Now, what you havin' today for you lunch?'

I groaned. It all looked so tasty. 'What's low calorie?'

'Maybe you try chicken for a change?'

Once I'd agreed on the chicken she turned to leave. But, surprisingly, this time it was she who returned to our original subject. 'I feel real sorry for her family. Husband and daughter. They both look so sad. So lost without her, you know. And Mr Clay . . .' She moved in closer, speaking softly in my ear. 'It my belief that he feels he failed her, somehow.' It was that word that alerted me to the fact that, maybe, Jalissa O'Sullivan wasn't quite as unsuspecting of her new employer as she'd initially implied.

I tucked her sympathy away. I couldn't quite join in. In my book Richard Clay didn't so much deserve sympathy as a pair of handcuffs nice and tight around his wrist. But Harriet . . . even with her nasty nosiness I did feel something for her. She'd lost her mother and for all I knew she might feel concern about her father's role. Questions might be storming through her mind as they were through mine. Could he have prevented this tragedy rather than joining in? He could have pretended to swallow a dose, waited, and called an ambulance. If he'd failed to convince his wife that she did not have a terminal diagnosis, why hadn't *he* insisted she be seen by a psychiatrist, a psychologist or at least someone with counselling skills who might disabuse her of her delusion? That might have prevented the tragedy. Relatives often offload their guilt on to the health services. Was blaming the practice a means of deflecting the attention away from the central players?

It's easier to blame an anonymous corporate business. Nameless and faceless. But how was I going to contact Harriet Clay without provoking her and exposing myself further to her hostility? In contrast walking a tightrope would probably be easier.

Jalissa was watching me with a very strange look, so I changed the subject and asked how the children were getting on at school, whether Charles had settled in. As usual anything pertinent to her children distracted her. 'Charles' teacher say he the brightest in the class.'

No surprises there. I'd always realized there was something special about Charles O'Sullivan. He had the intelligence and insight of a child years older than five. I revelled in Jalissa's pride in both her children. The surprise came when she asked about mine. 'How are your children?'

I laughed. 'Not exactly children. But Lara is coming again next weekend. And with the boyfriend.'

That was when, hand on hip, she stepped over the line. 'And will they be meetin' your new man?'

Now I really was astonished. 'How the heck . . .?'

She stood up and patted my shoulder. 'You think you can keep anythin' secret in this town? I don't think so, Florence.' And she sidled out of the room, hips swinging, leaving behind a big belly laugh rolling around the surgery while my mind had snagged on something else she'd said. *You think you can keep anythin' secret in this town?*

Someone was.

THIRTY-FIVE

Tuesday 17 October, 11 a.m.

I wore a navy mac over my uniform.

I don't know what I'd expected. After all, the situation was awkward. The grieving widower, the survivor, his daughter looking for someone to blame, were the chief mourners. And practically the whole of Stone would show up 'out of sympathy', they'd say, while I would argue 'out of curiosity'.

The ceremony was to be held at the crematorium in Stafford and I arrived with time to spare. The weather – grey, bleak and cold – reflected my sudden feeling of depression. The image of Christine was vivid in my mind and at the front of the building the pictures of her in happier days further reminded me. In the pictures she was serious as a child, holding a woman's hand – the aunt, at a guess. In others she was laughing, holding a baby, in still more she was in medieval dress holding a chalice to her lips, taking part in an am-dram production. Not a great choice, I thought, considering. I studied the pictures carefully, wondering what had turned her into that cowed, submissive appendage to her husband. That disruption in her childhood? Then I turned my head as Richard and Harriet followed the coffin to the front of the room, a coffin that seemed too small. Harriet's eyes were on her father but I couldn't read her expression. Then when she drew parallel to me she turned her focus on to me and I felt its power, but whether anger, hatred or something else I couldn't interpret.

As the coffin reached the front we all sat down.

The person leading the ceremony managed to walk a narrow line, skipping past all the sensitive subjects: suicide, mental health, missed diagnoses and a surviving partner who'd joined in a lethal pact and stood in front of him.

Richard (head bowed) hardly looked up as a few eulogies were uttered, one from a neighbour who described her as unfailingly good. 'And brave through her illness,' she added, heaping wood on the fire of speculation that Mrs Clay had or had not had cancer. That was left swinging in the air and I could hardly stand up and shout, 'No, she bloody well didn't.' The next eulogy was offered by a reluctant ex-employer who gave a rather stuffy, almost begrudging tribute that *Dear Christine* had been a brave (again that word) and faithful employee.

There followed an awkward silence.

Throughout the service I kept my eye on Richard and his daughter, studying their body language. They were side by side but so obviously apart, both in spirit and physically. Which made me wonder: as she spent time with him, was her blame focus shifting? Was she now blaming *him* for her mother's death? Or at least seeing the part he'd played rather than turning the blame on the surgery? If so, could she possibly work as an ally? In her thick black coat, she was leaning away from him towards a thin, severe-looking woman with short hair dyed a uniform and unnatural looking lilac. Pink, plastic earrings swung from her earlobes which seemed a minor rebellion against funereal expression. The two women (aunt and niece perhaps?) appeared to be exchanging a whispered argument while Richard sat, upright as a monolith, scrawny neck poking out of a dark sweater and stiff-looking blue shirt collar. He looked straight ahead, distancing himself from the people in the church, rising above their whispers, his lips moving. In apology? Supplication? Criticism?

What was he saying? I wondered.

The final eulogy was delivered by a priest who rather laboured the point, repeating himself with words like 'tortured', 'suffering', 'sick' and 'unhappy' making frequent appearances. The hymns were predictable, 'The Day Thou Gavest' and the dirge-like 'Abide With Me' tinnily playing on an electric organ while the gathering did their best with tentative, plaintive singing.

And afterwards, an unavoidable line-up, where again no one seemed able to vary the phrases as they shook hands or kissed Harriet's cheek. 'I'm so sorry.' And, 'How are you bearing up?' Repeated over and over again.

When it came to my turn, I would have avoided them both and slunk past, head down, hoping neither of them would see me. But Harriet Clay blocked my exit.

'I wondered if you'd come,' she said in a stiff, awkward manner.

I shrugged. There was no suitable rejoinder.

She grabbed my arm then. 'I need to talk to you.'

The phrases 'speak to my legal representative' or 'talk to my lawyer' came to mind. Even holding up my hand – talk to the hand – however inappropriate and rude, flashed through my mind. I was tempted. Instead, I simply regarded her with a face cold with suspicion and hoped she'd recognize my response as wary, if not overtly hostile, so she'd realize I was on to her journalistic tricks.

'Please,' she said, her attitude shifting. 'The whole thing . . .' She started again. '*This* whole thing. It's so wrong. Something's wrong.' There was a heavy appeal in her voice and her hand was gripping my arm so tightly I couldn't have escaped. Her eyes left me to sweep towards her father. 'I don't understand what happened.'

That was the first time I wondered if it was possible we could be thinking the same thing.

If only I could read that letter. I held the thought back. We weren't on that sort of footing yet.

Even through the sleeves of my mac I could feel her nails biting into me. Sharp.

'You didn't know my mother.' She was shaking her head. 'Not really. Few people did.' She put her head close to me so I could smell coffee on her breath. 'She was a woman of many layers.'

I had no idea what she meant.

I could see Richard, in his dark clothes, tall and skinny as death itself, on the periphery of my vision. No one was shaking *his* hand now. The collected crowd, having sucked the drama out of the situation, had drifted away leaving him standing alone.

Harriet and I too were an isolated island. And I didn't know what to say to Christine's daughter. I'd already swallowed back the retort that obviously I *had* known her mother. That wasn't what she'd meant at all. There had been a hint of a twisted, dark side to her mother's character. Now I was curious. And I could feel that curiosity biting into me. What exactly was she hinting at?

Thankfully, realizing her words had grabbed my attention, she'd released my arm. 'She wasn't what you think, Nurse Florence,' she said with a small smile. Then her eyes swivelled towards her father. 'Neither is he.'

'Harriet.' The lady with the pink earrings was touching her shoulder while regarding me with overt hostility. She had a sharp, commanding voice which diverted Harriet's attention. She stared at me for a moment, frowning and shaking her head, as though she'd lost her train of thought. Or an actress who'd forgotten her lines. 'Will you come back to the house?' she asked finally, her voice low and still confused.

I shook my head. 'No. I have to get back to the surgery.' I managed a smile and she turned away from me.

Which was when I felt a tap on my shoulder and turned around. Jalissa was smiling at me. 'You lookin' very far away, Nurse Florence,' she said. 'It is sadness or somethin' else?'

'Not sure . . .' I still had that awful feeling I was making a mess of this and while I was trying to work out how to respond Will seemed to appear from nowhere and we were both under Jalissa's all-seeing dark eyes, bright with humour under their fringe of curling black lashes.

'So,' she said cheekily to Will, 'you comin' here too to the funeral.'

'It's customary,' he replied, his eyes twinkling at her. 'And polite in cases of unexplained death.'

I addressed *him* then. 'I didn't see you inside.'

Will glanced back at the crematorium. 'Slipped in just behind you,' he said quietly, adding, with a slightly mischievous smile, 'didn't want you distracted.'

That almost made me giggle. But the black tie and rather smart grey suit distracted me. I was about to say, 'You look nice,' when I realized that Jalissa, with her thirst for drama and romance, was drinking the whole scene in.

So I gave up on them both. 'I have to get back to the surgery.'
'I'll walk you to your car.'

Running the gauntlet of Jalissa's all-seeing gaze, I accepted.
I knew he had something to tell me and didn't want any ears
flapping in our direction.

THIRTY-SIX

He waited until we were out of earshot before speaking.
'We've discovered the source of the OxyContin.'

I turned my head, unable to suppress a slight gloat.
'So you've accepted the fact that we didn't prescribe it.'

He nodded and couldn't resist defending himself. 'You understand all these secrecy laws seem designed to confound us.'

'Confidentiality,' I corrected.

He dipped his head – the only apology or correction I was
going to get, but the side of his mouth twitched in a smile.

'So . . .?'

He looked awkward now. And I knew that look too. Mark's
face had been plastered with it when he was about to leak a
secret he shouldn't have while swearing me to secrecy. Will went
one further. He even leant his head towards mine and covered
his mouth – as though anyone was lip reading.

'There's a local connection.'

'Well, I guessed that.'

'No,' he said, 'those guys that Ryan's in with are just keeping
the county lines in order. Making sure they know what's to be
done if anyone of their little tribe steps out of line.'

'So . . .?'

'The stuff is coming via various routes from somewhere in
Germany.'

'And before that?'

'We think possibly the USA.'

'County lines,' I picked up. 'In other words, kids. The guys
Ryan was with were not kids.'

'They're keeping everyone in order.' The expression in his

eyes changed. He looked sad. 'Ryan seems to be in charge of recruitment.'

'Oh no.' All thoughts of the Clays, the recent funeral and my doubts about the 'true version' vanished. I knew what happened to the kids who were recruited to 'help' distribute anything illegal whether it was prescription drugs, illegal cigarettes or pornography. What seemed tempting to the kids – easy money, a wad of twenty-pound notes, a pair of expensive trainers or the 'friendship' of the older guys, all of it, every blood-soaked penny – would cost them. From being 'useful kids' who 'helped' they quickly became a liability and were dealt with accordingly.

Once they were hooked.

Which was probably one of the ways Ryan, with his honest blue eyes and engaging personality, had been recruited in the first place. And look where it had got him. A four-inch knife wound which had near as damn it severed a nerve. And nerves rarely knit easily. Like lives, I suppose.

I was disappointed – and worried. But then I understood. Maybe Ryan had tried to redeem himself, wriggle free. And that was why the knife wound, the reluctance to attend hospital, instead sneaking into the surgery heading for treatment from me. I felt suddenly akin to the boy he'd once been. Ryan had tried to hit back.

It was against the rules of the NHS but I had to tell Will – who was looking at me strangely.

'You're really fond of the guy, aren't you?'

I nodded. 'I know his background.'

'I know some of it. The rest I can guess.'

But another of Mark's sayings had been resurrected. 'It doesn't matter how good their core is. If they're mixed up in organized crime it will soon wear thin and the crimes they'll join in will escalate, each step taking them nearer to a life sentence. And however much the public bleat that'– he'd wriggled his fingers – 'life should mean life, it's long enough to turn them into the most hardened of criminals. While anything good that was once in them dissolves as though it was immersed in an acid bath.'

I struggled against Mark's pessimism and tried to steer the conversation back to the Clays.

'So if you have the source . . .' I hesitated. 'Who actually bought it?' Then I held my breath.

Will's mouth had tilted into an even wider smile. 'What would it tell you, Florence?'

'It might . . .'

He was still looking at me. 'Drop it,' he advised. 'Leave it to us to investigate.'

I could feel the chilling of our friendship, the coolness in my voice. 'But you're not, are you?'

Silence.

'The inquest is next Monday,' he said. 'It'll be opened and adjourned.'

We both chimed in with the next line. 'Pending police investigation.'

'The coroner's officer might ask for a written statement from you,' he added, 'but I doubt you'll be called as a witness.'

And that was that. A statement which would be read out in court. Possibly the last service I would ever be able to perform for my patient.

I climbed in my car and returned to the surgery.

THIRTY-SEVEN

3 p.m.

The message came through on my computer as I was talking to a patient undergoing a well woman check.

Can you please ring Harriet Clay on this number? She says it's urgent.

The number was a mobile – not the Clays' landline.

I was wary. I read the message through twice and decided forewarned is forearmed.

Tell her I'll call her back.

Ten minutes later I was free.

It was only a couple of hours since she'd watched her mother being cremated. But I'd sensed the lady with the pink earrings had held her back from speaking to me. She hadn't wanted any confidences overheard.

Now I was curious.

I dialled the number and the phone at the other end was picked up on the first ring. As soon as I'd spoken my name she started talking in a state of hysteria quite the opposite of the hard-nosed, cold woman who'd practically threatened to expose me as an uncaring charlatan. What on earth had wrought this volte face?

She launched straight into her explanation. 'I didn't know who else to call. Honestly.'

And she'd called *me*? Right.

I felt even more wary, tightly guarded, telling myself this could be a ploy. Luring me to believe she and I were on the same side.

I repeated to myself her very blunt threats. But I couldn't have guessed the reason for her panic.

'He can't wait to get rid of me.' Her voice was high-pitched. Panicky. 'He wants me to go. God, I'm his only daughter. His only child,' she corrected. 'You'd think he'd want me to stay and, maybe, comfort him.' Even she sounded dubious at this version but, regardless, she ploughed on. 'Instead, he wants me gone. Every day he asks me when I'm going. Every. Single. Day.'

Hmm, I thought. Maybe he was worried she would pick up on something that would make her realize what a fake job the whole suicide/failed suicide had been. Maybe, knowing her talent for such things, he worried she would sniff out the holes in his narrative. Naturally I could say none of this to her so instead asked, 'Your friend's still with you?'

'Dekina?' Her voice was squeaky. 'The one he calls my lesbian *frau*.'

Even I didn't know what to say to this.

'He's hiding something.' Her voice was spiteful now, her desire to get back at her father floating on the top of her words like rancid fat on cold water.

I was still at a loss how to respond. Not only because her profession polluted my mind, but also because I was shocked at her about-turn. Previously her attitude towards her father had been protective. Now it was blatantly destructive. She wanted him down. This is when secrets come bursting out like a squeezed pustule.

Protecting Dekina had changed her loyalty to her father.

Or was there something else? Had she picked up on something else? I was desperate to know, while at the same time I worried that she was using this as a ploy, a trick, to lure me into trusting her, confiding in her, hoping to uncover indiscretion on my part. She could even be recording this conversation which she could then use as a quote.

I don't trust you yet, I thought.

'I'm sorry about your mother, Harriet, but—'

She forestalled me. 'Please, Florence. I think my father . . .'

I heard the desperation in her voice. She was drawing me in.

'I understand the inquest's next Monday,' I said stiffly. 'If you have concerns maybe the coroner or his officer would be the best one to talk to.'

'Yeah,' she said, scepticism oozing out of her voice. 'Yeah, and let the whole world know I think he might have—'

It's the world you and your ilk created, I thought, a world full of suspicions and litigation. But I said nothing, which was fortunate because, almost belatedly, I wondered how she would have finished the sentence.

Her next utterance was softly confiding as though we were terrifically good friends. 'I'll be glad when it's over.'

When it's over?

I didn't want to disabuse her of her comfort blanket. And I was itching to remind her we weren't bosom pals or secret sisters but adversaries.

I dropped back into neutral. 'I'm sure,' I said, in my best nurse-voice, fake sympathy oozing out of every pore. It sounded as shallow and meaningless as the ubiquitous 'take care' or 'not a problem' or even 'have a good day', the empty phrases that are spat out numerous times a day.

There was a moment's pause. Maybe she'd seen through my insincerity. For a moment I felt ashamed and rushed to fill it. 'So when do you intend returning to London?'

'Tonight,' she said huffily. 'I may as well. There's nothing I can do here except hang around with a long face, getting in my father's way, annoying him and tripping over voyeurs.'

Again, she was hinting at an alternative version but I wasn't going to take the bait.

'You're not staying for the inquest?'

'No point,' she snapped. 'It won't tell us anything we don't already know.'

Privately I had to agree with her but, as it seemed she was abandoning her mission to expose more flaws in the NHS, I felt I ought to say something. And I did want to learn the truth behind her mother's fatal misapprehension, learn the source, and find out what exactly Richard Clay's role in this tragedy was. And so I added, 'If I can be of any help, Harriet' – more sincerely this time – 'just pick up the phone. And, Harriet,' I continued, 'I really am sorry.'

There was a pause between us. I was wondering how I could swing the subject round to the letter. Her response was ambiguous. 'If you do learn something, even if you imagine I won't like it,' she said, 'you will let me know, won't you?'

I gave a blanket response. 'Of course.'

The relief I felt when she'd hung up was immeasurable. I revised the words I'd used.

Nothing there that she could use to accuse me.

I was temporarily cheered by a text from Will accompanied by a love heart emoji. *What are you up to next weekend? Hoping we can get together? X*

Texts have their shortcomings and Lara had intimated she and David might come up again for a visit. She'd actually mentioned that she might see if her dad was around. And I was dying to know what the situation was between Mark and Vivien. I didn't want to hurt Will or put him off, but I wanted to delay Will meeting my daughter and her partner as long as possible, at least until I was more certain this would be a long-term relationship. And, as usual, Lara had been vague about her plans.

I scanned the message again, reading in it optimism and hope. To respond by text wasn't appropriate. I should speak to him face-to-face, explain why I wasn't jumping at the chance of more time together. I sat for a while wondering how best to manage the situation. I didn't want to hurt his feelings. Finally I came up with: *Will, I would love to spend more time with you but I have family stuff going on over the weekend. What about one night in the week?*

His response was curt. *Sorry, working.* No kisses, no love heart emojis, no suggestion of a substitute date. I was beginning to realize this late dating game was awfully tricky.

After watching the screen for a minute or two (no typing . . .)

I gave up and returned my phone to my bag, staring around the walls of my clinic room and facing the problem. Middle-aged love had so many difficulties, so many more obstacles to manoeuvre around, so many taboo subjects. An ex, ex in-laws, kids, finances, bitter truths, hidden pasts, ugly scars and previous disappointments. Realism has no tidy pigeonhole in modern day, second-hand romance. Like searching for the perfect fit in a charity shop, you're lucky if you find it.

I pulled my phone out and read through the texts a second time, reading his optimistic, romantic initial suggestion, my own response (which now looked pretty off-putting) and felt a mirroring stab of disappointment. I'd blown it.

I knew I'd hurt him, pushed him aside. What could have been an opportunity to bind us together had resulted in increasing the distance. He would imagine I had some happy reunion with Mark (past forgiven).

I was sorry I'd handled it clumsily. But I was convinced I'd done the right thing.

Family comes first. But I'd strangle Lara if she didn't come after all.

THIRTY-EIGHT

Wednesday 18 October, 9.30 a.m.

The day had been set aside for a training day connected with a new bariatric service which was being set up at the hospital, but at the last minute it was cancelled as the new consultant had been double-booked and we were the losers. Or winners, depending on your take.

It meant that I had an unexpected free afternoon which bore even more unexpected fruit.

I was still a bit down after the failed date with Will. Should I have explained why I wasn't free for the weekend? Was I wrong to have simply said I wasn't available with the excuse 'family stuff'? Whatever, it was too late now to backtrack or revise my text. I sat and moped for half the morning but I couldn't do that all day.

There is nothing like a water-walk to pick up your spirits, so I put my jacket on over my uniform and headed for the canal. But this time instead of heading south along the Trent and Mersey Canal towards Aston Marina, I turned north towards Barlaston where I planned to have a coffee at the Wedgewood museum and then head home.

And who should I bump into – almost literally – but Dr Morris Gubb, our retired senior partner. Morris had been gone less than a year and I still missed him. When I'd worked alongside him I'd sometimes cursed; he could be annoyingly naive, at times failing to read between the lines. Wanting to find the best in people he often failed to recognize their worst. But he was one of those doctors whose core values were good. He prioritized patients and their needs over all else and his life had been lonely since his wife had died a few years back. He had aged overnight and it had been sad to watch him slip into old age and retirement, with just his black labrador, Doric, for company. But here he was, walking briskly towards me, his arm slipped into his companion's arm. She was a lady, possibly in her fifties, maybe early sixties, with neatly cut, short, blonde hair, a fitted scarlet designer jacket, skinny black trousers and tan leather boots. Doric was sauntering comfortably ahead of them, nose down, searching for olfactory stimulus. Maybe he recognized me because he ran up to me, sniffed me and gave a short, welcoming bark. Or maybe it was the familiar scent of antiseptic, which seems to cling to health workers long after they've left their workplace, that he'd recognized. Whatever, his tail was wagging so hard it created a draught.

Morris gave me a wide, happy smile tinged with obvious pride. 'Florence,' he said delightedly. 'This is Eirlys.' I looked into a pair of well made-up, sparkling blue eyes and a smile which displayed a set of natural, even, white teeth.

Morris turned to her and introduced me. 'This is Florence, the nurse I used to work with at the surgery.'

I was studying him, noting the fact that he looked ten years younger than when I'd last seen him, only a year or two ago.

He seemed to think some explanation was called for because he continued, 'I met Eirlys' – he turned to the woman at his side – 'on a cruise. I was very brave.' He chuckled. 'I'd gone on my own. Eirlys was with a group of friends.'

'Who adopted this brave, isolated man,' Eirlys picked up with a smile. 'And so Morris and I became acquainted.'

Acquainted? That was what they called it?

I was so happy for him. Too many GPs work and work and work. Then they retire and die. Many don't survive long enough to draw their generous pensions and enjoy their retirement and, when Sylvia, his wife, had died, I'd feared that would happen to Morris. His sole offspring – a son, also a doctor – worked for MSF and spent little time in the UK with his dad.

So this . . . I met Eirlys's bright eyes. This was wonderful. 'Where are you heading?'

'Thought I'd show her the Wedgewood museum,' he said.

'And I was planning to have a coffee there.'

'Wonderful idea.' Her enthusiasm was infectious. 'Mind if we join you?'

'No.'

So the three of us – with dog – stepped along the canal towpath and enjoyed a burst of autumn sunshine, while I learned more about Eirlys. She too was widowed although she didn't say what job her husband had done. A profession, I guessed. She was witty and funny, poked gentle mockeries at Morris who took it all with affectionate grunts.

When we reached the coffee shop, naturally our talk turned to our times in the practice and our patients.

Which was when Morris's face changed. 'I heard about the Clays,' he said. 'Awful. Simply awful.' He looked reflective. 'I can hardly believe it. I treated them for years. Although . . .' He frowned. 'They were a couple who kept themselves to themselves.' His frown deepened as he looked into the distance. 'She changed,' he said. 'She was different before, but afterwards she changed.'

I was alert. 'Afterwards?'

'Old scandal,' he said, trying to dismiss it. 'None of it proved but I never quite trusted her afterwards.'

Never trusted *her*?

'There was no proof, of course.'

'Morris,' I said, exasperated, 'what on earth are you on about?'

Eirlys was looking intrigued, her face bright with curiosity. 'Do tell, Morris,' she urged. 'Sounds like scandal.'

But he looked awkward. 'It's not important,' he said, 'or relevant.' He lifted his coffee cup to his lips, gave a noisy sip and set it back down on the saucer.

I knew Morris Gubb and his famed stubbornness. Once he'd decided that a patient's past was pure gossip, he would button up his lips and keep schtum.

We dawdled all the way back. The afternoon was dropping into a dull dusk. Less than a fortnight and the clocks would go back. The evenings would lengthen and I would come home to long, dark, lonely evenings because already I was beginning to realize how friable mine and Will's relationship had proved. In the end it had taken so little – nothing more than an awkward, clumsy phrase, a badly chosen implication, the word 'family' shutting him out and it could have crumbled into dust.

I headed home, despondent, still puzzling over Morris Gubb's cryptic hint.

THIRTY-NINE

Friday 20 October, 5 p.m.

Lara had rung to finalize details of their flying visit. It had been on the tip of my tongue to ask whether she had paid a similar visit to her father, but I knew whatever answer she gave it would make me conscious that our daughter appearing to have found the love of her life was something Mark and I would have shared. We could have swapped impressions post visit, as we would have shared premonitions pre visit, and bask in our daughter's joy. If their relationship worked out we might have helped plan a wedding, celebrated together on the actual day and afterwards we could have, maybe, looked forward to grandchildren. But now I felt strangely lonely. I had no one I could share the happy news with, just as I had no one with whom I could confide my darker moments and fears.

I could hardly expect Will to share both my joys and fears when he didn't even know her, whereas Mark and I had known Lara since before her birth.

And so, instead of being wholeheartedly excited about Lara's new love, I fretted.

There were gaps in my knowledge of David Abrams which would slowly be filled, learning a little more each time I met him or my daughter and I chatted about him. One thing had already struck me. Handsome as he was, he was at least ten years older than my daughter – at a guess in his forties. A man of that age had to have a past. Nothing of that had been mentioned but I wondered what that past might hold. An ex? Children? I didn't know where or how she'd met him – through the Internet, media, friends, work? All blank spaces so far, waiting to be filled in.

I simply had to focus on the fact that my daughter loved him and so I should banish my doubts and accept him as my daughter's partner.

From Will I still heard nothing. I checked my phone too many times that Friday, making sure my answerphone was working, searching through my emails in case I'd missed one, but there was nothing, adding to my feeling of despondency and insecurity. In the end I realized it hadn't taken much to shed my comfortable optimism as completely as a lizard sheds its skin.

I felt surprisingly down considering and scolded myself. I had a weekend ahead to enjoy with my daughter and her partner, but I also had a shadow hovering over me. Just before I'd left for the weekend I'd had a call from the coroner's officer. In nicely couched terms his message was clear. While I probably wouldn't be asked to make a statement at the inquest on Monday into the death of Mrs Christine Clay, I would be required to attend in case questions were asked.

And so a locum was hired to manage my Monday surgery. Who knew how long the inquest would last.

There was one benefit to this. If *I* was asked to provide a statement so would the police. I might learn something which helped me understand the sequence of events. In preparation I printed out each consultation I had had with the Clays over the past year, realizing that Christine Clay had had only one appointment with her GP – Jordan Bannister. I read it through recognizing his cursory style.

Patient complaining of:
Tiredness X one year.
No previous H/O same.
Physical check appeared NAD.
? Some element of anaemia.
Plan: Sent for blood tests including FBC (Full Blood Count)
Ferritin levels.

And later:

Practice Nurse suggests referral to psychologist.

It was all I would have expected from him: cold, factual and efficient whereas my comments were open to interpretation: 'Patient appeared . . .' and so on.

And every time the phrase 'accompanied by husband'.

Except that last time, which even I had failed to pick up on the point.

My worry was that I might be expected to voice an opinion on Christine Clay's mental state. I agonized over this. But with Richard Clay sitting on the front seat, any mention of coercion or the powers of suggestion would be unwise. I only hoped that I might learn something. Possibly all or part of Christine's alleged suicide note might even be read out. Some reference would almost definitely be made to it.

I wished Christine had been seen by Ruth Carroway. She would have been in a much stronger position to make some reference to the Clays' marriage and in particular Christine's mental state. But, of course, she'd never had the chance.

Now, instead of looking forward to the weekend and beyond, I was nervous and apprehensive.

FORTY

L ara hadn't specified a time, loosely saying after lunch, but as the afternoon drew on I started to fret. I could have called her mobile but that would have seemed as though I was criticizing her for being late.

Twice I went online to check for road delays or accidents but for once the motorways between London and the Midlands appeared clear. The M6 was behaving itself.

I'd expected them before evening, having promised them a meal on arrival. I'd thought maybe tea, but the time was heading towards dinner.

And so I fidgeted, with everything ready: salmon wrapped in foil with herbs and slices of lemon, new potatoes the size of tiny pebbles, fresh broccoli and baby carrots buttered and a homemade Hollandaise sauce – one of my few culinary talents. However, I'd bought a bread and butter pudding from Marks & Spencer. My culinary skills have their limits.

Finally they arrived at seven thirty, climbing out of a white Tesla, still laughing, looking the picture of love and happiness. Standing on my doorstep, greeting both with a kiss, I surreptitiously cast my eyes around the cul-de-sac and was gratified to note faces in windows and curtains twitching, including Eve Miller whom I'd noticed the other day was pregnant again. I only hoped this pregnancy wouldn't be accompanied by her previous pregnancy's drama. After a quick wave and the broadest of grins, the pair of them fumbled around in the boot of the car, bringing out flowers, wine and a small, single, overnight case.

Which answered one of my questions. Lara was tossing her head and laughing as she threw her arms around me. 'Hello again, Mum.'

I thought that they both looked glowingly happy, lit up from the inside in the way that only a young couple in love can look.

I greeted her back then looked past her to David.

'Hello again, Lara's mum.' He dropped another kiss on to my cheek before handing me a bunch of white roses and a bottle of wine. I closed the door behind us and we decamped to the kitchen. 'I hope you're hungry.'

'Starving.'

I'd noticed that it was David who'd responded and I turned around, my heart just beginning to flutter. As a teenager Lara had suffered (and I mean that word) from anorexia with frequent bouts of bulimia. She'd always been picky about her food but during that period she'd become positively skeletal. And then she'd headed for university where her condition seemed to stabilize while I'd remained wary. Now I was alert again, whipping around and reading the hollowed-out cheeks together with something else that made my heart beat faster. While many of us wear clothes to disguise unwelcome bulges, during that dreadful time Lara had worn oversized clothing, trying to disguise her vanishing body. Today she was dressed in a loose sweater two sizes too big for her and a pair of very baggy cargo pants. I shot a look at David, trying to alert him. Something did pass between us, but I wasn't sure he realized the potential seriousness of her condition.

If she'd read any of the subtext David and I had exchanged mutely, Lara provided the conversation with gusto. 'So now you've met my hard-working mother.' She opened her eyes wide. 'Twice.'

We were all holding our breath for the natural sequitur – her dad – but it didn't come. Instead, David started asking me about my job, whether I agreed (broadly speaking, of course) with nurses striking, before we moved to more general topics and the moment passed.

Thankfully.

They praised the meal while I watched my daughter eat and silently praised myself for hanging back on mentioning Mark, though the subject lay dormant between us, like a dead animal. Finally, over a glass of very fine Rioja (the wine they'd brought,) I bit the bullet, deeming David the safer option to address my query to.

'So have you met Lara's father?' I'd tried to keep my tone light but I wasn't convinced I'd pulled it off because he shot a very penetrating look at me.

'I haven't,' he finally conceded quietly. 'I understand he's about to become a father again.'

Lara hiccupped and put her hand over her mouth. I remembered those hiccups. When she'd been about to vomit a meal she'd often started with a bout before dashing off to the toilet.

So now I had a reason for her current weight loss. I turned my attention back to David and tried to keep my response light.

'So I believe.' I gave a laugh that sounded insincere. 'Not sure how he'll respond to that.'

Lara hiccupped again. We looked at each other and I read the fact that we were all troubled by Mark's approaching parenthood. Finally Lara managed an answer. 'Thought I'd wait until the "happy" event is over before we go and see him and . . .' Her eyes filled with tears and she stared at the tablecloth.

I felt terrible. I'd focussed on my own loss without really considering its effect on Lara.

She couldn't even say the woman's name. I reached across and touched her hand, noticing that David had done the same.

But at least mentioning the taboo subject had got it out of the way.

We chatted through the evening. I tried not to interrogate David but I still learned a few facts. He was the only child of a barrister who'd died of cancer a few years before. 'My mum's had a difficult time adjusting,' he said with an apologetic smile. 'But she's getting there – albeit slowly. It's helped that she's sold the family pile and bought a much smaller Victorian cottage on the edge of a village in the Cotswolds. She's joined loads of clubs and things but really I think she should go back to work.'

'What was her job?'

'She was a professor in a university.'

'Wow,' I said, slightly overawed.

'But she gave up when I was born.' He gave a rueful smile. 'So it's a long time ago that she had that post. To be honest, Mrs Shaw . . .'

I did the almost obligatory: 'Florence, please.'

And he continued seamlessly, 'She was a sort of . . .' Again, that apologetic look. 'Wife and mother.'

Though we shouldn't have responded, all three of us seemed awkward at this description. And were silent.

Until the conversation started up again.

I went to bed early and finally fell asleep, hearing soft conversation from the spare bedroom.

We spent Sunday walking in the Staffordshire Moorlands, climbing over The Roaches, finally descending into Thorncliffe where we ordered a hearty meal at The Reform Inn.

And then, all too soon, it was time for them to leave and return to London. I gave my daughter a hug, feeling the bones beneath her clothes and when I hugged David I whispered in his ear.

'Look after my girl, won't you?'

He nodded and exchanged a look that partly reassured me. I felt this was a man I could trust. Or at least I hoped I could, because I had felt the fragility in her.

I closed the front door as their car sped out of the cul-de-sac. Now I had my own difficulties to face and nothing to distract me. Tomorrow was the inquest.

I'd already answered the questions the coroner's officer had posed, mainly about dates, times and frequency of surgery attendances, but I wanted to be clear in my responses if asked, so I revised my notes to have them fresh in my mind for the morning.

I went to bed where, finally, my thoughts turned to Will. I only hoped my awkward brushoff over the weekend hadn't cost me the only real possibility of a relationship I'd had since Mark had gone. I recalled his curt response to my suggestion we meet in the week.

Maybe he really had just been busy with work. I reread through his initial message to me as well as my dismissal unpicking his enthusiasm and my tame attempt to patch up my initial refusal.

First thing tomorrow, I vowed, I was going to contact him. Then I remembered. He might be attending Christine Clay's inquest.

FORTY-ONE

'd made the decision to attend the inquest in uniform. Nurses engender sympathy and, if things went wrong, I might need it by the bucketload.

Also, in uniform I thought I would look more professional, any statement given gravitas, trusted rather than questioned.

Besides, I'd been summoned as a nurse.

A coroner's remit is actually quite simple – determining who has died, when and where, how and why, before giving a verdict: unexplained, misadventure, murder by persons known or unknown and, the one they try hard to avoid because of the grief it causes the living as well as potentially cancelling any life insurance payout, suicide. While witnesses stand and swear, most of the statements have already been made, usually via the coroner's officer. As I had. I had also told the coroner's officer I'd been unaware that Mrs Clay believed she had cancer which, of course, had been completely disproved by the post-mortem. Darren Holmes, the coroner's officer didn't quite look the part. He was in his mid-forties, with a shaven head, a gold sleeper in his left ear and a sleeve tattoo on his arm (which he hid by wearing long sleeves). He'd focussed his questions on fact rather than conjecture deflecting my comments about the Clays as a couple. Which I'd thought were highly relevant as it was Richard's dominance over his wife which had probably resulted in her suicide.

The coroner may well release the body for burial before the inquest is held, which at least means the relatives can hold the funeral. On other occasions, the inquest may be opened and adjourned pending police enquiries.

Not in this case. I had the impression police enquiries were more likely to focus on the sources and suppliers of OxyContin rather than focussing on the actual events of the night of the fourth of October.

What I hoped was that some reference would be made to Christine's suicide note because I suspected the change in Harriet's attitude towards me was something to do with that.

I wondered if she would change her mind about returning to London and turn up after all.

I'd also prepared myself to face Will Summers again. He might have been asked to attend – if only to assure the coroner that there *was* an ongoing police investigation.

And yet it was difficult when I entered the courtroom to see him sitting on the front row, but a pleasant shock when he turned and grinned at me.

I smiled back, feeling warmth creep into my eyes and curve my mouth into a smile too wide and inappropriate for a nurse's attendance at a coroner's inquest into what was a tragic death.

My eyes slid along to Will's right and found the thin shoulders of Richard Clay, topped by his bony neck and wispy white hair. He seemed to age every time I saw him. On Richard's right was his daughter, again dressed in deep black. So she *had* changed her mind. As I scanned the room I recognized various other people, some of whom I knew, finally resting on the broad shoulders and thick neck of someone I had known since he'd been a boy, 'Pants' aka Police Constable Robert Pantini, who had been in school with my son Stuart. What was his connection, I wondered.

We all quietened as the coroner entered.

Like many coroners Suzanne Fletcher was both a lawyer and a doctor. In her early forties, she was short, with a pair of strong, stocky legs and an undoubted presence – albeit competent and calm. Today she was wearing a well-cut grey suit which looked expensive, the material having a slight sheen on it, the skirt reaching just below her knees. She had shoulder-length, shining, dark hair which I guessed she was rather proud of as she stroked it frequently while listening to her officer's opening announcements. A pair of steady grey eyes which gleamed behind black framed glasses completed the air of calm professionalism. She exuded authority and a no-nonsense approach, a little like a school headmistress – trusted and reliable.

She gave a nod in Will's direction – at a guess the two had

worked together before – and another kindly nod towards Richard and Harriet. Then she settled back in her seat and opened the proceedings, which was when PC Rob Pantini played his part.

In a monotone, his eyes fixed on some faraway point, he recited his lines. 'At eleven thirty p.m. on the fourth of October I was summoned to number fifty-two Newcastle Road by a neighbour, a Mrs Sheila Stanley, of fifty Newcastle Road.'

I sat up straight. This was the first time I'd really thought about this. How had the Clays been found? When had they been found? Who had raised the alarm at that time? Why?

I listened intently.

The woman to my left had given a little twitch of excitement when the name had been mentioned. I swivelled around to take a good look at her. Mrs Stanley, I presume?

She was a plump lady with a happy, smiley expression on her face, now pink with anticipation and breathing quickly in excitement. As PC Pantini gave his statement she sat up even straighter, looking around her expectantly as though she hoped someone would realize the significant part she had played in this drama.

No one did.

And after a couple of minutes she shrank back into her seat, her shoulders bent, her part seemingly over.

While Pants continued in his droning voice until the coroner hurried him along, interrupting in her sharp voice, 'Why had the neighbour called the police, Constable Pantini?'

'She had heard some noises from the house next door and when she went to take a look the front door was open.'

Again. Suzanne Fletcher hurried him along. 'What sort of noises? Please be explicit.'

PC Pantini was unfazed. 'She described it as a sort of weak cry, so she went to take a look and was worried when she saw the front door open.' He looked up and scanned the room.

The woman to my left started forward as though to contradict him but then, again, she sank back in her seat.

Maybe PC Pantini had picked up on her movement. He corrected his careful statement. 'Groaning. She didn't want go in on her own. She was nervous so she rang the call centre, asked if an officer would go and see if everything were all right.'

'And what did you find?' The coroner's voice was gentler now, coaxing his statement forward.

Rob Pantini blinked. 'The front door,' he said, frowning as though he didn't quite believe it himself, 'was ajar. I called out and pushed the door open.'

I held my breath, waiting for the detail.

Somehow the droning monotone of his voice injected his statement with more drama – not less. I looked around and realized the combined courtroom was joining me, holding its breath.

'And?' the coroner interjected again. Moving him along.

Constable Pantini cleared his throat and continued. 'I found the owners of the property, later identified as Mr Richard Clay and his wife Mrs Christine Clay. Mrs Clay was lying on a large' – he swallowed, still suffering from the memory – 'red sofa. Mr Clay was on the floor, near the door.' He'd finished the description quickly, galloping through his statement as though once he'd spoken the words he would be rid of them forever.

'And?' Again Suzanne Fletcher prompted.

'I called for an ambulance. Mr Clay was lying on his side. He was unconscious but had a faint pulse. Mrs Clay was lying on her back. I tried to . . .' He gulped. 'But . . .'

The coroner took pity on him. 'Thank you, Constable. You may sit down.'

Pants stumbled back to his seat, flushed and uncomfortable.

The coroner next called on the ambulance paramedics who were more concise and less affected by their memories. They described both their patients as 'unresponsive'. But while Mr Clay's vital signs were present, Mrs Clay had no pulse and was not breathing. 'We cleared her airways and attempted CPR but . . .' The lead paramedic shook his head. 'We transferred Mr Clay to the ambulance but left Mrs Clay where she was as it now appeared a . . .' For the first time he looked awkward and was avoiding the centre of the front row where Richard and Harriet Clay sat. He didn't complete the sentence.

Over to the police doctor who had attended the scene at one a.m. and pronounced Mrs Clay as 'deceased'.

'And did you form an opinion as to the cause of death?'

He nodded. 'I believed that an overdose of some opioid was likely. Her lips were blue, she had pinpoint pupils and considering the fact that, according to the paramedics, her husband had shown the same symptoms—'

'Thank you,' the coroner interrupted sharply. I knew why. No one wants conjecture in a court. And subsequent blood tests would soon confirm or refute his opinion.

All through this Richard Clay sat, immobile, staring straight ahead, the only movement his Adam's apple jerking each time he swallowed.

As for me, my questions were piling up. Such as, if both were unconscious, who had been making the noise? I glanced across at Mrs Stanley but she was spellbound as she listened.

I tried to put myself inside that house. Richard on the floor; perhaps he had been the one to open the front door? She on the same red sofa that I had sat on when I'd visited.

And then came the drama.

FORTY-TWO

Looking back, I should have anticipated it. After all, I knew the remit of a coroner.

Suzanne Fletcher looked at her most business-like, pulled her glasses off and pinned her gaze on Harriet Clay. Her voice was soft as she addressed her.

'I believe there is evidence as to Mrs Clay's intent.'

For the second time the whole court seemed to hold its breath.

Suzanne Fletcher addressed the entire court now. 'It appears – rather tragically in this case – that Mrs Clay had the erroneous belief that she had a terminal illness and feared the consequences.' She stopped for a while. 'I have here the post-mortem result.' She nodded at a short, plump man with a rather pink face and curly dark hair. 'No need for you to get up, Dr Parry.' She lifted her head. 'Apart from some irrelevant details I will read out the pathologist's summing up. "Death caused by respiratory failure due to narcotic overdose. No evidence of malignancy".'

She waited for everyone in the room to absorb this fact. I

glanced across at Harriet. Her head was bowed, hands clenched together, as though she was praying.

'I have no intention of reading out the entire letter Mrs Clay left, addressed to her daughter . . .'

I felt a twinge of disappointment.

'. . . but some phrases deserve to be read.' Surprisingly she now looked directly at me and I felt myself grow hot under that cool, appraising focus. She struck me as a fair woman but I would not like to get on the wrong side of her. '"I need you to understand why I'm doing what I'm doing and why your father is involved. I don't have long to live. And the end will be so cruel that the doctors and nurses can't even be honest with me".'

Suzanne Fletcher paused while I worried I would be in for a scolding.

'"I'm sorry to leave you".' Again, Suzanne Fletcher hesitated.

'"I have tried to dissuade your father but . . ."' And now the coroner appeared thoughtful. She stopped reading and looked around the courtroom. 'I have already spoken at length to Mr Clay and he confirms both the contents of the letter plus his own actions, which might seem incomprehensible to many of us. But he was faced with a terrible dilemma and made a decision.' Then she dipped her head and read a final sentence. '"Think of this as my goodbye".'

The entire room fell silent.

But I was thinking. This was too much of an explanation. Something theatrical, staged. Too neat and tidy. Were I writing a scene from a suicide pact I would have spelt out just such an explanation, covering it all.

I held my breath now, expecting I would be called, but the moment passed – to Dr Jordan Bannister. He was sworn in, as one would expect, and gave two pieces of information concisely and in quick succession.

'Mrs Clay attended the surgery to see the nurse on numerous occasions but in spite of extensive testing no evidence of serious disease was ever found.' He certainly was not suffering from any pangs of guilt. He moved on quickly. 'We were not aware that she had this erroneous belief. At no time was there any mention of a malignancy either with myself or Nurse Florence Shaw whom she saw with increasing frequency, attending surgery on ten occasions in the last year. Had she either mentioned or persisted in this misapprehension either one of us would have tried our best to persuade her otherwise. Had she *persisted* in her conviction either one of us would have referred her for counselling. In fact, because of her frequent attendances at the surgery we had already referred her for some counselling. However' – an apologetic smile here – 'our psychologist's waiting list is long. Mrs Clay was not deemed a suicide risk.' He looked pleased with himself, aware that he'd made a good account of himself and, I grudgingly admitted, he'd done the same for me.

Got me off the hook.

Dr Bannister then produced a list of the deceased's medication to prove that she had never been prescribed an opioid and was not being treated for chronic pain.

He said this in such a firm voice, while looking around in that confident, condescending way he had, that no one would have dared contradict him. But just to be sure, he added, 'The prescribing of opioids, in particular OxyContin, which is, I believe, highly addictive and is the drug in question, is against practice rules except in cases of a terminal diagnosis.'

The coroner nodded and Dr Bannister sat down.

There was a pause and then Suzanne Fletcher settled back in her seat and addressed the room while focussing her gaze on the front row a feet away from her. 'This appears a tragic case of a wife and husband who decide to end their lives together. I have interviewed Mr Clay at length and he confirms this version of events: having failed to disabuse his wife of the conviction that she would soon suffer a prolonged and painful death, he decided to join her.'

Not on your Nelly, I almost screamed.

I couldn't see Richard's face; it was turned to face the front, but I felt sure he would have managed a convincing job of pasting on an expression of suffering, anguish and genuine grief.

I wanted to stand up in that courtroom and address everyone there. *You have it wrong. This was manipulation and a false narrative.* I wanted to point the finger at him and make the allegation loud and clear. *He. Killed. Her. He murdered her and now you're letting him get away with it.*

I wondered how Harriet's face was looking.

Needless to say, I actually said nothing. However powerful my emotions and certainty that this was the true version, I couldn't say a word. Because . . . I had no proof.

Perhaps the coroner sensed my uproar. She seemed to shake herself free of something. 'In the light of the evidence combined with the statements I have no option but to find the death of Mrs Christine Clay the result of suicide while the balance of her mind was disturbed.' She looked at Will. 'I understand police enquiries are ongoing?'

Will Summers half rose from his seat. 'That is correct. We're looking into the source of the illegally obtained drug used in this case.'

So I'd been right.

'In which case,' the coroner continued, 'we shall wait for the results of the ongoing police investigation.' She put her glasses back on to read her final statement.

'The pathologist has submitted his report and given the cause of death as respiratory failure due to opioid ingestion. There was no sign of malignancy.'

Now she did address Richard and Harriet. 'I extend my condolences for this tragic situation. I understand the funeral has taken place.'

Both nodded.

And that was the end of it.

FORTY-THREE

3.50 p.m.

I felt gutted. We'd all swallowed Richard Clay's narrative and he was going to get away with it. I watched his thin frame leaving the court, a few people stopping to offer their condolences. But he seemed like a man in a dream, nodding, shaking his head, stumbling forward. Maybe he was just beginning to realize what he'd done – or more likely what he'd just got away with. Harriet was by his side, catching his elbow when he foundered. I watched them both until they'd exited through the main door. And then I caught sight of another familiar face. Ryan Wood was sneaking out of the back exit, hoodie turned up, head down into his shoulders, getting out as fast and anonymously as he could. But I recognized him. I would have gone after him but Will had caught up with me. And the width of his smile wasn't something I was going to ignore.

'Florence.' His grin broadened. 'I wondered if you'd still have to attend once you'd made your statement.'

With him I could be honest. 'I would have come anyway – just to hear the outcome.'

He nodded, as though he understood. But did he? I still wasn't sure.

'Thank goodness I wasn't called,' I continued. 'I would have been so nervous.'

'It's not so bad,' he said, grinning widely, an ear-to-ear job now. 'You just work out what you need to say and then say it. At least there's no cross-examination or prosecution lawyer trying to make you out to be a liar.'

'It still felt pretty intimidating to me.'

Silence as I waited for what I sensed he was about to say. 'We're getting to the heart of this,' he said, putting his hand on my arm. 'We're not finished yet, I promise you.' He rubbed his forehead. 'Things don't quite add up.'

I watched him carefully as I waited for him to explain. 'I don't suppose . . .' he began. Then he changed that to: 'I wonder if . . .' And then: 'Is there any chance you could, maybe, have a bit of a word with Richard Clay?'

I watched him uneasily. 'To say what?'

He heaved out a long sigh and I began to read his subtext. 'To ask what?'

'To ask what really happened.' He looked to his right. In the car park people were either clustered in gossiping groups or else climbing into their cars and accelerating away. Richard was just opening the door of his daughter's Audi, bending his head and dropping into the bucket seat. Will, watching him, was shaking his head. 'Whatever part that bloke played in his wife's death, we don't know the half of it. I just hope' – he turned back to me – 'that at some point we find out exactly how and why that poor, tortured woman died.'

Maybe it was the words 'poor' and 'tortured' that hit a nerve. 'Will,' I said, 'when you looked at the crime scene . . .'

His eyebrows had shot up at my words.

'OK, then, when you got to the house. What did you find?'

'Two wine glasses.'

I waited and he drew nearer. 'Both had both their fingerprints on, in case that's what you're wondering.'

Again, I waited for him to continue. 'The one he'd drunk out of had half the level of OxyContin than the other glass did.'

'The one *she'd* drunk out of.'

He nodded. 'It had a smear of lipstick on it.'

'Lipstick?' I was frowning, conjuring up every image I held of her. 'She didn't wear lipstick.'

Except at that one consultation. I remembered now. It had been a peach colour, pale and quite flattering. I felt my curiosity shift.

'Both were in nightwear,' he continued. 'She was wearing a cotton nightdress, he a pair of pyjamas.'

Both in nightwear, late at night and she'd swallowed double the dose that he had. And he'd had enough to send him to sleep while she . . .?

Will was scrutinizing me. 'Florence?'

I shook my head. 'Did you not think there was something very strange about that note?'

'In what way?'

'Explaining in such detail.'

Now he was looking harder at me. 'Suicide notes comes in all shapes and sizes. Some are garbled, others offer an almost forensic explanation.'

'Like this one.'

He nodded.

And now Will was looking thoughtful. Moments later he excused himself and crossed the floor to speak to the pathologist.

FORTY-FOUR

4 p.m.

I had a clearer picture of how the bodies, or rather body, had been found that night but I'd left the inquest feeling even more confused than before. I shuddered, realizing I'd sat on that very same sofa only days after Christine had died on it. And I also now realized it hadn't been subjected to forensic analysis. The police had never really taken the case seriously, had made up their minds pretty quickly. Which could have been a mistake. Not only do crime scenes degrade but they become contaminated and/or deliberately tampered with. By whom? I wondered next. Whom did I really suspect? Richard had been in hospital for a day and a half following his wife's death. Harriet? Really? As far as I knew she had driven straight to the hospital when she'd received the news, and stayed there until her father was discharged.

Nevertheless. it continued to bother me as I crossed the car park through a drizzling mist that refused to either rain or stay dry. And then I spotted Pants. He was standing alone, not part of the groups of people who were still discussing the case. I could tell from his stance that he was lost in his thoughts, motionless and frowning. And I knew the scene he had described in the coroner's court had affected him. He always had been a soft-hearted sort of a guy – unlike Stuart who had been the tough one of the pair of them. And yet they had remained friends right through school – from primary to sixth form. For all I knew they could still be in touch.

He looked up as I approached and gave me a shaky greeting. 'Stuart's mum,' he said, and I was immediately back in that time when Stuart would say, in his newly broken voice, 'Pants and me – we're doing a geography project together so he'll be over in a bit.'

And I had provided a Coke and a packet of cheese and onion crisps to aid their creative juices.

The memory quickly faded as I studied him. He was looking pale, almost sickly, but managed a wan smile. 'Saw you in there.' He jerked his head towards the court.

'Must have given you a shock,' I said, 'coming across that.'

'Absolutely it did,' he responded. 'Been giving me nightmares.' He gave a weak grin and attempted humour. 'Don't think I'll ever be buying a red sofa.'

I was struggling to remember his rarely used first name before, thankfully, it came to me. 'Rob,' I said, 'was Mr Clay deeply unconscious? Would he have been able to crawl to the front door, open it and call out as Mrs Stanley reported?'

He thought for a while.

Now, one of the things I'd always noted about Rob Pantini was, even as a schoolboy, he'd been incapable of any flight of fancy. He was one of the most pedantic, literal fellows I'd ever known. His imagination box was empty. In fact, the police force was the ideal career for him because any statement he made would not take a single step outside the truth.

'I don't know.' His voice slowed. 'He'd sort of . . . fallen over near the door.' He looked at me. 'He was sort of mumbling.'

'Could you make out what he was saying?'

He shook his head.

I pressed on. 'And Mrs Clay?'

'She was sort of tucked up,' he said slowly. 'She had a blanket on her. And there was sick on it.'

He was warming up now, the memories less damaging as he related them to me. 'I could tell she was dead. She was white-pale. But he was breathing. Making a funny noise.' He gave an unexpected grin. 'Like snoring.'

The scene he was describing made sense as I processed the images.

'She was lying on her back?'

He nodded.

I was thoughtful. Opioids can make you sick. She could have died of inhalation of her own vomit. I thought back to the patholo-gist's report. Respiratory failure. No mention of inhalation of vomit. Besides, there was the suicide note.

Poor lad, I thought, tempted to give Pants a hug and hoped he wouldn't come across too many more gruesome scenes.

He quickly recovered when he spotted a squad car rolling into the car park. 'Think I'd better be going.' He grinned at me now, the harrowing events already receding in his mind. 'Give my best to Stuart.' Maybe he picked up on something in my face. 'He's all right, isn't he?'

'Yeah.' Then I added, 'I don't see a lot of him. He's in Manchester.'

'Tell him I said hi.'

Any further conversation we might have had was abruptly stopped by a blast on the horn from the impatient driver of the squad car.

And Pants was gone.

I spent a moment reflecting on how attending a scene like this can impact on a young, naive police officer before getting into my own car and driving away, trying to relegate Stuart, whom I hadn't seen or heard from for months, to the back of my mind. It didn't quite work and I felt a momentary sadness at the disintegration of our family until I cheered myself up with the image of Lara and David.

I returned to the surgery to see a few patients who'd been booked in for the afternoon. No one had had much idea how long the court case would take so the bookings were sparse in case one of the other nurses had had to absorb my caseload. I was thoughtful and distracted, working like an automaton, my mind sifting through the statements of the morning until just after five I received another message on my screen. Harriet Clay was at the front desk asking to speak to me.

I groaned. Quite honestly I'd had enough of the whole scenario. Christine Clay's death had been bad enough when I as good as knew her husband had been gaslighting her. Those numerous appointments had been a cry for help. And I'd done nothing. Ultimately I'd let her down. And, realistically, what chance did I have of convincing the police of Richard's role in his wife's death? Gaslighting is impossible to prove. Too subtle to pick up on tiny hints and comments made between two people when alone. No witnesses. And now I had Harriet the Terrier on my tail whom I didn't trust in spite of her appeal. I'd seen bits of her programmes on YouTube and soon realized their remit: nurses, doctors, health staff hiding under blankets, refusing to give interviews, trying to 'escape' the hounding of the press, darting through back entrances like killers leaving the courts, exposed to social media vilification, having to justify every sentence uttered, every note consigned to the permanent, unforgiving memory of a computer.

The thought terrified me the more I considered it. It could erase my entire life's work.

So I scanned through the brief message with fear rather than curiosity. I could anticipate the impending confrontation. I should have a witness, so I switched my phone on to record and hid it behind the window blind, then responded with a weary capitulatory, *OK. Send her in.*

It turned out I was wrong – on all counts.

Her footsteps might have been light as they tapped along the corridor but I heard every step and her knock was firm, authoritative and uncompromising.

I felt sick. I shouldn't have agreed to see her. I was walking into a trap. And I could hear the tension in my voice. 'Come in.'

Her head came round the door. The look she gave me was flinty. At least she wasn't pretending we were friends, I thought.

'Thank you for seeing me.' It was as ungracious a thanks as I have ever received so I didn't bother returning the unpleasantry.

'I thought you might like to read it,' she said, without specifying to what she was referring.

Then she handed me the letter, nodding to indicate that I should read it.

It was handwritten on a sheet of A4.

Darling Harriet, I need you to understand why I'm doing what I'm doing and why your father is involved. I don't have long to live. He's explained that. But the end will be so cruel that the doctors and nurses are in denial. They won't come out with it. They won't tell me.

I looked up, straight into Harriet's eyes, but was unable to guess what she was thinking. Her face was as impassive as the sphinx.

I continued reading.

I'm sorry to leave you. You have made me so proud. But the time has come. Think of this as my goodbye.

I aimed another sly glance in Harriet's direction and thought, as I had at the inquest, that something about the tone of the letter felt staged. I read through it again and the instinct was stronger.

It didn't sound like either of the versions of Christine Clay that I had met.

'Is this your mother's handwriting?'

She nodded.

'You're sure?'

She nodded again. 'Is this the sort of letter your mother would write?'

'Well, she was under duress, *wasn't* she?' Her tone had been slightly sarcastic but there was a question in its tail and, considering her track record, I wasn't quite sure how to respond. I reminded myself, Harriet Clay was no fool. She would know that the fact I'd asked the question implied that if her mother didn't write it I had to be pointing the finger at her father.

She looked confused. I sensed she didn't know which way to turn. In a vague way I realized her history as a journalist might be getting in the way of her duty as a daughter. She was used to asking leading questions. As she'd know I'd be cautious in my responses. Then she seemed to gather her thoughts, shaking her head. 'I guess,' she said slowly, 'that as we now know my mother *wasn't* ill . . .' She stopped right there before adding, 'She must have been deluded.'

Again, I waited, expecting her to move to her father's role. But she didn't.

'There's something else,' she said, flipping a mobile phone on to the desk. I looked at her, confused. It was a small, basic model – not hers, I surmised. Surely an investigative reporter would have a smartphone?

'It's my mother's,' she said. 'Look at the calls.'

There seemed only one number. But it had been contacted plenty of times.

'I rang it,' she said. 'It went through to a consultant's secretary. A Dr Farquar.'

I knew the name. 'He's an oncologist,' I said, now thoroughly confused.

'I know,' she said.

'So . . .?'

'Dr Farquar's secretary said that my mother kept ringing asking about an appointment.'

'But she was never referred to an oncologist,' I said. 'There would *never* have been an appointment letter sent to her.' I threw caution to the wind then. 'I did wonder whether your dad . . .' There, I'd said it, avoiding anything incriminating.

Her response was calm, surprising me. 'Initially that's what I thought,' she said quietly. Then she repeated the sentence she'd said before. 'You didn't really know my mother.'

I suppressed the instinct to blurt out, *Of course I do. I've known her for years. I know her well.* I could almost have imagined adding, *Probably better than you.* But something held me back. She was telling me something and so I watched and waited while she pierced me with those hard, flinty eyes. 'She was complicated, Florence. There was another side to her. One she kept carefully hidden. Think about it.'

She waited for me to absorb this statement before, without another word, she stood up and left.

And with relief I switched my phone off. At least I had a record of the conversation.

FORTY-FIVE

7 p.m.

I was just emerging from the shower, wondering whether to change into a pair of comfortable jogging pants and T-shirt, when my phone pinged up a message.

After such a day the message was welcome.

Fancy a takeaway Chinese? It'll go well with the news I have to deliver. I'll bring wine too. And the emoji was a hopeful face.

I sent back a tick and a love heart and watched as he responded with a thumbs-up.

Since coming home I'd sat in the quiet, pondering Harriet Clay's final words to me before moving back to that last, strange consultation with Christine Clay. Harriet had been hinting at something she could see but I could not. I struggled to unravel the knot but I couldn't. A Chinese takeaway with Will would be the perfect distraction.

So instead of the sweatshirt and pants I fished out a T-shirt dress and a pair of wedge-heeled sandals.

He arrived almost an hour later.

'Bearing gifts,' he said, holding out brown paper bags containing trays of food, a bottle of rosé tucked under his arm. I took it from him and we nestled into the kitchen.

'Forgot this,' he said, kissing my cheek.

'You're very chipper this evening,' I said, spooning rice on to the plates, and setting out the food with serving spoons in.

'I am,' he said, 'but I'm also hungry. Let's have our food and I can tell you the news as we eat.'

Needless to say, I was agog. And delicious as the food was, I couldn't wait. 'So?'

'We've arrested two guys,' he said, 'on charges of possessing with intent to supply.'

'OxyContin?'

He nodded. 'And the rest of the pharmacopeia as well as a few that have escaped any legal use. Luckily your friend Ryan wasn't actually with them when we tracked them down to a shabby little hole in Stafford. You remember the guy I almost knocked down when he ran in front of the car?'

I nodded. 'How could I forget?'

'He was one of them. The car parts were just a sideline – something they couldn't resist as they had a ready market for certain parts of certain cars. We've bust the entire operation – until the next time,' he finished soberly. He forked some of the chicken satay into his mouth and chewed for a while. But my fork remained empty, my appetite for the story exceeding my appetite for food. And he knew that. He looked across at me, grinning while chewing his chicken and couldn't resist a tease. 'Not hungry, Florence?'

I smiled back at him, playing his game of pretend calm, resisting the urge to press him.

'Romanians,' he said thoughtfully. 'Not people we've had much problem with before. Ah,' he said, picking up a morsel of seaweed with his chopsticks. 'It's the way it is these days. One minute it's the Albanians we're having to watch out for. Now it's Romanians.'

I was perfectly aware he was watching me out of the corner of his eyes, waiting for me to prompt him. But I was still resisting. Finally I broke. 'Is there any link to the Clays?'

'We-ell . . .' And then he gave up. He set his chopsticks down and looked me in the eye. 'Here's the thing,' he said. 'The guy . . .' He gave a wry smile. 'Once he realized he was copped he couldn't have been more cooperative. He said it was a woman who approached him.'

'A woman?'

'That's what he said. Mind you' – he gave a heartfelt sigh – 'they're not exactly the shiniest buttons in the box. Hanging around the middle of a high street, like that. I mean it'd be difficult to miss them. They might as well have displayed a drug dealer's flag.'

'Is there one?'

Will looked at me suspiciously, bursting out laughing, when he realized I was teasing him. He reached for my hand and squeezed it. 'Skull, crossbones and a few tablets scattered around?'

We both laughed at that. Out loud. And now we'd started neither of us could stop.

When we'd simmered down, he added, 'There's something else.'

My ears pricked up.

'It was six months ago.'

Now I was puzzled. The extra fact only seemed to complicate matters. But then the gaslighting had continued for around two years by my estimation. This was only part of the planning.

But later, as we made desultory conversation, my mind was stumbling over the fact that it was a woman who had bought the OxyContin.

Even so, it took me a while to point out the obvious. 'They must have lots of customers. They could have been mistaken.'

His response was quiet. 'They recognized her from the picture in the paper.'

'No,' I said quietly. 'No.' And then I remembered the first time I met the Clays and the problem they had presented with: sleeplessness. Might Christine Clay mistakenly have bought OxyContin illegally in the hope that it would help her sleep? It was still possible that she was the one who'd purchased it while her husband had been the one to give it to her? Or had I been wrong all along? Was this actually the double suicide bid that was the official version?

Immediately the thought formed I rejected it. Richard Clay was not the sort to join his wife in a suicide pact. He was the controller. Not she.

'Will,' I said slowly, 'what's the police version of Christine's death?'

He was silent for a moment while I was remembering, with shame, the milksop advice I had handed out to my suffering patient, to avoid coffee and alcohol, keep bedtimes regular, a ten-minute read of a book unlikely to cause nightmares (nearly as unhelpful as counting sheep), maybe a milky drink at bedtime. And if that failed, I'd said, we could refer her to a clinical psychologist – she'd probably get seen within months – and, as a last resort, a trial of Zopiclone.

'She came to me a year or two ago complaining of sleeplessness,' I said, hearing shame in my voice. 'I doled out the usual advice. She'd have to have seen a doctor to get a prescription for insomnia.'

I couldn't read the expression on Will's face. 'She never followed up on it,' I continued, hearing the defence in my voice now. 'She didn't ask again. Just kept coming in with other various ailments. How was I to know it would lead to . . .?' I said instead, 'If patients don't return to ask for different treatment or advice how are we to know?'

Will gave me a sharp look. 'I hope you're not blaming yourself, Florence. And you did connect the frequent attendances with an underlying problem.'

I was trying to rub the frown lines out of my forehead. 'Of course,' I said, appreciating the softening of his eyes as he moved in closer. 'Hey,' he said, leaving his chair to put his arm around me and drawing my head towards his. 'Hey. You can't blame yourself.'

'We all played a part,' I said, feeling dismal. 'And there's something you should know.'

I told him then about the phone calls to Dr Farquar's secretary.

'He's an oncologist,' I said. 'But she was never referred to an oncologist. And as we know, she didn't have cancer.'

Now we were both confused.

FORTY-SIX

11 p.m.

In normal times I would have loved Will to stay the night, to wake up in the morning beside him, to have him to cuddle if I woke in the early hours. But I felt a sense of heavy responsibility mixed with confusion. I needed to be alone. Fortunately Will seemed to realize that. He helped me clear away the remains of the Chinese, screwed the top back on the bottle of wine, and wordlessly hugged me, rocking me on my feet. It felt good. He felt strong, stable, reliable. It felt comforting and at the same time it released me from any obligation. There was no sex or lust in the actions. It was the action of a friend. An understanding friend, who had absorbed my emotions and responded to them.

When he'd gone I showered and made myself a cup of tea then sat up in bed, drinking it and thinking. Reading that letter had confused me. It seemed to be Christine's confession. Harriet had confirmed it *was* her mother's handwriting but something still felt off. I hadn't yet grasped either his or her role in the drama that had been set up. And that was the point. It was a set-up. I knew that. But I was going to have to be very careful as Harriet Clay would be dogging my every footstep. She might have returned to her flat in Fleet Street or Mayfair, or wherever she holed up with Dekina, but sure as eggs were eggs she would be peering over my shoulder, at whatever I was at. Once or twice when she and I had locked eyes, I had even wondered if she could read my mind.

A few days passed when nothing happened. All was quiet. I almost wondered whether I had imagined the entire scenario, invented a drama where none existed.

To add to my sense of peace Harriet really had gone. I'd passed the house in Newcastle Road on a couple of occasions and there was no Audi parked outside. In fact, number fifty-two almost looked abandoned. Curtains were permanently drawn, the old Merc stationary, gathering dust and falling leaves.

I'd tried to find things out from Jalissa but it was obvious Richard Clay practically drowned in sympathy from her. 'Poor man,' she said. 'He grievin' some.'

I found out she was doing his shopping for him. 'Not that he eat much,' she said. 'He got no appetite at all.'

As autumn winds blew even the garden of number fifty-two started to look neglected. Obviously Richard hadn't the heart to do any tidying up there either. The drive was speckled with the leaves of an ash, an ancient warrior that stood guarding the property. I felt frustrated. I needed to uncover the true facts, learn the real movement behind closed front doors. I tried again with my secret source.

Friday 27 October, midday.

I asked Jalissa again how her new job was going or, more specifically, how her new employer was and this time my digging bore fruit.

'Oh,' she said, shaking her head as though she hadn't expected this. 'Obviously, Florence, he is such a sad man.'

I'd heard this before so my response was automatic. 'Naturally.'

'No,' she said, tugging my arm. 'It is more than that. It is as though the bottom drop out of his world.'

That was not what I had expected to hear. Richard had what he wanted – surely?

'He's mourning his wife,' I said sharply. 'It's natural.'

Jalissa moved in closer as though she worried someone might

hear although there was no one else in the room. 'He is lost without her.' She banged her hand across the left side of her chest. 'His heart be broken.'

I actually pulled back because I wanted to contradict her, point out the real truth. But Jalissa wasn't finished.

'He like a lost person. He blame himself.' She gazed sentimentally into the distance while I was trying to thread the facts together. Jalissa was intuitive and quite penetrating in her observations. So what did she mean by this statement? I looked sharply at her. Was she being hoodwinked by fake grief? Because, before this, I'd never seen him display anything but irritation towards her. And this was the precise moment when the embryo of an idea started to form in my mind. And, like a fertilized egg, once I'd allowed the thought to multiply, it started to grow arms and legs.

I was seeing a different scenario from the one I had been nurturing. Jalissa had a shallow smile on her face as she picked up her basket. 'You need to take a reality check, Florence,' she said. 'That poor man is as much victim as his wife. *He* act like the dead one.'

I stared at her, realizing she was being sincere.

It was only later as I ate my sandwich that I chewed over her words. Jalissa was no fool. And I didn't believe Richard would affect grief to convince his cleaning lady. He was the sort of arrogant man who wouldn't care what she thought. And Jalissa was perceptive enough to make her own judgement, which didn't exactly fit in with the narrative I had built up around the Clays' tragedy.

I remembered something else – Harriet's insistence that I hadn't known her mother. I stopped chewing my sandwich and took time to think. Surely I *had*? I remembered my first impressions of them as a couple. He, impatient, she, submissive. What had I based those judgements on? Clothes, body language and the way they'd related to one another. But what about that one strange final consultation? The one when she had attended alone? What had been the point of that? Or maybe I should be asking how had she slipped the net? Escaped her husband's scrutiny? Why had she made that visit? Nothing had been achieved by it. Or had it?

I scrolled through the consultation. Bit by bit.

I realized she had skirted around her cancer fears, referring to it obliquely without actually uttering the words. She had deflected my offer to discuss the subject of sleeping tablets with her doctor. Another point that struck me now was her avoidance of seeing her GP, sticking to me for consultation after consultation, knowing that I would have to go through him to refer her for any expert psychiatric opinion. And that would mean delay.

And lastly? Again. to reinforce something – my opinion of the dominant, controlling nature of her husband.

I could see things more clearly now.

I forced myself to consider the possibility that, if Christine had acquired the OxyContin six months ago, a drug-induced paranoia could have caused her conviction that she had cancer. But I realized now, like the photograph displayed at her funeral, Christine Clay had been playing a part.

If Richard was less villain than victim, why had *she* killed herself?

I ran through things again. The tablets had, presumably, been in the house. He could have slipped them to her. I pictured the two glasses of wine standing side by side on the coffee table. I scrolled back to the consultation when she had mentioned sleep-lessness and at my extensive notes. I'd been so thorough – it was almost a textbook consultation.

I sat back, allowing my mind to wander. The trouble with opiates is that their side effects are legion – as well as practically impossible to list. Almost anything can happen when a patient self-medicates with long-term drugs or is surreptitiously dosed with them – particularly when the dosage is given without the subject's knowledge. Will said that the Romanian gang had claimed Christine had bought the drugs six months ago. Plenty of time for the seeds of mental disturbance to germinate.

But there was another aspect I should at least consider. When the drugs themselves are illegal they can contain just about anything. They might say OxyContin on the label but the tablets inside are not regulated.

And then I reflected. We'd never prescribed Christine any sort of mood-altering drug and certainly no opiates; their emergence on the streets of Staffordshire had been insidious. I couldn't remember when I had first noticed the Romanians. Certainly by summer they had been noticeable – that gang of six or seven youths. And at some point Ryan had joined them. When did *she* first start taking them? Was she addicted? And if so, who had introduced her? Again, I turned full circle. Had her husband been even cleverer? Made her a surreptitious drug addict?

Which brought me round neatly to Ryan. According to Will he was lying low. Maybe it was time to unearth him and test my latest theory.

FORTY-SEVEN

Monday 30 October, 6 p.m.

Now the funeral and inquest had passed the newspapers found other stories to fill their pages. Even in the town it had been little more than a two-day wonder. Local headlines shifted to pollution found in the River Trent, plans for yet another new-build housing estate on the outskirts of the town and a boy who had suffered a head injury when he'd been knocked off his bike. His parents had no intention of allowing their son's accident to be relegated to an inside page – they flooded the local paper with tragic pictures of their ten-year-old son hooked up to a ventilator, tubes in his mouth, a nasogastric tube coming out of his nose and a tracheostomy pipe protruding from his neck through which the ventilator worked its steady rhythm.

From my point of view, I had one – no two – consolations. The first being that Harriet, thankfully, stayed in London, quiet and out of the way. The second? I almost feel coy. Will and I were growing ever closer. Friends, confidants and now lovers.

Oh, and there was a third which I hadn't thought to mention. I'd asked Rowena to stop sharing Vivien's Facebook posts so I couldn't keep up with my ex and his pregnant mistress's daily life. Mark was well out of the picture. I'd heard nothing from him since the flowers which I'd replaced with Will's roses and chucked them away, feeling another stage of the goodbye when I'd dropped the lid on my brown bin.

I couldn't prove that Richard Clay had somehow administered his wife's fatal dose while he had swallowed just enough to make it look like a suicide pact. And I was beginning to think I never would.

I was determined to get in touch with Ryan, though. I kept a lookout for him but he was doing a good job of staying out of sight. I looked on the bright side. At least he hadn't turned up at the surgery with another knife wound. And these days no young men clustered outside the hotels along the High Street.

Will was chipper as the police gathered the case against the Romanian gang. Almost every day he grew more and more confident of getting a conviction for trafficking drugs as well as appropriation of expensive car parts – although so far Gillian's catalytic converter hadn't turned up in any of the multiple warehouses they'd stormed. What made his pleasure intensify was the fact that, through Interpol, they were managing to close down the entire operation.

'Job done,' he'd said, rubbing his hands.

Watching his glee in having solved this case I could hardly keep whinging about Christine Clay's death. Besides, even if Ryan said it was *Richard* who had bought the drugs, I couldn't go to the police and say I had a secret source that contradicted theirs. I was going to get nowhere. It was best Ryan laid low for a bit.

However . . . I sent him a text.

Hi Ryan, wondered if we could meet up for a drink? Florence. (The nurse from the surgery.)

But when, hours later, he hadn't responded, I began to worry. Will had told me enough about the gang to know they may have rounded up most of them. but there were probably still fringe members who might take a stab (literally) at Ryan if they suspected him of 'grassing them up'. Maybe Ryan was astute enough to realize there was something behind my invitation and that was why he was ignoring me.

The end of British Summer Time marked for me the beginning of the dark season. I came out of surgery to a heavy, damp darkness. The town, which by daylight, in summer, seemed virtually on the surgery doorstep, could now only be reached by traversing a dense black area, crossing both a river and the canal. The surgery car park was almost empty, the paved area lit by only one orange lamp; two of the lights meant to make us feel safe had been damaged, leaving corners dark and large enough to hide an elephant.

And this was the moment when I inconveniently recalled one of the receptionists had been assaulted a couple of years ago by an angry patient who'd knocked her to the ground in a fury for her manner which he'd described as 'rude and offhand'.

She'd fallen heavily, breaking her wrist, and had never returned to work.

The patient had been struck off our list but a charge of ABH had been dropped after his solicitor entered a list of mitigating circumstances including documented depression and 'challenging' home conditions.

But the result was that we staff felt unprotected. CCTV had been installed but it could hardly identify anyone in such darkness. The two broken bulbs seemed like a deliberate act to spring another assault, so I was always wary until I was safely inside my locked car. This evening, rainy and dull, seemed tailor-made for another assault. I walked quicker than usual.

Two steps from my car I felt a meaty hand on my shoulder.

I didn't have to turn around to know that this wasn't Ryan. But it was his phone that was being held – right in my face.

'What you want see friend for?'

The voice was foreign. I turned to face it. Took in a shaven head, fleshy face, big shoulders and the stink of sweat. I screwed my eyes up, waiting for a blow, a push, a shove, or, remembering the knife slash along Ryan's arm, something worse. I'd taken in enough to know he wasn't one of the gang I'd seen with Ryan. Was he 'Mr Big'? One of the suppliers who'd slipped through the net? I had no way of knowing. I took a risk, blurting out, 'I wanted to ask him something about one of my patients.'

'Really?' He looked . . . interested. And a tiny part of my fear melted.

In the dim light I watched his face, trying to read what was going to come next. But his face was now impassive. Not a muscle twitched; his eyes stayed steadily fixed on me, the pupils neither expanding nor contracting. I stared back trying not to let him know how much he was frightening me. I'd only had one real experience of dealing with a man like this. An ex-patient who had always unnerved me with his hard stare. Two years after leaving our list he'd murdered a young couple he'd taken exception to when they'd been guilty of nothing but some heavy petting outside a nightclub. The woman, he'd claimed in court, reminded him of his ex-wife so he'd 'lost his rag'. He'd served ten years in prison as his solicitor claimed he'd been 'provoked'.

But *something* had triggered this man's interest. 'And what is it about one of your patients?'

I was in no position to waft the confidentiality clause in front of this insane guy. But I was desperate to know and so made an unwise decision.

I smelt beer as I moved in – overriding the instinct to back off. 'I think one of my patients might have killed his wife.'

That shocked Mr Baldy. His mouth curved into a smile. 'And you investigate, hey, with our friend Ryan's help?'

I nodded. Honestly, I was feeling too sick to do much else.

Then he jerked his head. 'You better go. Trouble is going to happen.' He gave me a missing-tooth smile. 'You don't want get caught in the crossfire.'

I wanted to ask where Ryan was but I didn't dare. Even mentioning his name – again – might put him in greater danger.

But at least I now knew why he wasn't responding to my texts.

I didn't need to be told twice. As quickly as I could I unlocked the car, started the engine with a shaking finger, put the car into gear and was out of the car park before I took another breath. I'd heard the screech of my tyres and the squeal of brakes as though another driver was behind the wheel.

But it was only me.

FORTY-EIGHT

6.28 p.m.

My finger was shaking as I tried to text.
Really need to see you.
He was waiting for me when I turned into my drive, standing outside his car. And the look of concern on his face would have melted a polar ice cap.

I tried to relate the whole sorry saga but, of course, he homed in on my original text to Ryan.

He gave me a stern look then smiled. 'I know you think we haven't looked into the Clay tragedy enough.'

I could hardly deny it.

Then he moved on to asking me exactly what had happened and I suddenly felt foolish. 'Nothing really,' I said.

'Did you find out where Ryan is?'

I shook my head. 'But at least I know he's not ignoring me,' I said. 'He just doesn't have his phone.'

Will looked thoughtful. 'Ryan's just small fry,' he said. 'But sometimes small fry get caught up in something much bigger than themselves without realizing it. It'd be better all round if he went on a nice long holiday.'

But my mind had reverted. 'The man in the car park,' I said. 'Do you know who he is?'

Will nodded. 'Tell me something, Florence. Did he have a sort of raggedy ear?'

'Yes.' It hadn't really registered at the time but now I could picture it, a torn pinna.

Will's smile was grim. 'He used to breed dogs for fighting,' he said. 'One of them more or less chewed it off.'

'If you've rounded up most of the people involved in the gang,' I asked, 'why is he still free?'

Will scratched his head. We were sitting side by side on the sofa, a bottle of wine opened and poured into two glasses on the coffee table in front of us. 'That,' he said, 'is just one of the anomalies in this case. We have nothing on him.'

'But he—'

Already Will was shaking his head. 'No,' he said. 'I get it you were frightened. I get it that you're worried about Ryan.' He paused for a moment. 'I even get it that your involvement with the Clays convinces you that Richard Clay gaslit his wife and convinced her to take a fatal dose of OxyContin while he took a lower dose – enough to support the story that this was a side-by-side suicide pact. But Florence . . .' He was looking at me earnestly now. 'How do you account for the suicide note in her writing?'

'I can't.'

He was shaking his head. 'There's no case to answer,' he said. 'And if you want my advice you'll leave well alone.'

Will had his arm around me now so it didn't feel like I was being ticked off.

'So why exactly did you want to speak to Ryan?'

'I thought maybe if it was Richard who bought the drugs,' I began, but Will was already forestalling me, shaking his head.

'Drop it, Florence. We know it was Christine. And anyway, what difference would it have made? They took the drugs both voluntarily and simultaneously.'

Then he paused, looking thoughtful.

'What?' I asked.

'There is one interesting thing.'

'What?' I asked again.

'Something that happened twenty years ago.'

'What?' I asked for a third time.

His arm around me tightened. 'It's nothing to do with this.'

'But . . .?'

'Mrs Clay was involved in a road collision. Ran over a little girl. Ten-year-old. Lost a leg.'

There had to be something more. 'And?'

'Witness statements.' He seemed to change his mind. 'It's nothing to do with it,' he said, virtually wafting it away. 'Nothing.'

I left it at that. But if I had the chance I might bring it up with Harriet.

I had to come out with it. I sat up straight and his arm dropped away. 'Will,' I said boldly, 'I know the police aren't going to follow this through. I'm perfectly aware that you're quite happy to accept Richard Clay's version of events that night. But I'm not. I won't stop,' I finished bravely.

Will's face was amused. 'And you think Ryan . . .?' he prompted, still gently.

'Knows something,' I insisted.

'And you'd swing the entire case on that?'

'I would.'

'Because?' His voice was still softly questioning.

'Because.' I'd sat up straight now. 'Because I know them. I know her.'

'Knew her,' he corrected.

'All right, knew her. And I do *know* him.'

'You're going to need a lot more than that.'

'All right. I know that. And I will.'

It was a very bold statement and caused Will to move his mouth in an attitude I can only describe as sceptical.

But first I had to locate Ryan Wood. And that meant a climb down.

'Do you know where Ryan is?' I'd tried to keep my voice calm but I could hear the shake in it.

So could Will. He gave me one of those warm, understanding smiles then nodded. 'Leave it with me.'

FORTY-NINE

Tuesday 31 October, 6.45 p.m.

I hadn't paid enough attention to the nugget Will had dropped. But now I recalled something else: Harriet Clay's firm assertion that I didn't really know her mother. 'Layers' was the word she'd used. I couldn't think what bearing these two sources might have but I knew I'd been skating over something of significance.

Two people knew Christine Clay's past.

Catherine Zenger, the retired practice nurse, whom I'd worked with when I had first started. Having worked in the practice for thirty years she knew everything about the patients on our list. And when I'd asked her about the Clays before I'd sensed there was something she wasn't telling me.

And Morris Gubb, who had also hinted at there being something in Christine's past. The accident? But close-lipped and loyal, he had kept it to himself. However, Catherine was not so guarded. If she knew something, particularly something scandalous, she would share it. Maybe even embellish it – a little. I didn't know whether this hidden secret had any bearing on my recent interest in the Clays, but it was worth finding out.

We met that evening, just giving me time to rush home and change out of my uniform. Somehow the sight of a nurse, drinking in a pub in her uniform, was something the gossips would easily turn into an alcoholic. Next time I advised any of my patients to cut down on their alcohol intake they would look at me askance, wearing a 'knowing' expression akin to a wink.

For a change we met in the town hotel, The Crown, which was quiet this early in the evening. I walked down; with comfortable shoes and a brisk pace it took around twenty minutes and meant I didn't have to worry about driving home having had one over the limit. Though there were few police parading around the town these days and nights, every now and then there was a clampdown on drink driving and, like drinking in uniform, being banned from driving would do my reputation no good. In fact, it could result in my registration and thus my career being rescinded.

Catherine was already sitting at a table, two glasses of wine in front of her. She looked delighted to meet up with me. And that was another thing. Catherine was well suited to her chosen profession. She had a warmth that enveloped completely. Friendship was something she treasured. I took a good look at her. She looked well – marginally slimmer (Catherine was on a permanent 'diet') and she was dressed in a navy-blue dress with a cream jacket and low-heeled court shoes. Positively smart for a meeting with a friend in a town pub. I raised my eyebrows and she gave me a cocky smile. 'Tell you all about it over a drink.'

Actually I was anxious to interrogate her about the Clays. But I thought she'd better spill her beans first – otherwise I sensed my dear friend would have burst.

'So,' she began, 'someone came to eye up the flats.'

Catherine lived in a very upmarket two-bedroomed maisonette close to the town. They were pretty, modern and well designed, with Juliet balconies facing the canal with its permanent view of brightly painted barges, dog walkers striding along the towpath and a distant vista of the town.

'So?'

She leaned forward. 'Lost his wife two years ago. Sold one of the big Victorian houses along the Barlaston Road and was looking for . . .' Here she managed to look both cocky and coquettish. 'A new direction in life.'

'And he found you.'

Now she looked unmistakably smug and nodded.

There was a brief silence while I said nothing about Will. It would have taken the wind out of her sails. Let her enjoy the moment, I thought, raising my wine glass with a toast. And so I listened, hearing that she and Gregory had a real 'connection'. They'd been to the theatre, the cinema, out for meals and were planning a cruise sometime during the winter. 'Maybe the Caribbean,' she said with more than a trace of triumph. My mouth fell open. I actually felt envious. It sounded like fun, fun, fun all the way.

But I hadn't come here to hear about her love life. I wanted to pump some detail out of her. I wanted to know what I'd missed. If Catherine did know something relevant I would have to steer her very gently in the right direction. She was no fool; neither was she disloyal or loose-lipped about her erstwhile patients.

I listened to all of Gregory's virtues for a good twenty minutes before I dared puncture the balloon and bring up the subject of the Clays. None too subtly as my attempt at a casual question, something about Richard Clay's business, resulted in a sharply penetrating look and an accusation. 'You're at it again, aren't you, Florence?'

I felt exposed. I tried shaking my head. 'Not really.'

But I could see from Catherine's look of amusement mingled with disbelief that it hadn't convinced her.

'The newspaper claimed that it was a suicide pact. Why can't you just leave it at that?' But her comment was accompanied by a look not of irritation but of curiosity.

I said nothing. My friend would draw her own conclusion.

'You don't believe it.'

'I'm just searching for the facts,' I said doggedly.

She raised her eyebrows.

'Which are that Christine died while Richard did not.'

She shrugged. 'I guess that happens sometimes.'

'Will told me the psychiatrist said suicide pacts are actually very rare. I looked them up. There were only two such cases last year. And in both those cases they were a murder and a suicide. A chronically ill wife was smothered while her husband overdosed on barbiturates. And in the other a husband was given an overdose of insulin while his wife slashed her wrists and survived.'

Catherine looked marginally more interested but I could tell really her head was still filled with her newfound romance.

I leaned in, elbows on the bar table. 'This seems different. And I don't know why.'

I saw something in her eyes then, a sort of light that danced. I just hoped she wasn't about to make up some story.

'Years ago,' she said, frowning, 'there *was* something about Mrs Clay.'

I started fishing. 'Will told me she was involved in an accident with a little girl.'

'That was a long time ago but there was something about it . . .' Disappointingly she was frowning, trying to retrieve a memory.

'Let me get you another drink.'

By the time I returned to the table, wine glasses charged, Catherine had remembered.

'The little girl,' she said, her face looking sad, 'lost her leg. But that wasn't it. Mrs Motello was bringing her in for dressings after the amputation. She said something that really disturbed me at the time. I've never forgotten it, Florence.'

I waited.

'She said, "Don't tell me it was an accident when Harriet and my little Cindy had had a big falling out a few months before. Cindy said she'd never be friends with her again".'

I was shaking my head. 'Kids fall out like that all the time. It doesn't mean anything.'

But Catherine stayed firm. 'I spoke to the Clays,' she said, 'and suggested they make up. I saw Harriet's face,' she said. 'She looked like murder. And as for her mother . . .'

'Her mother?'

'She looked pleased with herself,' she said, shuddering. 'And the two girls . . .' She looked at me. 'They never spoke again. Mother and daughter are vindictive, Florence. And that accident was no accident. But no one would believe me at the time.'

Catherine's words resonated inside me.

Her face grew even sadder. 'I had some long talks with poor Mrs Motello. She felt doubly aggrieved because the police warned her to stop making allegations, that there was no evidence that it was anything but a tragic accident. They told her *she* could be in deep trouble if she started spreading rumours. She moved away soon after. Couldn't bear the thought that she might bump into one of the Clays.'

'What do you think?'

Catherine shrugged. 'Put it like this. I got it that Mrs Motello was upset. But I watched Mrs Clay. And I haven't forgotten that smug look on her face. I never trusted her after that.'

I was startled. 'You're sure?'

She nodded. And I was speechless as I realized Catherine's perceptions of Christine Clay were the opposite of mine. I saw her as a victim; she as an aggressor.'

I moved on. 'Tell me about him.'

Surprisingly she giggled. 'He owns a pottery firm.'

'And that's funny?'

'Sanitaryware,' she said. 'Toilets, basins. Bidets. I think he did a lot of travelling before he sold the business.' She frowned. 'For quite a lot of money, I think. I don't really know much about . . .' She stopped. 'I didn't know *him* well. *She* used to come on her own.'

'What for?'

'Oh, the usual, well woman checks, that sort of stuff.' Her face was far away now before she gave a merry smile. 'He used to be quite attractive.'

I thought of the bloodless, skinny creature who'd accompanied his wife to the surgery. 'Attractive?'

She looked annoyed then. 'Stop parroting me. He was a catch. Not my sort. Too skinny and pale but some of the receptionists found him appealing.'

I was incensed. 'Well, time hasn't been kind to him,' I said crossly. 'He's a bully!'

'She had a troubled childhood so was a bit flaky. She mentioned a few times that Richard was away – again. I think she thought—'

I was convinced she was making this bit up and skewered Catherine with a look. 'What?'

'That he had another family tucked away somewhere.' She moderated that to: 'Well, maybe a mistress.'

While that might explain why, out of spite, Christine could have wanted to make sure her husband died too, I still wasn't absolutely convinced Catherine was telling the truth. Until she added, 'Said he'd been up to no good with their neighbour.'

'Which one? There are two, one either side.'

'Number fifty, I think.'

Number fifty, I thought. Mrs Sheila Stanley, the plump lady who'd alerted the police to the strange noises, the front door standing open? At past eleven o'clock at night?

I'd thought the story sounded strange at the time.

So had Christine been right? Or was this another indication of her paranoia? Or was Sheila Stanley part of the plot?

And then there was the odd aspect of repeated phone calls made to the oncologist's secretary which actually supported the story of the spurious cancer diagnosis.

My head was spinning now. I couldn't thread all the facts together. I couldn't make any sense of any of it – yet.

'So,' Catherine asked me now, eyes bright for scandal. '*Was* she suicidal?'

'No,' I said firmly, but honesty compelled me to add, 'I didn't think so.' I realized I still wasn't sure. 'And Harriet? Did she go to school here?'

Catherine shook her head. 'After the accident she went away to school. Somewhere in Kent, I think. Boarding school. But you know she's a really famous documentary maker now.'

'I know.'

She carried on blindly. 'She did something on undercover cops, I think.' Her tone was vague and I suspected Catherine was making another part up. 'It was really good.'

'I don't know about that, but she has made some documentaries on short fallings in the NHS.'

She realized the implications right away. 'Oh shit,' she said.

She started fumbling with her bag – always a sign she was ready to go. 'Letters came from Harriet's school,' she said, not looking me in the eye now. 'All her jabs and illnesses and stuff,' she finished vaguely. 'That's how I know.'

I stood up and gave her a hug. 'I'm really glad about you and Gregory. You deserve something nice in your life.'

'As do you, Florence,' she replied with sincerity. 'So stop digging up shit. Eh?'

I walked her part of the way home until she was within sight of her flat. We hugged again and parted ways.

On the way home I chewed over the points I'd learned from

the evening. Coming up with an indisputable fact. Richard held the answers. But would he talk to me? I pictured his face, uncompromisingly hard and strong. I very much doubted it. I would have to find another way.

FIFTY

Wednesday 1 November, 3 p.m.

Will texted me, trying to sound casual, but I sensed some tension behind his invitation.
Fancy a drink or two at The Wharf? Could do with talking to you X
I know when someone is anxious. I smiled and sent back, *6? X*
And got a heart emoji in return which felt rather nice, a feeling which lasted right through the squawking that inevitably accompanied my afternoon baby immunization clinic, heading home, showering and changing into a dress. Right up until we'd arrived at The Wharf and were sitting in his car outside where he broke his news, an anxious eye out for my response.
'We're not making any charges against Richard Clay.' He was watching for my reaction, which was muted. I'd searched the charge of assisting a suicide online and hadn't been surprised that there were few convictions. Most of those had been given a suspended sentence, including the case I'd quoted to Catherine of the woman whose husband had 'apparently' overdosed on insulin while she had survived, which had resulted in the charge being dropped. And the evidence against her had been much stronger – her fingerprints on both the insulin bottle and the syringe. It still upset me that I was letting Christine down, that Richard was going to get away with it, but I was starting to realize that there were things about both him and his wife that changed the perspective. And the neighbour? What part had she really played, because I didn't believe that at that time of night she had investigated a noise which couldn't have been very loud. Christine was dead, her husband hardly conscious. I made a note to question Jalissa

(casually, of course) about the relationship between Richard and his neighbour. I realized both Jalissa and Catherine saw Richard through a different perspective. More victim than villain. These were two women whose judgements I trusted. Was *I* the one looking through the telescope from the wrong end?

I realized I'd based my judgement on the consultations I'd had, swayed by my dislike of him, impressions formed of his wife's demeanour. What if his impatience and irritation was a result of frustration at being unable to shift her conviction that she was ill? Neuroticism, I knew from experience, is an incurable, intractable condition. Trying to convince someone they are *not* ill is, actually, harder than convincing a patient that they *are* ill when you have visible proof – scans, X-rays, blood tests.

'Florence . . .' Will had been scanning my face for a sign of guilt or regret but he had his hand on my arm now. 'Let it go as a suicide pact. Accept that. She obviously had some mental problems. He just happened to survive and she didn't. It can't do any good keep going over it.'

'And you're happy to accept that as the truth?'

He looked at me even harder, shaking his head. 'We have to.' His lips were pressed together. Uncompromising. 'We have no evidence to make a charge against him.' He knew he had this as a get-out. 'The CPS would never be happy for us to proceed.'

I stared at him and changed my question, putting my face close to his. 'Was Christine's life insured?'

He shook his head. 'No. Only Richard's was.'

That was one of my theories put to bed. 'You don't really *want* to know the truth, do you?'

He didn't quite know how to answer this very direct question, but blinked and then smiled and linked his arm in mine. 'Time to get a drink.'

While I hadn't made up my mind whether to thank him for telling me all this in person or feel furious at him for not seeing the fable of the Clays' suicide pact through to the end, I capitulated, feeling cheated by the system as well as disappointment in that, ultimately, I'd let a vulnerable patient down.

I got it that the Romanian gang deserved a higher priority but simply brushing the Clay case under the carpet made their lives seem less deserving.

I had a sudden blurry vision of Christine, vulnerable, weak, her quiet voice dominated by her loudmouth bully of a husband. It was the picture I'd had of them since I'd first met them, each subsequent consultation reinforcing that image. But now it was out of focus, blurred, and I was wondering whether I'd been wrong, misled somehow.

Will was still watching me, a little nervously by my estimation. 'Florence?'

And, strangely, I wasn't sure how to respond but shook my head.

We walked into The Wharf, found a table in a booth where no one could eavesdrop on us. I waited until we had drinks in front of us and shot my last bolt.

'I need to speak to Ryan. Do you know where he is?'

He gave a slow nod, then broke into that warm, all-encompassing smile. 'Can we just eat first?'

I'd thought things were back on track but now I sensed he was holding something away from me. Halfway through my fish pie I put my knife and fork down.

'What is it, Will?' I demanded. 'You didn't just bring me here to run through the case, did you? Is it us?'

He shook his head and I saw the light had gone out of his eyes. At the same time my heart sank. He was breaking up with me? Before we'd even got going?

FIFTY-ONE

'Rumour has it,' he said reluctantly, the words dragging out of him as though pulled by a weary animal, 'that Mark and Vivien have split up.'

I looked at him and couldn't bite back the one word that shot out of me. Rapid as a bullet. 'So?'

'She's given birth to a daughter. Premature.' He still couldn't look at me.

'There's more?'

'There's something wrong with the baby.' He was frowning now. He held his hand up, shielding me. 'I don't know what but it seems things . . .' I realized he was trying to break the news gently. 'Things aren't good,' he said quickly, glad to have got the words out in the right order.

I was gaping, my emotions in turmoil and I wasn't sure which dominated: pity for the child, pity for Vivien whose amorous adventure had turned so sour, or anger at Mark for having jumped into a tiger pit. And, shamefully, a touch of triumph, which I quashed as soon as I'd felt it rise. I tried to say something decent, something good. 'Many babies born with problems are the most loved, adored, beautiful children. Plus,' I added, gathering strength, 'it can be difficult to assess just how much the child will be affected. These days . . .'

I stopped because he'd covered my hand with his own and locked his eyes into mine, boring right into my soul. 'Do you want him . . .?'

'No.' Again the word shot out of me, a second bullet. 'No. But I do want to meet up with him. He has an obligation to both Vivien and his daughter.'

And now DC Will Summers was smiling. 'Phew,' he said, and took a long draft of his beer.

We spent the rest of the evening in happy, comfortable companionship. He left me at the door with a long kiss before returning to his car. 'Early start in the morning,' he explained, adding, 'I'll try and persuade young Ryan to make contact.'

And then he was gone.

10.45 p.m.

I let myself into the house and sat in the dark for a while, my mind dealing with the confusion Will's revelations had provoked.

And I lectured myself. This was not my problem. It was Mark and Vivien's.

Unlike Christine Clay's death. And I knew why it stuck with me. Only if I understood what happened that night could I learn the part I'd played in the tragedy. And only then could I even hope to absolve myself of responsibility. I had to find the truth for my own peace of mind. It was a selfish instinct rather than loyalty to my patient.

I sat very still and tried to turn my mind around.

What if I started believing Richard's version of events? The letter that Christine had written proved that Christine had intended to die. *She* had been the one to buy the drugs illegally. Enough for herself and her husband, presumably. Six months ago. I stared across the room.

How was that significant? *She* had been the one to persuade him to take a near-fatal dose. No, no, I thought. That didn't fit. Richard a dumb victim? Swallowing a near lethal dose of drugs – because she'd persuaded him? My mind drifted some more. Poison, they say, is a woman's weapon. The weapon of the weak against the strong. There was an alternative. She *could* have slipped the drug into his tea or his dinner or that glass of wine. I closed my eyes and saw those two glasses, side by side, on the coffee table, right in front of the sofa where I had sat and she had died. But if he had been poisoned by her, why hadn't he said when he'd woken up that his wife had tried to kill him? Had he truly forgotten? Had his mind erased an unpalatable memory? I tiptoed through the theories, that caveat always present. I would have to be very, very careful. Any hint that I was making false accusations, which was how Harriet Clay would see it, would result in one of her 'investigative documentaries' and the result of that would inevitably result in my losing my job, possibly suspension of my fitness to practice. I would never be able to work as a registered nurse again. The stakes were high but I *had* to know what had happened for my own peace of mind.

And then I turned to the other revelation of the evening. Mark, Vivien and this child. I'd worked in the Special Care Baby Unit which dealt with nenonates with congenital abnormalities, so I had some experience of babies born with various congenital conditions. Many are so minor they can practically be ignored. As the child grows the condition becomes less and less significant. But some carry a disability right through their lives. I had enough patients at the surgery with various defects to be all too familiar with the daily grind of caring, worrying and planning for a child who has problems. Mark could be selfish. Yes. But he was not cruel. And this might seem a strange pronouncement about a cheating husband but Mark was not inherently dishonest either.

He had been caught in the last fling of a dwindling sexual prowess. Flattery and, no doubt, some effort by a younger woman, had won him over. Not the first and he certainly wouldn't be the last.

Ah well.

Then I thought about Will's revelation about the life insurance. Which meant my theory about a wadge of money being behind Christine's death was wrong.

A text came in from Will.

Ryan will call in the surgery tomorrow. Tell him he's a lucky boy to have got off scot-free.

This was further followed by kisses. *XXXXXX*

Six!

I sent a smiley face and a love heart back. Sometimes emojis say it all. No need for words.

Right, I thought. Tomorrow . . .

FIFTY-TWO

Thursday 2 November, 7 a.m.

I still searched for something to support my original theory but I was running out of ideas. Fast.

7.30 a.m.

I was in the shower when I heard a knock at the door. I turned the water off and peered out of the window to see DC Will Summers grinning up at me.

'Thought I'd catch you in,' he called up while I was glad the lower bathroom window was frosted, wrapped a towel round me and ran downstairs. 'You put the kettle on. I'd better get my uniform on.'

Fifteen minutes later we were sitting in the kitchen, drinking companionably. His face was soft with a look of humour, both quizzical and curious, but he stayed silent, his eyes trained on my face as he watched thoughts trickle through my mind.

He didn't interrupt but seemed happy just to observe – and drink.

And then he did speak. 'You there yet?'

I shook my head.

He chewed his lip. 'We've closed the case, Florence. I've already told you that.'

I put my mug down on the table, harder than necessary. 'And I've already told you that Richard Clay never discussed his wife's belief with us, not once. He could have come to the surgery alone and confided in us. Had he done that we could have tackled her underlying problem. As it was, we were working in the dark.'

Wait a minute, I thought. This cancer phobia. The only evidence we had of it was in that letter – that helpful letter, and those repeated phone calls to the oncologist's secretary.

I cradled my mug of coffee, aware that Will was watching me.

'Hypochondriacs,' I said. 'They're a nightmare.'

Then I thought of something else. 'You asked Richard where he thought the OxyContin had come from. Of course.'

Will was wondering where I was going with this. 'He assumed his wife had been prescribed it by one of your doctors.'

'He never checked though he had plenty of opportunity. He could easily have asked us as he was always in at the consultations.'

Why didn't he check? I was thinking. Because he already knew? Or because it was a fabrication?

There I went. Round and round, trying to wrap up the story in rope so thick it would not break, knotted so well the harder you pulled it the tighter it bound. Rope so long you could not find the beginning or the end.

Will put his mug down. 'Thanks for the coffee.' He leaned forward, touching my lips with his own. It was not a proper kiss. Too perfunctory. 'Time I headed for work.'

'Before you go, did Ryan say what time he'd be in?'

'Around two, I think he said.' He dropped another kiss on my cheek. Then hesitated, seeking reassurance and finally giving the reason for his early morning visit. 'Any more thoughts about Mark?'

'Ahh,' I said, shaking my head. 'Not a single one.'

'Good,' he responded and now his grin was genuine, his eyes caressing.

Moments later I heard the front door slam and his car start up before heading out of the cul-de-sac. I hoped the neighbours were spying now and at the same time, as I stood in front of the mirror, brushing my hair and applying what I called my 'work' make-up (basically a light coating of foundation, a more generous application of mascara and a light lipstick), I reflected how strangely things were turning out. Two years ago I had been the abandoned wife. Today I was abandoned no longer.

It was hard not to aim a smile into the bathroom mirror until I remembered the child who might find itself abandoned – at least by her father.

FIFTY-THREE

8.20 a.m.

D riving into work that morning I realized a few things. One was this relationship I had with Will was not on quite such an easy footing as I'd thought. While our parting had been warm, undercurrents swirled around from our past. I knew Will wished I would drop this investigation into the circumstances surrounding the Clays' suicide pact. Not so much because he felt I was pointing out a certain sloppiness in the police's handling of a death. I got it that they had to prioritise serious cases where they were most likely to secure a conviction and skate over others. It made sense. More because he worried I would never let it go.

He couldn't realize I would – when I'd teased out the truth. I wasn't there yet but I was inching closer.

I still had a few stumbling blocks. Chiefly the letter.

I'd read two suicide notes before, both tragic cases, misunderstandings combined with depression. Both had illustrated a blind, desperate state of mind. Not this structured rationality which scratched at the back of my mind like a rat behind the skirting board.

I wondered if I could turn Harriet into an ally or if that was too dangerous a strategy, but I didn't see how else I could move these uncertainties along. However, she would have a deeper understanding of her parents' relationship and might be able to provide some missing answers. She was intelligent and insightful. And so must have formed her own narrative of her parents' suicide pact. If only she would share it with me without pointing the finger of accusation. If I talked to her and learned nothing else, if I was careful, I would, at least, have a chance to stand at her side and peer into her mother and father's actions that night.

I was still trying to picture it.

To kill his wife he had risked his own?

I was still shaking my head when I reached the surgery. That was not it.

But I was moving closer.

However, my next thought led straight into an unwelcome third.

The only way I would learn the whole truth would be to talk to Richard. I shrank from the thought of facing that skull-face, pale skin stretched taut over bones like the head of a drum. I might owe it to his dead wife to expose the truth but it might lead somewhere I didn't want to face. The frustration was that I believed I had almost all the facts. I was simply failing to put them in logical order.

And then there was the Mark issue which obviously haunted Will, though it seemed an imbalance when I considered I knew nothing about *his* past except that he'd had a long-term relationship that had fizzled out. That was the version he'd given me.

And I'd accepted.

And lastly, finally, I needed to put Mark, Vivien and the baby out of my sphere and stop worrying about them. They were not my problem. I needed to focus my time and energy on my relationship with Will because . . . And here I smiled, recognizing the unmistakable indulgence. Simply because I wanted to.

I left the car, locked it and headed for the front door, stopping by the receptionists' hatch to tell them I was expecting Ryan to turn up around two p.m. that afternoon.

However, the morning seemed not to want to dance to *my* agenda but to its own.

10.40 a.m.

Halfway through my morning surgery my phone pinged a message through. And it was from Harriet Clay suggesting we meet for lunch. Lunch? That's what friends do. I hesitated over a response, finally acknowledging I might learn more of the truth and it was worth taking the risk. And so I texted back.

One o'clock? At the coffee shop in the square?

I got a thumbs-up.

When Jalissa called in later that morning, her basket of sand-wiches swinging from her forearm, I told her I didn't need her sandwiches today as I was meeting up with someone. Her face, hangdog since both her children were at school, brightened up. 'That nice policeman, Florence?' There was a mischievous twinkle in her eyes as well as a suggestive twist to her mouth and a quick wiggle of her hips.

'Sadly, no.'

'Who then?' And for some reason I was reluctant to tell her. However, she obviously had problems of her own because she flopped into the chair at the side of my desk.

'I thinkin' of havin' another baby,' she said.

'Really?'

'Yes. I am so lonely without a little one to cuddle.' Her eyelashes were damp with emotion.

I know I could have suggested she 'take up a hobby', 'enjoyed her little bit of freedom' or 'joined a club' but I held back. This was something she and Brett needed to sort out for themselves. It was not for me to intervene, but I was worried how this was affecting her. The Empty Nest Syndrome is a reality, sometimes for both parents.

I wanted to ask her about the relationship between Richard Clay and the next-door neighbour. But I sensed today was not the right day. So I gave her a pat on the shoulder and watched her leave, shoulders drooping, slow, slow steps, nothing now like her usual hip-swinging rhythmic walk, almost a dance to a tune no one else could hear, though the rhythm was always unmistakably reggae.

I worked my way through the morning heading up to the square at one.

Harriet looked even more severe in trousers and a black jacket. She was already sitting at a table, her eyes firmly fixed on the door so she spotted me straight away managing a tight, cold smile which I couldn't interpret. But as I slid into a seat opposite her I picked up on something else – genuine grief and uncertainty.

'You all right?'

She threw her hands apart in a 'what to do' gesture, then waited while I got myself coffee and a sandwich.

'It's my dad,' she said, then paused, while I tinkered around with those two words. *My dad.*

She had my full attention now. 'I'm really worried about him. He's gone into a shell since Mum . . .' She stopped while I wondered what word she *would* have used had she completed the sentence.

Instead, she continued on another vein. 'He's hardly eating and spends his time just staring at the floor. It's as though he's switched off. I don't know what to do with him.'

I tried a neutral sentence. 'We-ell, he has just lost his wife.'

She was shaking her head. 'No. It's more than that. And he hardly speaks to me. We used to be so close.'

I tiptoed towards her opinion rather than voicing my thought. *Guilt?* 'So . . .?' I was staying in neutral. 'Why do *you* think he's become like this?'

She sighed and fiddled with the muffin in front of her, crumbing it without eating a morsel. (No wonder she was so thin!) 'I don't know, Florence. But he looks wretched. Crushed. I can't get him to snap out of it. I'm frightened to leave him. I worry whenever I have to go back to London in case . . .'

I thought I knew what she was about to say. But I couldn't say the word either. I had a repertoire of phrases to comfort patients on such an occasion: 'just be patient' or 'these things take time' or else 'time is a great healer'. Any of those great phrases would have been appropriate but I'd picked up on her very real fear. She didn't say it, but it hung around in the air like mustard gas.

He might try again.

And it didn't take me long to realize this was my opportunity. 'Would you like me to call and see him?'

She raised her head, pretended to consider my suggestion before nodding, her expression still wretched, showing no relief. 'I couldn't bear to lose them both,' she said, grief etching her face with signs of worry. 'Not in such dreadful circumstances.'

I gave an understanding nod and she continued. Confiding now. 'You knew Mum well. I guess they trusted you.' But her voice wavered, a question still vaguely audible. It was time *I* asked something.

'Harriet,' I said, then, realizing I might sound a bit forward replaced that with, 'Miss Clay.'

Something startled in her eyes made me realize she *was* wary but this was my perfect opportunity. I couldn't let it pass me by.

'You implied that there was something . . .' I couldn't find the words. 'Something I didn't know about your mum.'

She gave me that intense look then. 'She could be . . . unexpected.'

Which told me nothing. I prompted her. 'You used the word "layers"?'

'She harboured grudges,' she said after a pause. 'Deep grudges which she held for a long time. And . . .' She scooped in a long deep breath, her eyes looking downwards at the table. I knew she was wavering, wondering whether she could trust me.

'Instead of them fading over time they sort of . . .' Now she was looking around the hot steamy coffee bar, the atmosphere thick with gossip. No one was listening. Everyone had a story of their own to tell. She leaned in to share a secret. 'They took on a life of their own.'

Legs, I was thinking. They grew legs. But Harriet's version was far more fearful.

'Her grudges grew wings and claws. Became the empowerment of nameless, faceless evil.'

I had no idea what she was talking about so retained my neutral face, intelligent and listening without any expression of judgement. 'They took on a life of their own?'

'Have you heard the name Cindy Motello?'

The second time in as many days, I thought, but nodded my confession. 'Yes.'

'God . . .' Harriet dropped her head into her hands. 'It was just a kid thing. She teased me at school. It was nothing. But I came home and told Mum about it. A month or two later . . .' Her voice trailed away.

I had to pin her down. 'Harriet, why are you telling me this?'

'I don't know.' Then she admitted, 'I'm frightened.'

'Frightened of what?' This I could not puzzle out.

She leaned in closer, urgency in her face now as well as her voice. 'The next-door neighbour.'

'Mrs Stanley?' I almost whooped.

She nodded. 'She and Dad had a bit of a fling. It was years ago.'

I wondered then if Harriet was thinking straight. It was her *mother* who was dead. What did any of these people, her father, Mrs Stanley, anyone else for that matter, have to fear?

'*Will* you go and see him?' she begged. 'Please?'

'Of course.' I didn't add that it fitted in with my plans perfectly. 'But tell me something.'

'If I can.' Her attempt at a smile was pathetic.

'Since this . . . fling, how were things between your mother and father?'

'That's the point,' she said. 'Everything seemed fine. Absolutely fine. But . . .' Again, she checked around the coffee bar. 'The more hideous Mum's plans were the sweeter she could be towards her victim. The day before she knocked Cindy over she asked her if she'd like to come to tea one Saturday. Said she'd bake a special cake. She found out about Dad's affair and just smiled and shrugged. Said boys would be boys. Nice as pie, she was. But almost a year later she practically wrote off Sheila's car. I saw what happened. It was deliberate.'

Six months, I was thinking. The OxyContin had been bought six months earlier.

Harriet was still speaking. 'Mum got out and acted so apologetic while Sheila was in bits. I would have believed Mum's apology. But when she got back in our car her face was so smug. "Well," she said. "That's shown her." Florence . . .' She grabbed my hand. 'Dad knew what she was like. He was frightened of her.'

No, I thought. It was the other way round.

I hardly needed to remind her again that it was her mother who was actually dead.

I responded stiffly. 'That was not the impression I had.' I could have added my own words: downtrodden, browbeaten, subordinate.

'Don't you see?' There was despair in her voice as though I hadn't listened, or else I'd completely failed to understand the point she was trying to make. 'She could play act. That's what I'm telling you.'

'And the suicide note?'

'A script.' She stared, shaking her head.

While my take on it was unchanged. Even if her observations were all true, the fact remained it was her *mother* who was dead and her *father* who was suffering.

Instead, I tossed the ball back to her. 'So what do *you* think happened?'

She countered that with a question to me. 'What do *I* think happened?'

We looked at each other, maybe not foes now, but we still skirted around each other, wrestlers in the ring, avoiding any contact. We still didn't trust each other.

'I want you to find out,' she finally admitted.

As I walked back down the High Street I remembered the words she'd used: wretched. Crushed.

The Richard I knew didn't square up to either of those descriptions. Neither did the picture she'd painted of her mother as an avenger who built up disproportionate punishments match with my image of a browbeaten wife constantly supervised by a controlling husband who took over her voice.

Except that last time.

I realized something else. Harriet Clay might be an investigative journalist with an impressive track record but she'd passed the baton to me and now she was free while I was having to adjust to different perspectives. Richard Clay was now playing the part of a grieving widower, his wife transformed into a vengeful Lady Macbeth.

Allegedly.

I reached the surgery, pushed open the door and reminded myself. Even killers can experience remorse.

FIFTY-FOUR

2 p.m.

R yan Wood had his own idea of sticking to appointment times. The receptionists had duly booked him in for two o'clock and left a message on his phone but whether he turned up then or chose another time of his own was anybody's guess. And that was if he turned up at all. A pack of cards thrown into the air landing in random order. That was the predictability of Ryan Wood.

However, when I returned to the surgery there he was, sitting in the waiting room, calmly leafing through an old copy of *The Countryman.*

During and just after the pandemic we'd stopped having magazines at the surgery, believing they could harbour 'the virus', but we'd soon realized that having them to entertain patients waiting meant fewer complaints about delayed appointment times. And so they were back. And Ryan appeared engrossed. In a blue sweater and clean jeans, I could have taken a picture of such sweet innocence. He lifted his guileless blue eyes from the copy and grinned at me.

'Nurse Florence,' he said. 'Fancy seeing you here.'

I couldn't help but return his smile. It was infectious. 'Ditto,' I returned. 'Come on then. Let's take a look at that wound.'

It was always better to maintain a pretence that this was a normal medical consultation while the two receptionists watched, exchanging glances, obviously wondering why Ryan Wood had been summoned to the surgery.

Armed with bland comments about the weather, Ryan trotted behind me along a corridor lined with pictures of partners past, the latest one being a smiling, benevolent Dr Gubb.

Ryan is not quite a villain. Or if he is he's a soft-hearted one with aspirations. He could go either way, become an empathetic social worker or end up in prison. Possibly both, one after the other. Ryan's greatest attributes was his eyes. Wide and blue, planted in a face that magistrates and judges found hard to convict, Ryan was a likeable character, with a soft heart, but he was also untrustworthy. The habits of his troubled life were proving hard to break. The odd thing was that, although he'd done badly at school with not a qualification in sight, he was bright. He had a memory for names and places, a certain agility in his thinking and, even amongst the local police force, according to Mark, their attitude was a sort of amused tolerance. Even respect – sometimes.

But that tolerance wouldn't do Ryan any good in prison, surrounded by violent criminals. And if he wasn't careful that was where he would, ultimately, end up. Because he still pilfered here and there, and now I feared he was unaware he'd swum into shark-infested waters, because Ryan had no real experience of major crime or violence. Light-fingered he was. Evil he was not.

He gave me a smile I can only describe as brave and closed the door.

And I realized my axis was still shifting, while I faced a fear that, due to my probing, Ryan the harmless was about to be harmed.

Again.

He cleared his throat. 'Sorry I missed your calls,' he began. 'Lent my phone to a mate.'

An obvious and unsubtle lie.

He continued, 'Detective Constable Summers thought it might be a good idea if I came and talked to you.' He was staring at the floor now while it had taken me a few moments to realize he was talking about Will.

'Do you know why, Ryan?' I asked gently. 'Why he thought you should come and talk to me?'

The corner of his mouth lifted in the beginnings of a smile that was heartbreakingly sweet and mischievous. ''Cos,' he said slowly, ''cos I was the one what got her the stuff.'

'You mean Mrs Clay?'

'She was desperate, see,' he explained while his smile widened. 'She couldn't get no stuff on her own.'

'Did she say why she needed it?'

He shrugged, a sharp movement of his shoulders. 'I never asked.'

His gaze dropped to the floor.

'I didn't mean for her to . . .' He stopped right there and I could sense his fear now. 'It was months ago, I didn't think there was any connection to . . .'

I reasoned with myself. Christine could have been the one to procure the OxyContin but it could still have been her husband who instructed her. She'd been malleable enough to obey. All the same I was aware I was still trying to bend the facts to fit my original theory. A theory which was developing holes.

I checked. 'You didn't ask why she needed it?'

He shook his head and gave a typically Ryan explanation that adhered to his own, unique moral code. 'Not my business, see?'

I changed tack.

'Have you told Detective Summers where you got the stuff from?'

He nodded, his shoulders twitching in fear now as he made an appeal. 'If they find out, Nurse Florence, I'm done for.' He gave me an anxious look. 'You know what I mean? They don't tolerate anyone grassing them up.'

I nodded. He gulped in some air, making plans now. 'I'll have to lie low,' he said. 'Detective Summers says they'll be banging the rest of them up before long. And he says they'll keep an eye out for me.'

I was only glad he hadn't mentioned a witness protection scheme.

I changed tack again. 'How's your mum doing?'

He looked nervously around even though he knew we were alone. 'Not so good,' he said. 'She gets down when she thinks I'm in . . .' He looked up, his face lined with worry. 'Deep shit.'

He seemed to think a small, added fact might help. 'It were months ago, Nurse Florence,' he said again. Which reminded me of one sentence Harriet Clay had used when describing her mother.

She harbours a grudge.

Another piece snapped into place.

But I had to still consider two possibilities. She might have bought it but possibly under his instruction. She could have bought it for her own use. Or – and this was a distinct possibility – Richard Clay had found his wife's stash and used it.

Ryan watched me process the information before giving me a grin which was ninety per cent cheeky but there was also that remaining ten per cent which displayed pure, neat, concentrated anxiety.

'Thanks,' I said. 'And maybe I *should* take a look at that arm. Just to prove I'm not a liar.'

We both chuckled at the shared conspiracy. His arm was fine, muscled and well healed, with hardly a scar where I'd stitched him up. He and I both looked at it, possibly our thoughts colliding. I was wondering whether one day other knife wounds might scar his arm further.

While he looked at me anxiously, he asked, 'We good then, Nurse Florence?'

I nodded. 'Yeah. We're good.'

He raised his hand and I gave him a high-five.

FIFTY-FIVE

The rest of my afternoon consisted of an asthma clinic. I could hear Sophie Anthony wheezing as she walked along the corridor. I opened the door watching her chest rise and fall in an effort to breathe. I sat her down, gave her some oral prednisolone and Salbutamol via a nebulizer. She was six years old and had had numerous severe attacks and a few hospital admissions. We would have to refer her to the hospital for a new treatment which, we hoped, would give her better control over her asthma. She was a thin child with a hollow, fearful face, her eyes pleading with me as I sat with her and her mother while we waited for the medication to take effect. Gradually her breathing rate slowed, the panicked look faded and the wheezing calmed. Her mother and I exchanged glances. We'd discussed her treatment over the years, waiting for her sixth birthday when the hospital could start her new treatment. At times we'd thought she wouldn't make it. But she had. Sophie was a fighter.

'You can take the nebulizer home with you,' I said, knowing her mother had watched her daughter fight off attacks before. She knew when to call an ambulance and when to come to the surgery. We exchanged glances and I watched them go, worried as always.

The drug was expensive, £250 a jab which Sophie would need twice a month possibly for ever. As I filled the consultation in on the computer my mind veered away from the Clays. I wondered if people might appreciate the NHS a little more if they knew the true cost of their treatment.

Yet another imponderable but a distraction nevertheless.

The rest of my patients that afternoon were much less dramatic and I was cheered by a smiling emoji from Will with a question mark after the word: *Tonight?* I texted straight back with a thumbs-up.

How about fish and chips? Chippie? Six o'clock?

I planted an X as my response.

And got a reply straight away in the form of a smiley face which transmitted to my own visage.

6 p.m.

Two minutes down the road from Endicott Terrace was a fish and chip shop to rival any. The newspaper wrapping paper might be gone in favour of polystyrene trays but the fish, chips and mushy peas were as traditionally tasty as ever. Bugger the diet, I thought. I was hungry. As was Will when he arrived. Some clothes enhance the appearance which was the case with Will's jeans and pale blue sweater. He gave me a kiss and a lop-sided grin, and together we put the fish and chips on warmed plates and tucked in. He too was hungry, apparently.

But as our plates emptied I could tell he had something to tell me and he wasn't looking forward to it. Finally he pushed back his chair.

'Florence,' he said, and I picked my head up. I know when something important is about to be said. I could hear the note of seriousness in his voice. I put my knife and fork down and waited.

I didn't prompt him.

'There's something you need to know.'

I dipped my head.

'Errrm. Just between the two of us. Some more detailed toxicology results have come back.'

I waited.

'Mrs Clay did have an opioid in her system but it had been adulterated.'

I stared.

'There was cyanide in her system as well as a whole load of other stuff. In other words, a knock-off.'

I tried to process that before asking, 'And Richard Clay?'

'Benzodiazepine. Enough to put him to sleep or in a coma, but not enough to kill him.' He tried to smile. 'He'd wake with nothing worse than a muzzy head.'

I was shaking my head as he spoke, trying to fit another oddly shaped piece into my narrative before realizing I'd held it upside down.

'He must have realized . . .' I didn't complete the sentence. Every time I thought I understood the man and his moves the pieces shifted. Had he been a chess player he would have won – every time.

'He just,' I mused, talking to myself, 'wanted to convince his wife of . . .'

There was only one way I could get any answers. I couldn't avoid it any longer.

It was time.

FIFTY-SIX

Friday 3 November, 7 a.m.

woke with a clear head, my thoughts put in order by a sound sleep. Will was sleeping peacefully beside me. The day was starting well.

I let my mind drift towards . . .

A picture of two wine glasses side by side on an oak coffee

table, a bright red sofa behind. A woman who harboured a grudge, her husband's crushing grief, a letter so explanatory and articulate. A dead woman, a living husband, a next-door neighbour hearing a noise at an opportune time (which no one had questioned), the preparatory purchase of illegal drugs.

I glanced across at Will who was just coming round and smiled. He said he'd requested the detailed analysis of the drugs because I'd pricked his conscience that he hadn't done the dead woman justice. His finding would point to justice.

Just not the justice I'd anticipated.

I was in a hurry to get to work and begin the day.

During the lunch break, I drove out to Newcastle Road and parked outside the Clays' house. For a moment I sat outside, reflecting. Victorian semis are spacious homes, with well-proportioned rooms, high ceilings and large gardens. Once I had envied the people who could afford these places. They made my small semi shrink. But all houses hide truth behind their doors: deceit, violence, ill health, unhappiness, bitter rows, proliferating grudges, looming poverty, worry about a future. Before Christine's death I had rarely visited this house. Now I had been here twice in just a few weeks. And I felt a strange reluctance to find out what secrets this house held behind its closed door.

Because I didn't want to face the truth.

However, moments later, as I stood outside, hand raised, ready to knock, I paused, because a new thought had struck me. The secrets contained inside were not only Richard's secrets. They were Christine's too. Secrets she had kept from me, deliberately leading me down a path of her own choosing. What good would it do to expose the truth now? I paused. Once I'd raised my hand to knock I would have set the train in motion. I briefly pondered this new angle. And there, on the doorstep, to add to my hesitation, I was further disturbed by a text from my one and only son.

Hi Mum, wanted to discuss something with you. Is it OK if I ring tonight around 7? He'd signed off with an X.

Stuart was my firstborn, thirty years old, two years older than his sister. And he had a barrowload of mental health problems. He'd attained a degree in accounting and finance in Manchester and had hung on there to work for a large firm where he was simply a number, sorting out numbers. He was stick thin –

fastidious about food – with a list of dishes he wouldn't or couldn't eat. Combine that with a degree of autism and a desert of a social life and you get a picture of an isolated, lonely, young man. Nothing like me or his father.

I didn't really want to spend the evening listening to his problems when I had psyched myself up to talk to Richard Clay and had so much else to think about. Besides I already had an idea what Stuart would be ringing about in which case I could have texted back: *If it's to plead your dad's cause don't bother.* But as we know all mothers are on call twenty-four seven. And so I messaged back, a neutral, *Yeah, of course, Stu. Speak tonight then.* And I ended with a double dose of XX.

And then I did raise my hand and knock.

For a moment it felt as though the house itself was holding its breath, and then I heard slow footsteps shuffling forwards.

It was only a week or so since I'd seen Richard at the inquest, but since then he seemed to have shrunk even further. He looked noticeably thinner and had aged another ten years. Even his hair looked sparser, pink scalp showing between wisps of hair. However, what faced me, rather than the crumpled face of grief, what I read was anger. Which seemed to be directed at me.

'Nurse Florence,' he said in his clipped voice while I wondered (hoped) I'd imagined a note of sarcasm in his tone. 'What can I do for you?'

I loosened my shoulders. 'I was just passing,' I responded, affecting a casual tone, knowing he wouldn't believe me. 'I just thought I'd pop in. See how you are.' I accompanied the statement with a bright smile.

'Did you now?' This time there was no mistaking his sarcastic, disbelieving tone. He fixed his eyes on me for a moment, as though he was trying to read what was really behind my visit. And then he smiled, flattening himself against the wall. 'Come on in then.'

This is the point where you scream at the film, *Don't. Don't go in. Don't be such a dumbbell. Can't you see? It's a trap.*

But I did. So now you change your line, spilling your popcorn and covering your eyes as you scream instead, 'OK then. On your head be it.'

And then I issued an instruction to myself that I could not afford to ignore: Don't be such a fool as to accept a cup of tea.

He led the way towards the sitting room in a pair of slippers, slip-slopping with a hesitant, shuffling step, pushing his feet along as though he was too old or too tired to lift them. By way of contrast, my steps sounded firm and decisive rapping along the tiled floor. I was a woman with direction, going somewhere, while he sounded like a man years older than his early sixties who had given up on life. I followed, my eyes focussed on those bent shoulders.

When we reached the lounge he continued with that polite mockery that I didn't quite trust. 'Do sit.'

I passed the sofa to sit in an armchair while he watched me and looked, long and hard, eye to eye. Steady and unblinking. Then he said, smiling, 'And if I offered you a cup of tea . . .?'

He didn't get to finish the sentence. I'd already shaken my head and produced a convincing excuse. 'I'll have to get back to the surgery. I have a clinic this afternoon.'

'Of course.' He was continuing with the sham politeness while an awkward silence made the air feel thick.

'Nurse Florence . . .?' he cued me in while I felt wrong-footed and grabbed at an explanation.

'Your daughter suggested I might call.'

He simply raised his eyebrows.

'She's worried about you.'

That produced a further, sceptical raising of the eyebrows.

'I think she thought I might help,' I added, floundering.

'I don't know why she thought you might supply any assistance,' he responded, his voice positively vinegary now. 'You could do little enough for my wife when she was alive.'

And then, quite suddenly, without any warning, it was *my* anger which erupted. Or rather exploded. 'Little enough,' I challenged, hearing steel in my voice. 'What would you have expected me to do for a state of mind I wasn't even aware existed?' Now I'd spoken I found it difficult to halt the flow. 'You never told me she had a cancer phobia, that she believed she was dying. If you had shared' – I used the word ironically – 'her phobia with us don't you think we'd have arranged an urgent consultation – even admitted her to a specialist psychiatric unit if we'd thought she might take her own life?'

I wanted to keep going, to accuse him of answering questions for her so she never had a chance to express herself. But I held back, peering over a cliff, sensing something else.

'She didn't.'

Before I had a chance to even open my mouth to ask him what he was referring to, he crumpled like a drinks can in a fist. Inwards, collapsing into himself.

And, peering down, at his side, I saw the truth, speaking it softly. 'Mr Clay, you can stop playing. I know what happened.'

FIFTY-SEVEN

We eyed each other up like a pair of wrestlers about to enter the ring, neither of us quite ready to relinquish our previous positions.

Then he spoke. 'Nurse Florence,' he said, testing the water now, 'do you have to tell anyone?'

'It depends.' We both heard the note of caution.

He drew in a deep, sharp breath while the thought passed through my mind that I'd broken the Lone Worker Agreement which was to always, always (no exceptions) let someone know when we were making a home visit and what time we expected to return to the surgery. No one knew I was here. I'd reasoned that this wasn't an official visit.

That wasn't the real reason. I'd also believed I was in no danger.

My eyes dropped to the cushions on the sofa, finding the marks. Pants had described her lying on her back, he on the floor. I searched for a stain on the carpet where he would have crawled, but nothing was visible there. Maybe Jalissa had been more successful erasing that mark than the other. He was watching me. While I looked back up at him, right into the cold eyes, I knew then. By stepping over the threshold I'd taken a risk.

'So,' he said finally, his voice quavering, 'what do you think you know?'

'She wanted to punish you, didn't she?'

He nodded. 'She never stopped wanting to punish me,' he said, speaking so calmly, so quietly, that I nearly asked him to repeat the sentence. He was looking straight at me. No fluffing of lines now. This was clarity and truth. 'The thing with Sheila . . .'

Ah yes, I thought. Sheila, the next-door neighbour who had stepped forward at such an opportune time.

'It was nothing really. A flirtation and it was years ago but Christine held it against me like a dagger, driving it deeper – but intermittently. I never knew when she would bring it up.'

He stopped for a while and I did not break the spell.

'I thought . . .' He looked across at me then. 'I thought when she practically wrote off Sheila's car that that would be an end to it. I hoped,' he said, holding his hands up, 'that it would be enough.' He shook his head as though words would be too difficult.

'You found her note, didn't you?'

He nodded and gave a ghost of a smile. 'It took me a while to realize its significance. When I did, I was forewarned. I knew something was coming. I just didn't know what.'

He continued, 'I never believed that version of that little girl's accident so I knew what she was capable of.'

He was still holding something back, so I waited.

'Years ago.' He drew in a long, deep breath. 'OK.' He'd come to a decision and looked at me directly. 'Sheila wasn't the first,' he confessed.

So he was a serial cheat.

'A couple of years ago I was having an affair with one of my saleswomen, a lady from Belgium.' He smiled as he recovered the memory. 'She was a young woman named Vanya.' He was still smiling. 'She was intelligent and generous and very beautiful.' Here he paused and, still smiling, he continued, 'She was my sales rep who covered most of France and Switzerland as well as Belgium. I loved her,' he said simply. 'I could easily have managed the business from the continent. Most of it was over there anyway. I planned to leave Christine and set up home in Belgium. The problems started when I tried to tell her. She became hysterical. Told me to get rid of Vanya.'

I shuffled around in my seat, trying to avoid an uncomfortable memory. In the early days I had asked – no, begged – Mark not to leave me. It had made no difference. He'd left.

'What happened?'

Richard's face had become mask-like, as though he had blocked all emotion to become an automaton. He drew in a breath deep enough to take him to the bottom of the ocean.

'She told me she had cancer.' His eyes were very far away now. 'She didn't have long to live. When she was dead I could be with Vanya. I believed her.'

He looked ashamed. 'I know,' he said. 'More fool me. But yes, I believed her.' He fidgeted with his hands. 'She said she had less than a year to live and I thought I could stick that out. Just – one – year. It was a clever ploy.' His mouth twisted. 'Not too long, you see, but not so short that I would quickly know it was a lie.'

'That was why you attended all her appointments,' I said, seeing a different truth.

He nodded staring ahead, refusing to meet my eyes. 'A year later Christine was, obviously, still alive and showing no signs of disease though she dreamt up one symptom after another.'

'All to keep you.'

He nodded. 'Vanya stopped waiting. She grew tired of my lame excuses. And then she met someone else. I think she knew we were never going to be together. I felt . . . defeated.' He'd taken some time choosing the word.

And his mouth was set now, hard and angry, his face suffused with hatred.

'You could have left your wife at any time.'

He shook his head. 'There was no point. Vanya had been the spark that inspired me to break free. Without her there was no incentive. I lost it and sold the business.' He waited. 'I hadn't realized how Christine could hold hatred in her heart and let it fester. I think part of her enjoyment was planning the punishment to fit the crime.' He looked at me, helpless now. 'The thing with Sheila . . .' He looked around. 'I had to have someone I could confide in. She told me to be careful, that Christine was vindictive and a consummate liar. She said the performance Christine gave when she practically wrote off her car would have earned her an Oscar. But she knew. Christine *accelerated* into her.'

'How did you alert Sheila that night?'

He smiled. 'Knowing what she knew she was always watchful.

I shouted and opened the front door before the drugs took effect and I crawled back into the sitting room. I knew it would be enough to alert her.'

He looked at me curiously. 'Do you know what actually happened?'

I nodded. Between us there was a strange, unreal sense of calm. Of anticlimax.

'You swapped the glasses.'

He nodded.

And my thought was it was as simple as that. He swapped the glasses so a planned murder became an accidental suicide while a failed suicide became a simple murder.

So simple I almost took my hat off to him.

'Perfect,' I said, tempted to clap.

'She was always greedy,' he said. 'She slurped hers right down to the bottom. I drank mine, opened the front door and called out to Sheila. Christine and I both fell asleep except she didn't wake.'

We were both silent.

'You understand,' he said, his grief showing through, 'my wife tried to kill me.'

And I realized he'd won – and lost – in the same moment.

FIFTY-EIGHT

And so I sat there with a dilemma while he watched me, our minds tracking towards what would happen next. While we both knew the answer. Case closed.

'But.' His voice was firm now.

I knew what he was asking.

'Harriet,' he began, and this was where his demeanour changed while we simultaneously acknowledged the weak link. Harriet was a truth-teller. She would be compelled to expose this. It was in her genetic code. This was what was bothering him. This was why he wanted me on side. Why he'd made this confession. I recalled Harriet's words about her mother and realized it all made sense now. Richard was watching me, waiting for my decision. Maybe he realized I'd met up with his daughter, formed some sort of loose, though guarded, relationship, tiptoeing around each other, neither quite trusting the other.

Which was where I fit in.

This was why he'd let me in. He thought I could convince his daughter that he was innocent. That her mother's death really was nothing but an accident – or rather a suicide attempt which had gone awry. He'd merely switched her mother's intentions. But we were all intelligent enough to ask the next question.

He was asking me how could he bend this version to make his daughter believe it.

That was my challenge.

He was still watching me but I couldn't figure this one out. It was time I left.

I stood up. 'You need to test your daughter's loyalty yourself,' I said and left.

FIFTY-NINE

I thought about Harriet Clay for most of the afternoon, wondering how deep her integrity was. Would she expose her own father or say nothing?

And then I switched back to my own problems. Stuart was going to ring tonight and I had a horrible suspicion I knew what his theme would be. My son tended to ring when he had a problem he wanted me to solve. And he always pleaded his father's case. Since he'd been a toddler he'd always sided with his dad. Mark's defection had had no impact on their relationship, as far as I knew. Manchester is marginally nearer to Stoke than Stone. Just a quick hike up the M6. They'd probably kept in touch, still met up. While I'd focussed on Lara's relationship with her father I'd not really thought about Stuart and his dad.

Seven o'clock precisely my landline buzzed. Stuart always had been a stickler for time. Which was how he'd ended up working for the civil service based in Manchester. Being on the spectrum for mild autism has its advantages. Precision being one of them. He'd told me a time or two exactly what he did, something to do with accounts, but I was pretty fuzzy about his precise role.

'Hi, Mum.' His voice was so like his father's, gruff, hesitant and questioning.

'Stuart. How are you?'

'I'm . . . all right.' I could hear the hesitance in his voice, the words dragging out of him. He hadn't wanted to make this call. Mark had 'persuaded' him. I felt angry. How could he use his son to plead his case, involve the boy when we both knew he had problems of his own?

'Good.' I paused. 'Work OK?' It was the only question I could think of. My son's life was a desert. As far as I knew he had nothing outside his work. That was it.

'Yeah. I think I'm in line for a promotion.'

That was another depressing area in the desert, the illusory oasis. Stuart always believed he was in line for a promotion. Except the promotions never came. But my heart tore at the hope in his voice.

I waited.

And finally it came after a bout of 'umming' and 'ahhing'.

'Heard from Dad the other day.' He'd tried to make it sound casual. It failed. 'He, umm he wonders if you fancied getting in touch.'

Honestly?

'Not really, Stu.' I'd reverted to his childhood name.

Still, he tried. 'He's not with anyone anymore, Mum.'

'Yeah,' I said. 'I heard.'

'He's, ermm, staying with a friend. Mum, he's sort of sofa-surfing.'

I wanted to say, 'And that's my problem?' But I kept myself in check.

'Any chance you could—?'

I cut him off there. 'No, Stu,' I said. 'There isn't.'

'Oh.' And there he gave up. And somehow the conversation had petered out which left me feeling sad. We'd never had much in common, but he was my boy. He'd been closer to his dad that too was true. But even that had not really been a close relationship. They'd never done 'boy stuff' together – not runs or bike rides, fishing or golf, tennis or Lads 'n' Dads, attended rugby or football matches supporting their joint favourite team. And now it was too late. Maybe we'd been a dysfunctional family all along – four separate people who'd happened to live under the same roof, share links in our genetic code? Are all families like this, linked by biology rather than sociology?

It was a sobering thought.

When he'd rung off, I consoled myself with the thought that at least Lara had dragged her boyfriend here. I'd met David before Mark had, so maybe our family was divided into the sexes – boys and girls – like public toilets. Except that wouldn't cater for the gender neutrals, would it? I was smiling until I started to wonder whether our future would always be divided.

And where would Vivien and the baby fit in? Anywhere or nowhere, simply a payment over a bank order? How things change, I mused, my pity now all for the baby and her mother who'd been abandoned at such a vulnerable time. My hatred for her, the husband-stealer, had dissipated.

But Stuart had used the phrase sofa-surfing. That wasn't fair. I was here in a house that we jointly paid for. Presumably he and Vivien had rented somewhere? I didn't know the details. But sofa-surfing? I returned to the phrase before looking around at my comfortable, warm lounge, central heating down low, gas fire sending out fake flames, making the atmosphere cosy. And call me a fool but I felt guilty. No wonder he'd sounded so desperate.

SIXTY

Monday 6 November, 1 p.m.

I'd had a wretched weekend. Will had been working – he hadn't told me on what – so I'd spent the time alone, full of uncomfortable thoughts. After the conversation with Stuart the guilt had stayed with me all weekend, so I'd been in a daze, picturing Mark homeless. Only one step down from sofa-surfing.

I knew I couldn't let that happen. But if I offered Mark a home here even temporarily, I would lose Will. I was certain of that. Mark's obligation was to his mistress (even if she was an ex) and his baby daughter – whatever might be wrong with her. It made no difference.

The situation surrounding the Clay family seemed less important than my own family circumstances, but they still lay, dirty and writhing, at the bottom of a pond.

Jalissa picked up that something was wrong and tried to pump me but I shook my head. 'I don't want to talk about it. Not about anything.'

She put an arm around my shoulders. 'Man trouble?' she asked sympathetically.

I nodded. 'In a way.'

'I am sorry.' She put a sandwich on my desk without even asking me what I would like. 'I have some news,' she said. That jerked me out of my torpor.

'You bin wonderin' who did the poisonin'.'

'Yeah. But . . .'

She put her hand in her pocket and drew out a bottle of pills. She put them in my hand. 'That answer any of your questions? They was inside the lavatory cistern, in a plastic bag. I guess the cops – they never found them.'

I looked at the label and my heart sank.

That was when I began to feel angry. Not just angry, furious.

I had trouble keeping my fury in during the rest of the afternoon. When I left I was still cursing. I drove out of the surgery, so immersed in my fury that I almost ran over a distracted Ryan. I slammed on my brakes and stuck my head out of the window. 'Sorry. Sorry.'

He held his hand up. 'It's OK.' He looked half drunk – or possibly high. He was reeling around, definitely not perpendicular.

'You OK?' Silly question as he was obviously not. But actually, Ryan wasn't really much of a drinker. At least not enough to have him reeling around in the street. He looked spaced out, pupils well dilated, face pale, sweating. I made a decision. Flung the passenger door open. 'Get in.'

He more or less tumbled into the passenger seat and sat passively as I clicked the seat belt around him. He looked weary – and frightened. I could guess why. I drove silently back towards the surgery, saying nothing and making no comment. Once or twice I sensed him turning his head and looking at me but he kept silent, saying nothing until I entered the surgery car park. Then he looked at me, sadly, and I turned to him. 'Ryan,' I said, in the tone of a head teacher, 'what have you got yourself into?'

His groan was hardly reassuring. Neither was the drop of his head into his hands.

But he said nothing so I continued, as though he had made a comment. 'More importantly how are you going to get out of it?'

He seemed to be gathering himself. He lifted his head and stared for a moment, through the windscreen, at the rows of parked cars, some haphazardly, others neatly between the lines. A couple of the spaces marked DOCTOR with yellow plaques. We nurses and all other staff had to take pot luck.

Realization is like a storm which begins innocuously enough, with a soft, intermittent patter of raindrops, one spattering, tentative spot followed by another and another. Then the clouds gather strength and power. They grow confident, darker and make their threat more powerful. The rate and ferocity increase until you can no longer ignore the sense of foreboding. It rages and threatens, terrorizes and bangs its thunder, dazzles with lightning.

And then it moves away and there is calm again and you are left with the knowledge that the threat has passed. Which was how I felt watching Ryan Wood's face. The realization had arrived, the clouds giving way to sunlight. I felt like sharing platitudes with him, by telling him all would be well, that every storm passes. But for Ryan, surprisingly naive, for all his minor villainy, I saw that that was not necessarily so. And when he looked at me, I saw he was arriving at that realization too. He'd been used.

When he spoke he lacked that jaunty confidence that had always marked him out. 'Your new boyfriend, he's a cop, isn't he?'

I gaped at him. 'My new boyfriend?'

'Yeah, the guy you was walking through the town with the other night.'

He meant Will – obviously. I nodded.

'Do you have to tell him everything?'

'Not necessarily.' I didn't like the way this conversation was heading.

He looked at me with those innocent blue eyes. 'I didn't mean to . . .' He dropped his head. 'I didn't know what it was. They didn't tell me.' He gulped. 'The boys made it into tablets that looked like Oxy. But they weren't.' He dropped his eyes. 'I know that now but I didn't then,' he added fiercely. 'They got me to do the label 'cos I was the one with the neatest writing.'

Neatest writing, I thought, finding it hard to keep it in. If things went wrong they'd set him up to be the fall guy.

He was watching me anxiously while I tried to fit this new fact into the narrative. Had she meant to scare him? Simply wanted to give him a fright. Punish him. Had she known that these were unreliable drugs?

Then I remembered the suicide note. The six-month plan. In the end I couldn't burrow into my patient's mind.

Ryan was watching me anxiously. 'What do you think will happen?'

'Honestly?'

He nodded.

'I have absolutely no idea.'

One feels a responsibility for one's patients. Not quite the shepherdess in charge of her flock beating off the wolves. But close.

And now my fear was for the patient who stood in front of me.

I would regret it.

But this was beyond my remit. I rang Will.

Who trusted me enough not to ask anything, simply saying, 'Ten minutes.'

He was with me in nine. Neither of us had needed to say the name.

'Thing is,' he said, looking past me towards my clinic room door, 'if he really does have something to say, something relevant that is, I'm going to have to caution him and take him down to the station for a proper interview.'

I nodded. 'I suspect he already knows that, Will. He's, ermm, pretty familiar with police procedures. You could say he's done his apprenticeship.'

'Hmm. Well, let's see. Can we use your room?'

I glanced at my watch. 'You're OK for around twenty minutes.' I risked a joke. 'If you haven't tortured the truth out of him in that time I'm afraid you'll have to try another way.'

'OK.' He went in and shut the door quietly behind him. Had I not been a nurse and blessed with a modicum of dignity I might have pressed my ear to eavesdrop, but I desisted and went upstairs to the staff room.

SIXTY-ONE

He was out fifteen minutes later. I peered into his face, searching for a hint but he was giving nothing away. Moments later Ryan followed him out looking sheepish but less frightened. Will nodded in my direction and gave a watery smile. 'Thanks,' he mouthed. 'I'll text you. See you later?'

I gave him a thumbs-up and returned his smile.

They disappeared together leaving me with a dilemma.

I could call on Richard on the way home, tell him there was some confusion over the drugs used, that it was possible his wife had tried to scare him – nothing more.

I could ring Mark and make sure he had somewhere to lay his silly head.

I could wait and see whether Harriet put her family loyalty aside and told the true story of her parents' suicide bid.

Or I could go home, close the door, leaving all my problems outside, climb into a bath full of oils and additives, shut my eyes and pretend none of this had really happened. That life was simple, not full of problems, difficult patients, sickness and cruelty, unhappiness and troubles.

However . . . I knew I would do none of these things. Because? Next patient, please.